BODY COUNT

SHAUN HUTSON
BODY COUNT

www.orbitbooks.net

ORBIT

First published in Great Britain in 2008 by Orbit

A CIP catalogue record for this book
is available from the British Library.

ISBN 978-1-84149-434-0

Typeset in Bembo by Palimpsest Book Production Ltd,
Grangemouth, Stirlingshire
Printed and bound in Great Britain by Clays Ltd, St Ives plc

Papers used by Little, Brown are natural, renewable and recyclable
products, made from wood grown in sustainable forests and certified in
accordance with the rules of the Forest Stewardship Council.

Mixed Sources
Product group from well-managed
forests and other controlled sources
www.fsc.org Cert no. SGS-COC-004081
© 1996 Forest Stewardship Council
FSC

Orbit
An imprint of
Little, Brown Book Group
100 Victoria Embankment
London EC4Y ODY

An Hachette Livre UK Company
www.hachettelivre.co.uk

www.orbitbooks.net

This book is dedicated to my wonderful wife,
Belinda and to my fantastic daughter,
and, trust me, it isn't nearly enough.

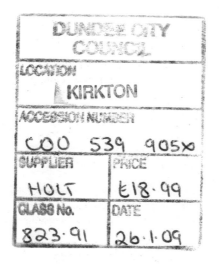

Acknowledgements

I just wanted to say thanks to the following people for different reasons (and because some of them like to see their names in print!). Everyone mentioned below should know why they're included by now.

At my publishers, Barbara Daniel, Andy Edwards, Carol Donnelly and everyone in sales, especially those 'on the road'.

My agent, Brie Burkeman and Isabelle and all those at the Buckman agency.

I'd also like to thank the following people for reasons too numerous, tenuous or trivial to list.

James Whale (and Melinda). Jason Figgis, Maria Figgis and Jonathan Figgis. Jo Roberts and Gatlin Pictures. Rod Smallwood, Val Janes, Hannah and all at Phantom Music. Steve, Bruce, Dave, Adrian, Janick and Nicko. Ian Austin, Zena, Terri, Becky and Rachel, Nicky, Hayley. Brian at the bank. Leslie and Sue Tebbs. All at Chancery. Martin Phillips. Graeme Sayer.

Cineworld UK, especially everyone at Cineworld Milton Keynes. Mark Johnson, Martin, Debbie, Martin, Paula, Keara, Terry, Fiona, Helen and everyone else who I can't remember or who's probably left by now.

Liverpool Football Club. Aaron Reynolds. Steve

Lucas. Paul Garner. Neil Davies. Tommy, Dave, Pete, Kevin, Brian, Paul and Phil.

As ever, I thank my mum and dad, for everything.

The last thank you I always reserve for my readers. Thanks you lot. You're the best. Always have been and always will be.

Let's go.

'You want justice, but do you want to pay for it?'

Bertolt Brecht

1

He was losing a lot of blood.

The piece of cloth he'd wound tightly round his left forearm was already soaked with the crimson liquid.

The knife wound that had opened the flesh was deep. He knew it needed stitches; the cloth was barely holding the ragged edges of the gash together. But, for now, it would have to do. He gritted his teeth and shook his head vigorously from side to side in an attempt to stop himself fainting. He wondered how much blood a human body could afford to lose before unconsciousness took hold.

As he ran he tasted blood in his mouth too. It was from the cut on the inside of his cheek but after the way he'd been running he wouldn't have been surprised if it had forced itself up from his ravaged lungs. He was gasping for breath now as he continued along the darkened passageway, glancing constantly over his shoulder.

He couldn't hear them behind him but he knew they were there. Somewhere in the shadows. Waiting for him to slow down. When he did, or when he moved out into the open, they would be upon him. Just like before.

He had no idea how long he'd been running, but his face was slick with sweat and he could feel his shirt sticking to his back and chest.

For a moment he paused, leaning back against the grubby wall to get his breath.

Inside the mask, his breathing sounded louder than normal, and more mucoid. Like the laboured snores of a slumbering drunkard. He knew there was no point in trying to remove the facial covering; he'd already tried a number of times and failed.

His injured arm brushed against the dirty plaster and left a red smear.

They would see the mark he'd left but, he reasoned, what did it matter? They would come this way eventually. What was the point of concealing his presence? It seemed that wherever he tried to hide they found him. And, when he thought about it, hiding would do him no good anyway. They would corner him. Surround him. Move in frenziedly and finish him.

No, he had to push on. Had to force his aching muscles to carry him a little longer. He had to gulp air down into his already overworked lungs. His heart was thudding madly against his ribs: a combination of his exertions and the fear that gripped him. Sometimes it threatened to overwhelm him completely. Especially when they got close to him.

He wondered how much further he would have to go.

At the end of the long corridor there was a set of stone steps.

He hurried towards them, almost stumbling over something lying close to the wall on his right-hand side. He steadied himself, unable to see what he'd tripped on in the gloom. Instead he moved on towards the five stone steps. He halted, gasping for breath.

4

To his left the corridor arrowed away into more darkness. At the top of the steps there was a wrought-iron gate. He could see through the bars to what looked like a deserted, but much wider, street beyond.

Out there in the empty thoroughfare there was just one light glowing sickly yellow. Everywhere else was in deep shadow.

He swallowed hard and wondered if he could make it across the street using the shadows for cover. There were more buildings on the other side of the road, including what looked like a church. He could use them as shelter for a few minutes at least. Get his breath. Redress his wound. Prepare himself for the next onslaught.

Again he glanced to his left and the dark corridor, but quickly decided the gate was his best option. He looked behind him, then climbed the steps and reached out tentatively to push against the barred gate.

It was locked.

2

For a moment he thought about shaking the gate but realised that the rattling would only alert his pursuers. He pushed against the metal partition once more; then, cursing under his breath, he ran back down the steps and darted off along the corridor to his left.

The gloom within this walkway was slightly less cloying than the darkness he'd just journeyed through. He blinked hard in an effort to see ahead, realising that the corridor turned in a gentle curve to his right.

He slowed his pace for a moment, wanting to ensure that no one lurked in the blackness ahead. Then, satisfied that his route was clear, he moved on a little more quickly.

Dull light was spilling into the corridor from the far end now and he could see that another short flight of steps led up to an open doorway.

He paused at the bottom of the steps, gazing out into the wide thoroughfare beyond. As he scanned his surroundings for any sign of movement a flicker of light ahead of him caused him to duck back into the gloom.

Another of the street lights had come on.

It flared feebly for a moment and then went out again. He waited, wanting to see if it burst into life once more. Sure enough, as he watched, it flickered a second time, bathing the street in a dull, yellow glow for about twenty yards in all directions. This time the light remained.

He cursed under his breath. The shadows would have been more welcoming. He would have felt safer crossing the open ground without the unwanted light from this second lamp post.

But he had no choice. He couldn't stay where he was.

They would be close behind him by now. He daren't even consider exactly how close. All he knew was that he had to make it across the open street to the buildings on the other side. Once there he could rest for a few minutes before moving on.

He pressed himself against the door frame, looked out into the street and saw no movement.

The only vehicle in view was a large white Transit van parked about fifteen feet to his right. It would offer cover.

A thought suddenly struck him.

It might offer a little more than just cover.

He took a deep breath and ran towards the van.

As he reached it he ducked down close to the driver's side, waited a second, then peered into the cab.

No keys in the ignition.

That would have been too easy, wouldn't it? he thought angrily. But there might be a chance to hotwire it if he had time before they caught up with him.

He swallowed hard, trying to make the decision. He'd stolen cars before. He knew the procedure. The van could be ready, its engine running, in a matter of minutes. He glanced back the way he'd come, straining his ears for any sound of their footsteps behind him.

There was only silence.

He pulled at the driver's door and slid in behind the steering wheel.

Now he had to work faster than ever before. Break open the steering column, expose the requisite wires, then twist them together to make the connection. Pump the accelerator until the starter motor turned.

Simple.

He wondered what he was going to split the steering column with. And how he could do it without their hearing him. The noise would give away his position as surely as if he'd put up a neon sign over the van. But he realised he had little choice if he was to have a chance of escaping them.

He looked into the back of the van, behind the worn and threadbare seats.

An empty bottle. That was it. Nothing else. No tools left conveniently for him to find.

He picked up the bottle and hefted it before him. It felt heavy enough to break the plastic housing on the steering column. He paused for a second, deciding that if the bottle shattered he would merely clamber out of the van and run for it.

He struck the steering column and the plastic cracked. Three more times he hit it, pausing after each impact to check around him for movement. When he was sure there was none he struck again.

When he saw the wires inside the column exposed he felt a brief, galvanising moment of joy.

He pulled the wires he needed free and bent low towards them, stripping away the plastic sheathing that covered the metal with his teeth. Then he twisted the wires together and pressed his foot down on the accelerator, waiting for the motor to turn.

Nothing.

Not even the groan of a flat battery.

Breathing heavily, he slipped the bonnet release catch, jumped out of the van and hurried round to the front of the vehicle.

He lifted the bonnet and looked beneath.

For a moment he smiled. He felt a laugh gathering in his throat. The laughter of the damned. It hovered there as surely as the sickness he felt rising in his chest as he stared beneath the bonnet.

There was no engine.

3

He dropped the bonnet despairingly.

The metal clanged loudly, the sound echoing over the deserted street, reverberating in his ears and bouncing off the buildings that surrounded him.

He spun round, looking into the shadows, glancing back the way he'd come, his initial despair now rapidly overshadowed by his fear that they would have heard the crash of metal on metal.

To his right there was a tall brick wall, well over twenty feet high and topped by razor wire. Even in the gloom he could see the blades glinting viciously. No way over that. Immediately ahead there was a narrow passageway, a walkway of concrete flanked on either side by high mesh fencing. To his left were the church and some other boarded-up buildings.

For interminable seconds he tried to decide the best way to go. To remain in this place would mean death. He had no option but to move on. Get as far away as possible from those who pursued him.

He moved towards the narrow walkway ahead.

There were small spotlights mounted on the tall wire

on each side, aimed down at the concrete below, providing more light than he would have liked as he hurried along the pathway. Darkness and gloom were his allies here, not the light. Brightness made him visible. It made it hard to hide.

Behind the fencing there were more buildings, but these were dilapidated and crumbling. Some had no roofs and he could see ceiling beams stretched skeletally between the walls. Rubble was piled high around the approaches, and the whole landscape reminded him more and more of a bomb site as he moved further into it. Even the concrete at his feet was now scored with deep cracks, as if it had been laid then immediately shattered with sledgehammers.

There was a wire mesh gate ahead and he ran towards it, praying that it wouldn't be locked.

He pushed it hard, relieved when it swung back on its hinges to allow him through. As he passed beyond it, his initial relief at being able to move on was suddenly tempered by surprise. The ground beneath his feet wasn't concrete any more. It was soft earth and grass.

He turned a corner and found himself in a wide, walled courtyard between four tall buildings. There were lights burning in the windows of one of them.

Were they waiting for him, he wondered? Had they somehow got ahead of him?

He looked around anxiously. The courtyard was dimly lit, illuminated only by wall lights placed high on the buildings surrounding him.

He wondered how he was going to find his way out. Could he escape through one of the doors in the walls or would he have to enter the buildings themselves?

There was a door near to him and he tried it.

Locked.

11

He ducked down behind an empty skip, wondering if he was being watched, even now, from one of the high windows.

He tried to control his breathing, wincing at a sudden twinge of pain from his slashed arm. He flexed his fingers, aware of a tingling in the tips of the digits. Perhaps it was caused by the blood loss, he thought. He began to wonder how long it would be before the entire arm went numb.

Keeping low, he moved towards an unpainted wooden door that led into the nearest building. He pressed his ear to the wood, listening for any sounds from the other side. When he heard nothing he bumped his shoulder gently against the partition.

It opened enough for him to squeeze through.

He found himself in a brightly lit hallway, which turned sharply to his right to form an L shape. From where he stood, he could hear someone talking.

They were ahead of him as well as behind him.

His entire body stiffened momentarily, his heart hammering frantically against his ribs. If he was caught in the middle he would never escape. He fought to control his breathing inside the mask, then peered carefully round the corner.

He had indeed heard a voice but, to his relief, it was a lone one.

The figure that walked slowly back and forth in the corridor beyond him was tall but thin. In a low, reedy tone, it was muttering words to itself. Not to another. Dressed in a T-shirt and jeans, it didn't seem to present much of an obstacle.

Except for the fact that it carried a machete.

The blade was fully twelve inches long, dull and rusted in places but wickedly sharp. Even if the cutting edge hadn't been as honed as it looked, the implement would have been perfectly usable as a bludgeon due to its weight.

He watched as the figure turned and headed back in his direction. The face was milk white, the bright red U-shaped mouth and bulbous red nose standing out starkly in contrast.

The figure carrying the machete was wearing a clown mask. Just like some of the others before.

The figure turned before it reached the corner and headed back the other way. How to get past it? Jump it now that its back was turned? Yes. Hit it from behind. Wrestle it to the ground, get the machete from it. Finish the job with that.

He nodded to himself, so intent on his next move that he never even heard the door behind him open.

Just as he never saw the automatic shotgun aimed at him.

The first he knew about it was the deafening blast and the thunderous discharge that severed his spine just above the hips.

After that, he knew nothing.

Probably just as well. Five of them entered the hall and stood around him for a moment before they stripped him of his clothes.

They used the machete to sever his head.

4

'It looks real to me.'

The words came from the youngest of the four detectives. Detective Sergeant Michael Bradley looked at the screen again, then back at his colleagues. 'It's the most realistic so far,' he persisted.

'It does look like the real thing,' added DS James Mackenzie. At thirty-eight, he was a year older than Bradley. Both men turned to look at the senior detective in the room.

'What do you reckon?' Bradley asked, chewing on a piece of bitten-off fingernail.

Detective Inspector Joe Chapman merely gazed at the screen.

'Joe?'

The question came from Detective Sergeant Maggie Grant, and Chapman nodded almost imperceptibly in acknowledgement

'Run it again, Maggie,' he instructed. 'I'm not convinced.' He looked at Bradley. 'And you shouldn't be either. Not until we've got more evidence.'

'Convinced about this one or the other three?' Bradley challenged him.

'Any of them,' Chapman insisted. 'You know what they can do with special effects these days. Where's the proof it's real? That could have been some fake head that was held up to the camera at the end.'

'What's it going to take to make you believe it?' Bradley wanted to know.

'More than we've seen here,' Chapman told him.

'You're not discounting the fact that this one and the other three could be snuff movies, are you, Joe?' Maggie asked.

'I'm sure snuff movies exist,' the DI conceded. 'I'm just not convinced that we've watched one here and now.' He reached into his jacket pocket for his cigarettes and lit one.

Bradley coughed as the bluish-grey smoke drifted in his direction.

'Does my smoking bother you?' Chapman enquired.

'A bit,' Bradley said, flicking the piece of chewed-off nail with his tongue. It had got wedged between two of his front teeth.

'Well, fuck off into the corridor until I've finished then,' Chapman told him.

Bradley shot him an irritable glance, then turned to face the screen once more.

'These settings look the same as in the other three films,' Maggie observed. 'Those steps down to the kids' playground and the video shop at the back are in all four of them.'

'Where are we thinking?' Chapman mused. 'Shot in London?'

'It could be any big city, couldn't it?' Mackenzie offered. 'All the shops are boarded up. There aren't any land-marks that are recognisable.'

'It must have been shot on some abandoned housing estate or something like that,' Bradley suggested.

15

'No names above any of the shops,' Chapman observed. 'No number plates on any of the vehicles either. That's weird, isn't it? If this was shot on some abandoned housing estate, why remove the number plates?'

'So we can't trace the vehicles,' Maggie said.

'Fair enough. There're no sounds of traffic in the background, though. No planes going overhead either.'

'Unless the background sound's been edited out,' Mackenzie cut in.

'That's a bit elaborate for your average snuff movie,' Maggie objected.

'Everything about this and the other three films has been elaborate,' Chapman reminded her. 'The way they're shot. How they're lit and staged. Everything. This isn't some bastard in his cellar with a camcorder and a spotlight.'

He blew more smoke into the room. It coiled and uncurled before the screen like a translucent snake.

'What about the masks?' Bradley said. 'Do you think there's any significance in the fact that all the victims and all the perpetrators are wearing masks in every one of the films we've seen so far?'

'Someone wants to keep the identity of the victims and their killers secret so we can't trace them either,' Mackenzie said.

Chapman nodded in agreement. 'All the films came from the same place?' he asked.

'They were all posted on the same Internet site within a week of each other,' Maggie said. 'But so far we've had no luck tracking down the source. Even the guys from the computer division say they've never seen anything like it. There's some kind of cloaking device or firewall that's been used and no one's been able to get through

16

it so far. We've checked with the vice squad but they've been no help because these films have no sexual content. We haven't got any idea who's putting them on the Net, let alone who's making them, or even *why* they're being put on the Net. It isn't for financial gain. There's no subscription fee to that particular site. Whoever created it didn't put these films on it because they wanted to make money out of them.'

'So why do it?' Bradley demanded.

'That's what we need to find out, dummy,' Chapman snapped.

Bradley again glanced at him with narrowed eyes.

'Are we going to watch it again?' Maggie asked.

Chapman nodded.

Maggie clicked on the play button and the film began to run again.

5

'I think there're at least six different cameras being used,' Chapman said, dropping his cigarette butt into a cup of cold coffee. It hissed then floated on the dark fluid like a dead fish on a rancid pond.

'Why go to such lengths if these aren't real snuff movies?' Bradley wanted to know. 'Why spend all this time and money to fake the deaths of four men?'

'He's got a point, guv,' Maggie said. 'As well as the victims there are anything up to twenty extras.'

Bradley snorted dismissively.

'What the fuck would you call them, smart-arse?' Chapman snapped.

'Extras makes it sound like Hollywood,' Bradley said.

Chapman gazed at him for a second longer before returning his attention to the screen.

'Whatever they're called,' Maggie continued, 'someone must be paying them. They're all accomplices to murder. We've seen them kill four men.'

'We think we've seen them kill four men,' Chapman corrected her.

'All right,' Maggie muttered. 'Let's assume that what

we've seen is real. It must have taken some organising. Four victims. Six cameras and, presumably, people to work them. The locations and those twenty or so guys in masks.'

'Perhaps we should interview Steven Spielberg,' Bradley grunted.

'Maggie's right,' Mackenzie said. 'That kind of set-up would take time and money. A lot of money.'

'It still doesn't explain why twenty people would agree to hunt down four men and murder them on camera knowing full well there was a chance they'd be recognised. Even with those fucking masks on,' Chapman said.

'If we knew who the victims were . . .' Maggie began, allowing the sentence to trail away.

'If they are victims,' Chapman reminded her. 'We still don't know if they're actually dead or not.'

'It doesn't make any sense,' Bradley said. 'If they're not dead why bother posting the films on the Internet?'

'Why bother anyway?' Chapman countered. 'Even if the victims are really dead we don't know why and we don't know who they are. Who the fuck would go to such elaborate lengths to kill four men and then expose themselves to possible discovery by putting the evidence on screen? If it's someone with money who wanted four guys dead then why not just hire a hit man? Get it done quietly. It doesn't make sense broadcasting it, making it so public.'

'If the killings aren't real, why is the source of the website impossible to find?' Maggie said. 'If what we've seen are just elaborate fakes, why would the maker be scared of being found?'

'She's right,' Bradley agreed. 'If these films aren't kosher, why go to such incredible lengths to keep their origin secret?'

19

'If they were fake and we found out who made them, what could we charge them with?' Maggie added. 'If you're right and no one's been killed, then they've got nothing to worry about. There's no reason why they'd want to keep their identity quiet. They'd only hide it if the murders were real.'

Chapman continued to gaze at the screen, watching again as the severed head was raised towards the camera by the figure wielding the machete. The image lingered for a moment longer, and then the screen went black.

'So, everyone thinks these killings are real except me,' Chapman said.

Maggie, Bradley and Mackenzie all turned to look at him.

'Find me some evidence,' the detective inspector insisted. 'Check missing persons. Let's see if we can match up some physical evidence to what's on these films.'

'They're all wearing masks,' Bradley reminded him. 'All the victims were wearing identical masks and almost identical clothes.'

'Then go over the films again until you spot something that stands out, something that looks individual about each victim. Give us something to work with.' Chapman got to his feet. 'Maggie, you come with me.'

She nodded and joined him as he walked to the door.

'What are you going to do?' Bradley asked, his tone insistent.

'We'll check out the website again,' Chapman said. 'See if we can find out who's been posting the films in the first place.'

'You know that's impossible,' Bradley said impatiently. 'No one's been able to find anything so far. Why should it be any different now?'

'We'll try,' Chapman said curtly. 'That's all any of us can do.' He left the room.

Bradley glared at the closed door. 'Prick,' he hissed under his breath.

6

'What have you got against him?' Maggie Grant skimmed some of the froth from her cappuccino and licked it from the spoon.

'Who?' Chapman wanted to know, gazing round at the other occupants of the café. He seemed distracted, unable to focus on anything for more than a few seconds at a time. Through the large plate glass windows he could see the towering edifice of New Scotland Yard thrusting upwards into the sky. The walk from his office inside that building to where they now sat had taken less than five minutes.

'Mike Bradley.'

'How long have you got?' Chapman asked humourlessly. He stirred his own coffee and took a sip, wincing when he found how strong it was. He tipped more sugar into it to try to alleviate the bitterness.

Maggie raised her eyebrows and lifted her cup.

'He's a cocky little bastard,' Chapman said finally, 'and he wants my job.'

'He's a detective sergeant, you're a detective inspector. Of course he wants your job. All of us do.' She smiled.

'He's too young.'

'He's thirty-seven.'

'That's what I said. He's too young. He's ten years younger than me.'

'I'm forty. You don't hate me too, do you?'

'You're different,' Chapman said, without looking at her. She was about to speak when he continued. 'I had to wait until I was forty-five before I was promoted.'

'That's not Bradley's fault.'

'What are you saying, Maggie? Do you want me to start sending him flowers? Just allow me my bitterness, will you? Let me enjoy it.' He took another sip of his coffee.

'I'm just saying that he wants to solve this case as much as any of us do,' Maggie said.

Chapman didn't answer, instead gazed distractedly at two young women who had entered the café. They were talking animatedly. One of them glanced in Chapman's direction, then turned back to her friend again as if reluctant to catch his eye.

'Why the sudden concern for Mike Bradley?' he said, still not looking at her.

'It isn't concern. I was just curious.' She sipped her coffee. 'Do you think I want your job as well? Are you threatened by me?'

'I'm not threatened by Bradley or you or anyone else,' Chapman told her. 'I just know him. I've seen his type a hundred times over the years. Arse-licking little fuck. He won't stop until he's Metropolitan Commissioner.'

'There's nothing wrong with a bit of ambition. You used to have some yourself.'

'That was a long time ago, Maggie. I had things to be ambitious about in those days. What the fuck is there now? All I've got to look forward to are prostate trouble and going bald.'

23

'You talk as if you've got one foot in the grave, Joe.'

He took a deep breath, then looked at her across the table. 'Was my ambition one of the things that attracted you to me?' he enquired.

'One of them,' she confessed.

'And what about your new bloke? What made him so attractive?' There was a note of scorn in Chapman's voice.

'Don't say it like that, Joe.'

'How do you want me to say it, Maggie?' he snapped. 'Am I supposed to be happy that what happened between us is over? That you're settled down with some guy?'

'Oh, come on, Joe, don't go over that again. What we had was only ever a fling. You always used to tell me that. You were the one who used to remind me you were married and you'd never leave your wife. I thought you might have been happy for me when Jason came along.'

'Are you going to marry him?'

Maggie smiled and ran a hand through her shoulder-length light brown hair. 'I've only known him five months.'

'He's got a kid, hasn't he?'

'A boy. He spends every other weekend with his mother.'

'How do you get on with him?'

'Fine.'

Chapman nodded slowly. 'Are you glad it's over between us?' he said, challenging her.

'I'm glad no one ever found out,' she told him. 'Especially your wife. I wouldn't have wanted to hurt her.'

'We had an affair for eighteen months and now you're glad you didn't hurt my wife?'

'I knew what I was getting into.'

'And out of.'

'We had to end it, Joe,' she insisted. 'Would you have left your wife? No, you wouldn't. What was I supposed to do? Hang around and never look at another guy on the off chance you might change your mind?' She flicked the handle of her cup with one immaculately manicured index finger. 'I'm just glad that no one at work ever found out. It would have ruined both our careers.'

'God forbid,' he said, acidly.

Maggie pulled up the sleeve of her jacket and glanced at her watch.

'I've got to go,' she announced, getting to her feet. 'Unless we've got any business to discuss. About the case.'

'I said all I wanted to say earlier on.'

'Are you going home now?'

'I might go back into the office for a couple of hours. Have another look at those films. See if I can spot something we missed before.' He took another sip of his coffee.

Maggie hesitated a moment. 'See you in the morning,' she said.

Chapman didn't look at her, merely nodded.

She turned and walked out.

He didn't watch her go.

Legacy

He wasn't a prisoner in the room.

It was just that he preferred not to leave it unless he had company.

In the summer especially he loved to walk in the garden. The feel of the sun on his skin made him happy. In the winter months he didn't like having to wear the extra clothes and the coat that kept him warm. When it was cold he would rather stay inside.

In his room.

He had a wonderful view from his window. He could see the big ornamental pond and he often sat for hours watching the large multicoloured fish swimming lazily about in the water. On warm days, he sometimes fed them himself, throwing handfuls of kibble to them and watching as they rose to the surface to collect it.

Once he'd tried to snatch one of them from the water but he'd been reprimanded and told to stay away from the pool for a week.

The nurse brought his food on a tray at the same times every day.

He wasn't sure what those times were but he knew that

the nurse would always come. With the food she brought his tablets. Two white ones and two blue ones in the morning (the white ones were big and difficult to swallow; he didn't like those). More white ones in the middle of the day and, before he went to bed, a smaller white tablet and two capsules. Red at one end and purple at the other.

Occasionally, there were injections too.

He hated those.

That was when they sometimes had to hold him down.

The nurse who was going to give the injection always arrived with two big men for company. They would stand on either side of him and sometimes grip his shoulders when she reached for the needle. They pinned him in a chair while the nurse tapped the inside of his elbow with two fingers then slid the long steel needle into his swollen vein.

The pain wasn't intolerable (he'd had much worse) but he still hated it.

Sometimes he hated it so much that he struck out. He could remember hitting one of the big men only days earlier. He still recalled the blood pouring from the man's nose and mouth. Then others had come, other big men. The nurse had stuck the needle straight through his trousers into his leg that day. The steel had broken off in his thigh and she'd been forced to ram another one into the muscle.

It had hurt.

He had spent the next forty-eight hours in a daze, barely able to move from his bed he was so heavily sedated. When he'd woken properly he'd found pinpricks and bruises in the crook of his arm. The nurse had said something about a drip but he didn't understand what that was. All he knew was that he was sorry for what he'd done.

27

Now he heard someone outside his door and wondered if it was the nurse. His stomach rumbled and he guessed that it must be time for food.

Rising from his chair, he stood up as the door handle turned.

His stomach growled loudly once again and he rubbed it with the flat of one large hand, smiling to himself.

He took a step towards the door as it swung open.

It wasn't the nurse. It wasn't food or medication.

He froze where he stood, his expression one of bewilderment now. Then he recognised the figure standing before him.

The figure took a step inside the room and closed the door.

7

Detective Inspector Joe Chapman swung himself out of the car and fumbled in his jacket pocket for his house keys.

He glanced up and down Corfield Street. The thoroughfare, like many others in this area of Bethnal Green, was flanked on both sides by semi-detached houses. They looked remarkably similar to Chapman. Only the colours of the front doors and window frames made one different from the next. Some, he noted, were in need of a paint job more badly than others, his own being one of them.

Perhaps the next time he had some holiday, he told himself, he'd give the paintwork a going-over. Freshen it up.

Yeah, perhaps. When are you ever going to take a holiday? It's been four years since you had one.

He locked the car and headed up the short path to his front door. There was a light on in the living room and he could see the glow of the television screen.

As he stepped into the narrow hallway he could hear voices. They were coming from the television too. One of the soaps was on.

There was always a fucking soap on.

'It's only me,' he called, wearily, as he closed the front door behind him. Then he pushed open the door to his right and stepped into the living room.

Laura Chapman smiled brightly at him from one end of the sofa.

'Good day?' she asked, one eye on the TV screen.

'Same old shit,' he told her. 'What about you?'

'Not bad,' she said. 'There's some lasagne in the oven if you want it. I saved you some.'

'I had something before I came home.' He stepped back towards the hall. 'I'm just going to have a quick shower.'

'Joe, you're not going out again, are you?' she asked, a note of irritation in her voice. 'It's nearly eight o'clock now.'

He didn't answer her but went up the narrow staircase instead. Laura followed him.

'What's the point?' she called. 'Leave it for tonight, Joe.'

'Don't start, Laura,' he said, moving across the landing into the largest of the three bedrooms.

'You've been out every night for the past week,' she reminded him. 'And what good's it done?'

Chapman hung up his jacket, then pulled off his tie and began unbuttoning his shirt.

'You won't find her,' Laura said.

Chapman continued undressing.

'She'll come home when she's ready,' his wife insisted, leaning against the door frame.

'Just like that?' he said flatly. 'Our daughter runs away from home and all you can say is "She'll come home when she's ready." What the fuck am I supposed to do, Laura? Sit here and wait for her to turn up? What if she

30

doesn't want to come back? And, in case you've forgotten, we don't know where she is, or who she's with. She might not even be in London now. She's been gone for seven days. She could be in another fucking country for all we know.'

'I doubt it. She didn't take her passport.'

'Very funny. How come you're so calm about all this? If you knew what happened to seventeen-year-old homeless girls on the streets of a big city you might not be so fucking smug.'

'I know what can happen,' she snapped. 'I read the papers.'

'Fuck the papers. I see it, day in and day out. Kids on their own. Nowhere to go. On the fucking game. Drugged up to the eyeballs. Being pimped out by Christ knows who.'

'She'll be with a friend somewhere.'

'Yeah, that little cunt who got her pregnant, no doubt.'

'If you hadn't threatened to make her have an abortion she might still be here.'

'Oh, right, it's my fault now.'

'We could have dealt with it, Joe.'

'We haven't been able to deal with her since she was fourteen.'

'We could have dealt with it as a family.'

'We haven't been a fucking family for a long time, Laura.'

She swallowed hard and looked at the carpet. Chapman ran appraising eyes over her and, for a moment, he wondered if she was going to cry. She looked more fragile than normal. Her skin was pale, her short blonde hair lank and lifeless. There were dark rings beneath her eyes.

'I'll be downstairs if you want me,' she said quietly, turning to leave the room.

31

Chapman took a couple of steps towards her. 'I can't leave her out there on her own,' he said, catching Laura by one thin arm.

She turned to face him. 'She won't think anything more of you for trying to track her down, Joe,' she said. 'And what if you do find her? What then? Drag her home? Make her admit she was wrong to run away? This has got nothing to do with Carla's welfare. This is all about your pride. That's why you wouldn't report her missing. There are people working for you who could have found her by now.'

'I can find her myself.'

'Then why haven't you?' she snapped.

'I will find her,' he said defiantly. 'I'll find her and bring her home.'

'I told you, she won't come even if you do find her. This has gone too far, Joe.'

Chapman's eyes narrowed slightly as he stared at his wife. Laura couldn't hold his gaze and shook loose of his grip.

'You know where she is,' he said flatly.

'She rang me two days ago on her mobile,' Laura admitted.

'Why the fuck didn't you tell me?'

'She only rang to say she was safe. She wouldn't tell me where she was staying. All I know is that she's still in London.'

He looked accusingly at her, unsure of what to say next.

'I know I should have told you,' she said quietly, tears welling up in her eyes.

'Fucking right you should,' he snarled. 'What kind of mother . . .' The words tailed off. He turned away and pulled open the wardrobe doors, taking out a leather jacket that he dropped on the bed.

'Carla asked me not to say anything to you,' Laura went on.

'I'm the one she's angry with, am I?' he rasped. 'That's why you didn't tell me she'd phoned.'

'Let her sort herself out, Joe.' She watched as he took off his trousers and pulled on jeans and a T-shirt. 'You're wasting your time,' she insisted as he fastened his trainers.

Chapman shot her an angry glance, then picked up his jacket and headed down the stairs, his feet thudding on the steps. Laura stepped out on to the landing, peering down into the hall in time to see the front door slam behind him.

Only then did she begin to cry.

8

Chapman rode the Central Line train as far as Tottenham Court Road. Each time the doors of the carriage slid open he looked up to inspect those boarding.

Yeah, because she's going to walk straight into your arms, isn't she? Just like in a fucking film.

The train from Bethnal Green had become busier with each stop. People heading into the West End for a night out. Those on their way to work a night shift. Some travelling further afield, to see relatives or friends perhaps?

Others looking for runaway daughters, maybe? Doubt it.

He glanced across the narrow aisle at two young men in their early twenties. They were smartly dressed and clean shaven, and their hair was immaculate. They were chatting and laughing.

Not a care in the fucking world by the look of it. *Little cunts.*

Another guy about his age was seated next to them. Big sod in a charcoal grey suit, white shirt and red tie reading a paperback. The man didn't even look up when the train stopped.

Probably travelled this route every day of his working life and would do until he retired. Knew every stop by heart.

What are you going home to? Empty house? Loving family?

Chapman unconsciously twisted his own silver wedding band two or three times.

A woman in a navy blue skirt and jacket had got on at Chancery Lane. Early thirties. Very attractive. She was holding a laptop in a leather carrying case. The earphones of an iPod were stuffed in her ears, running from her expensive handbag.

Professional type?

Chapman had offered her his seat but she'd merely shaken her head and looked towards the other end of the carriage.

Fuck you then. Stand there in your three-inch heels.

He could see that the skin on the back of both her heels was red.

You could have accepted the seat, couldn't you? Feminist bitch. Probably don't like doors being opened for you either.

The detective brushed past her as the train pulled into Tottenham Court Road.

He made his way towards the escalators and rode one to street level, glancing at those on the other side descending towards the platforms. He glanced at the tall, skinny guy strumming an acoustic guitar in one of the underground walkways, but he didn't throw him any loose change.

The DI left by the Oxford Street exit and stood there for a moment gazing across the street in the direction of the Virgin Megastore. It was still busy in there. The pavement was crowded, too, just as it was outside the McDonald's next door. There was a man lying motionless

35

on some cardboard next to the exit of the fast food outlet. Chapman glanced perfunctorily at him before turning away.

He had his route worked out in his head, just as on every other night. He knew where to go. He'd already decided on the places he had to visit. Digging his hands in the pockets of his jacket, he turned the corner and began to walk down Charing Cross Road.

To his left, the huge concrete and glass edifice of Centre Point thrust upwards towards a cloudy and overcast sky.

Rain might be a good thing. It forces people inside. Off the streets.

There was a queue of people crowding into the Astoria, all in their teens and twenties, it seemed to the detective, and all apparently dressed in jeans, leather jackets and various band T-shirts.

MEGADETH and Guests, the plastic lettering over the door proclaimed.

Could Carla be in there?

Was it her type of music?

You don't even know, do you?

He ducked right, glancing at the faces in the queue as he headed into Soho Square, and then started walking down Greek Street.

He looked at his watch.

9.03 p.m.

Another five minutes and he'd make his first stop.

Lipstick Encounters was on Peter Street, sandwiched
between a Korean restaurant and a small hardware store.

Chapman stepped over a couple of split bin bags that
had been dumped in the shop doorway and walked up
to the entrance of the club.

It was like any of the dozen or so other clip joints in
Soho, gaudily painted in various unmatched pastel shades
in a colour scheme that assaulted rather than attracted
the eye of passers-by. On either side of its arched entryway
there were menus in peeling, gold-painted frames which
showed that a glass of orange juice would cost fifteen
pounds. Bottles of champagne could run to more than
a hundred pounds. The glass over one of the two frames
had been cracked and there were pieces of it lying on
the pavement.

A flashing yellow neon sign above the entrance boasted:
Erotic Girls

Chapman stepped inside the doorway.

A tall, dark-haired girl in her early twenties stood
sentinel there. She was dressed in an impossibly short
skirt and teetered on heels so high they looked as if

they'd been designed by a steeplejack. When she saw Chapman she hurriedly took the cigarette she'd been smoking from her mouth and rolled her eyes.

'Hi, Monica,' the detective said flatly. 'How's business?'

She rolled her eyes again and shrugged.

'Anyone in?' he wanted to know, nodding towards the club beyond.

'No. Well, only two,' she told him, her voice heavy with an accent he recognised as east European. Chapman noticed that she had a large spot on her left cheek which she'd tried unsuccessfully to cover up with foundation.

'Do you want to see Paul?' she asked. 'He is in his office upstairs.'

'You might be able to help me,' Chapman said, digging in his back pocket. He pulled out a photograph and pushed it towards Monica. 'Have you seen this girl in the last few days?'

Monica glanced quickly at the photo and shook her head.

'Have a better look,' Chapman insisted. 'Otherwise I might decide to come back tomorrow and check your work permit and your passport.'

'Why should I see her?' Monica protested.

'Has Paul taken on any new girls in the past week?' the detective wanted to know, still holding the photo before Monica.

'He wouldn't tell me if he did.' She took a drag on her cigarette then looked Chapman up and down appraisingly, her gaze settling on his trainers. 'You are not on duty?'

'No.'

'Then why are you here now asking questions?'

'Have you seen the girl or not?'

Monica shook her head again. 'Why you ask me? Why not ask girls at other clubs round here?'

'Because not all the other clubs round here take in runaways and employ them.' He pulled the photo away but still held it in his hand. 'Runaways. Illegal immigrants. Girls with drug habits. Paul specialises in those, doesn't he?'

'He helped me,' she said quietly.

'By giving you a flat no bigger than a fucking shoebox to live in and share with two other girls?' he said challengingly. 'By forcing you to strip every night and paying you a hundred quid a week? Is that how he helped you, Monica? Or did he help you into prostitution? Seven days a week with your legs spread or he sends you back to where you came from. Has he helped this girl the same way?'

Monica took a drag on her cigarette, her hand shaking slightly. 'I told you, I not know her,' she said. 'Who is she? She is a pretty girl.'

Chapman nodded. 'Yeah, she is. Her name's Carla. She's someone I know.' He wrote quickly on the back of the picture. 'If you see her you ring me on either of those numbers.'

Monica nodded, and Chapman turned to walk away.

'Don't you want to speak to the other girls?' she asked, hooking a thumb over her shoulder towards the club entrance.

'Would it be worth it?'

She shook her head.

'Tell Paul I was here,' he said, and walked out of the door.

Monica waited a second then screwed up the picture and dropped it, kicking it into the street. A gust of wind blew it into the gutter.

39

Empire

The house stood on a slight rise in 226 acres of Buckinghamshire countryside.

The original building dated back as far as the seventeenth century but successive owners had added rooms, renovated, redecorated and modernised until the entire edifice now resembled the shape of an E, two wings having been added by the current owner no more than eight years ago.

In front of the house there was a huge maze. Privet hedges, immaculately cut, formed the walls of the puzzle. At its centre, only reachable by the gravel paths that cut through the hedges, there was an open area complete with wooden benches for anyone who cared to make the tortuous trek to reach it.

To the east and west of the house, past carefully trimmed expanses of lawn, there were paddocks where horses had once run free. The paddocks and the stables within had been unused for more than a year now.

To the rear of the house was a flower garden, more lawn and some copses of trees. Even an orchard.

The house itself was on three levels. Sitting rooms, library, kitchen, games room and other reception rooms were on the ground floor, bedrooms and bathrooms on the first. More bedrooms, an office and some servants' quarters made up the second floor.

The roof of the east wing was accessible from a small staircase on the second floor. Anyone who wished could, in the daylight, walk out and see over virtually the whole of the estate.

The house was reached via a pair of metal gates leading off from a narrow country lane. After entering a six-digit code in the keypad next to this entrance, visitors gained access to a driveway that snaked through well-kept and, in places, heavily wooded grounds for just under half a mile before the building itself was visible. The entire estate was enclosed within a twelve-foot-high wall topped with razor wire and broken glass.

The dark blue Transit van that now approached the metal gates slowed down to allow the passenger out. As the driver kept the engine idling, the man punched in the required code and the gates swung open, allowing the Transit access. The passenger swung himself back into the cab as the driver pulled away.

The van sped along the driveway, the man behind the wheel flicking his headlights to full beam, so total was the darkness on either side of the drive this far from the house. Only when the building itself became visible did he dip them again.

He didn't park in front of the house but aimed instead for what looked like little more than a dirt track close to one of the disused paddocks. The Transit bumped over the ruts in the track, swallowed up once again by the night.

Hidden by a thick hedge, a fox watched silently as the vehicle passed. The animal waited a second before continuing with its nocturnal business.

10

Chapman took a sip from his mug of tea, sat back on the seat and fixed his eyes on the café entrance.

From where he sat, he could see not only everyone who entered the eatery but also across the street towards the front of King's Cross station.

Inside the café, three of the tables were occupied. Two youths in their teens sat talking quietly over hamburgers and fizzy drinks. Both, the detective noticed, had grubby rucksacks propped on the seats beside them.

Just arrived into the station? Just about to leave on one of its trains?

Close by them, two other youths were playing the fruit machine near the main door. They were feeding coins into it, cheering when they won something and banging hard on the machine when they didn't. More than once the owner of the café looked warily towards the duo. He even took a step from behind the counter when one of the lads kicked the fruit machine in irritation.

At another table a man in his fifties sat alone, a copy of the *Standard* spread out on the table before him. He was running his index finger along the lines of print on one particular page, occasionally stopping to scribble in the margin with the pen he held.

Studying form? Looking for a job vacancy? Somewhere to live?

The man was dressed in a pair of faded jeans and a sweatshirt that looked in need of a wash. He had no laces in his trainers, Chapman noticed.

However, as the detective sipped at his tea, it was the other table that interested him most.

It was occupied by two girls in their teens and they were in conversation with a youth in his early twenties. Chapman had only caught snatches of their conversation, the odd sentence here and there, but he was sure he recognised the youth. Half-caste. Tall and thin. He wore a Burberry cap and a faded leather jacket. His mobile phone was lying on the table close to him. It had rung a couple of times during his conversation with the girls and he'd held up a hand to silence them as he spoke, smiling and nodding.

Chapman finished his tea, got to his feet and walked across to the table. He slid into the seat next to the youth, almost knocking his mug of coffee over in the process.

'Hey, what the fuck, man?' the lad said, looking angrily at the detective. 'What you doing?'

'I want to talk,' Chapman told him.

'I don't fucking know you, man,' the youth said. 'Fuck off.'

'Yeah, fuck off, Grandad,' said the older of the two girls in a broad Yorkshire accent.

'Seeing as I'm off duty,' Chapman began, leaning towards the older girl, 'I won't arrest you for soliciting, right? Even though I know that's what you've spent most of tonight doing. You look at this photo, tell me if you've

44

seen this girl and you can walk out of here now.' He reached into his inside pocket.

'You ain't a copper,' the girl said.

'You want to try me, you little slag?' Chapman rasped. 'Now look at the fucking picture.' He pushed another copy of the shot of his daughter towards her. 'Look at it. Have you seen her before?'

Both girls inspected the photo and shook their heads.

'Right, now fuck off,' Chapman said, retrieving the picture.

The girls hesitated, looking at the youth as if awaiting permission.

'I said go now,' the detective repeated. 'Unless you want to spend the night in the cells.'

They both got hurriedly to their feet and made for the door of the café, disappearing into the stream of pedestrians beyond.

'Now, what about you?' Chapman said, turning to face the youth. 'Have you seen her?' He pushed the photo across the Formica-topped table towards the lad.

'I ain't saying nothing to you, man,' the youth snarled. 'If you want to arrest me then fucking do it. My lawyer will be here as soon as I ring him.' He reached for his mobile phone but Chapman slammed his hand down over it first.

'Your lawyer?' The detective smiled. 'You'd be lucky if you could get a fucking plumber to come out if you called, you little prick. I know who you are. Your name's Rio Richardson and you're too far down the food chain to start shooting your mouth off at me. Now look at the fucking photo and tell me if you've seen that girl.'

He picked up the youth's mobile phone and cradled it in the palm of his hand, inspecting it. It was brand new. The latest model. State of the art. 'How much did this cost you, Rio? Two, three hundred?'

'I thought you wanted to know about the girl, not about my fucking phone,' the youth protested.

'I do. Have you seen her round here recently?'

'No, but I can get you a girl like that if you want.'

'Yeah, I bet you could,' Chapman said through clenched teeth. He pulled a pen from his inside pocket and wrote two phone numbers on the back of the picture. 'If you see her, you call me, right? Her name's Carla.' He leaned menacingly towards the youth, who slunk down in his seat. 'If I don't hear from you in two days I'll come looking for you. And I'll find you, too.'

'If I see her I'll fucking call you, man.'

Chapman got to his feet and turned to look at the youth. 'Good,' he said. 'When you do, you'd better use a payphone.'

He dropped the youth's mobile phone into his coffee.

'You fucking cunt,' the younger man wailed, dipping his fingers into the hot liquid in a frantic attempt to retrieve the Nokia. He knocked over the mug in his desperation, the brown fluid pouring out over the table top, some of it spilling on to his legs.

Chapman headed for the door and out into the night.

Preparation

He pulled the length of rubber tubing tightly round the top of his emaciated arm.

Working quickly with hands that had performed the same routine many times before, the youth tapped the crook of his left arm with the first two fingers of his right hand. He watched as the vein pulsed a little. Not as much as it should have done, perhaps, and he tapped it again, smiling when he saw it filling, swelling beneath the skin like a pulsing worm.

The needle was ready. The point had been immersed in the bubbling liquid, the fluid sucked up into the barrel.

He reached for the syringe and gripped it in his right hand, steadying it between his middle and fore fingers while his thumb settled over the plunger.

The others watched hungrily, knowing their turn would come.

The youth was the oldest of the group. Twenty-two. He was dressed in black jeans, heavy boots and a grey fleece. Almost by way of deference to his seniority, he was allowed access to the needle before the others.

He steadied the point of the needle over his skin for

a second then pushed the sharpened steel through his flesh and into the pulsing blood vessel beneath.

The vein punctured as the needle pierced it but the rubber tubing wound so tightly round the top of his arm prevented it from deflating. He pushed the needle deeper, pressing the plunger, ensuring that every last drop of the heroin was pumped into his system. Then he pulled the hypodermic free, ignoring the tiny spurt of blood that wept from the fresh hole. He discarded the needle and hastily undid the tourniquet.

Within seconds, the familiar rush swept through him.

Christ, that felt good.

He felt as if his head was swelling and he exhaled deeply, his eyes closed.

The next youth reached for the needle.

The others waited their turn.

11

As Chapman walked the short distance from Bethnal Green tube to his house he dug one hand in the pocket of his jacket.

His hand closed over his mobile phone.

Almost unconsciously he flipped it open, scrolling through the address book. *Maggie–mobile* was illuminated.

For precious seconds he slowed his pace, gazing at the name glowing before him.

He wanted to talk to her. Wanted to tell her that his search for his daughter had again been fruitless.

You just want to talk to her, don't you? It doesn't matter what you say. You just want to hear her voice.

But he knew she didn't want to hear his. Why should she? She was tucked up in bed with her new bloke by this time, wasn't she? She wouldn't want to talk now. Why should she give a fuck anyway?

He snapped the phone shut and dropped it back into his pocket.

This is the way things are now. Get used to it.

Chapman walked up to his front door and selected his key, letting himself in as quietly as he could. There were no lights on anywhere inside the house. Laura must be in bed, he assumed.

He closed and locked the front door behind him and peered briefly into the living room.

Empty.

So was the kitchen.

Chapman trudged slowly upstairs, glancing at his watch on the way.

12.34 a.m.

The stairs creaked loudly under his weight and so too did the landing as he crossed it to their bedroom. He pushed open the door and looked in.

Laura was asleep. He could hear her breathing slowly and evenly. He hesitated on the threshold for a moment, then backed out and headed towards the room opposite.

The door stuck slightly as he opened it but he pressed his shoulder to the wood and it swung back enough to allow him access. He flicked on the light and looked around.

The walls were painted lilac. They had been for the last six years. Having her room decorated had been Carla's reward for doing so well in her eleven plus. He could still remember her smiling face when she'd announced her results. Her grade had ensured her a place at the local grammar school and, they all thought, a bright future.

How fucking wrong could you be?

He looked round at the walls of the room, festooned with posters. Pop stars and celebrities stared blankly back at him. On the pouffe beside her bed there were copies of *OK* and *Hello!* magazines.

There was make-up on a small dressing table. Clothes hanging up on the door of her wardrobe. The stuffed cuddly monkey and dog that sat on her pillow looked curiously incongruous beneath a poster of Eminem. CDs and DVDs vied for space on a bookshelf. He saw more make-up too. On a noticeboard next to the bookcase the stubs of gig tickets had been pinned in place with tacks.

Chapman stood in the doorway for a moment longer then backed out of the room, flicking off the light again.

He looked towards his own bedroom, and in the quiet of the night he could still hear Laura breathing as she slept.

The detective headed for the spare room. He'd sleep in there tonight.

Performance

The tables were creaking under the weight of the weapons.

Six wooden trestle tables, each one eight feet long, had been arranged end to end.

Upon them lay knives that had been honed to razor sharpness. Baseball bats, some with nails driven through their heavy ends. Hatchets, the cutting edges sharpened until they could split bone effortlessly, lying alongside wickedly curved sickles. Knuckledusters glinting in the dull light. Hammers, ranging in size from those that could be held easily in one hand to sledgehammers that would need to be hefted by a powerful pair of arms.

There were chisels. Cut-throat razors. Machetes. Screwdrivers. Darts.

And then there were the guns.

Revolvers and automatics. Sawn-off shotguns.

Ammunition was on the last table in open boxes waiting to be collected.

Somewhere in the distance, the sound of furiously barking dogs could be heard.

It was time.

12

'There's a new snuff movie on that site.'

DS Maggie Grant stood in the doorway of Chapman's office, watching as the detective got immediately to his feet.

'Bradley's downloaded it,' she continued. 'He's got it ready to go on his computer downstairs.'

They both headed briskly down the corridor, Maggie forced to increase her speed to keep up with her superior.

'When was it posted?' Chapman asked.

'In the last four hours as far as we know.'

'How many victims?' the DI enquired, hitting the call button on the lift.

'One obvious one, as usual. But Bradley thinks there could be two others as well this time.'

The lift doors slid open and they both stepped inside. Chapman jabbed the appropriate button and the lift began to descend.

'Same set-up as the other four?' he asked.

'All the participants are in masks,' Maggie said, nodding. 'The settings look the same, too.'

'Is Bradley convinced all the deaths are real?'

'The one at the end looks pretty conclusive, Joe.'

'We'll see,' Chapman muttered as the lift bumped to a halt. He and Maggie walked out and along another corridor to the door they sought. Chapman pushed it open and stepped inside. Seated at the desk were DS Michael Bradley and DS James Mackenzie.

Both men looked round expectantly as Chapman walked in.

'Let's see it,' the DI said, seating himself.

Bradley pressed the required key and the screen lit up with images.

'Same alleyway as the others have started in,' Chapman muttered, leaning forward in his seat.

The figure on screen, clad in a white mask and what looked like overalls, moved slowly down a dark, narrow alley, occasionally feeling his way along the brick walls the visibility was so poor. He emerged in a deserted street littered with abandoned cars.

'No number plates on any of the vehicles again,' said Maggie, her attention riveted to the screen.

The masked figure ducked down behind a car with its back wheels missing, waited a moment, then sprinted across the open street towards what looked like the entrance to a loading bay. There were several discarded shopping trolleys close to the stone steps that led down into the bay itself. The figure onscreen hurried down the steps.

'What's that?' Mackenzie mused, getting out of his seat and moving closer to the screen. He was pointing to a painted red arrow that had been splattered on the wall close to the entrance to the loading bay.

'They're obviously told which direction to go,' Chapman said. 'We've seen those arrows in the other films too.'

'And he keeps touching his right ear,' Maggie added. 'They've done that in the other films too. Perhaps it means something.'

'Perhaps he can hear the others coming,' Mackenzie offered, seating himself once more.

More figures suddenly appeared on the screen. Also masked, they hurtled out of the right-hand side of the frame and began to chase the solitary man.

Chapman could see that two carried knives. He could also make out the unmistakable outline of a claw hammer in the fist of another. Another of the group was carrying what looked like a javelin.

Indeed, as the detectives watched, he flung the shaft at the fleeing figure.

The pointed missile hurtled through the air and thudded into the left shoulder of the running man. It stuck in the flesh and muscle for a moment, then fell away. The man screamed in agony.

'You still think it's special effects?' Bradley said, a note of disdain in his voice.

Chapman didn't speak. He merely continued to look at the screen, where the first man was now clambering over a wall. He dropped down on the other side, landing on a pile of cardboard boxes and other refuse. The heap of rubbish broke his fall and, despite the wound in his shoulder, he leapt to his feet and ran across a small court-yard towards some more stone steps.

'Check for any labels on those boxes,' Chapman said. 'There might be addresses on them, something we can pin down the location with.'

On screen, the running man crashed through a rotten wooden door at the top of the steps and blundered into a darkened room beyond. He slumped in the deep shadows in one corner and sat there gasping for breath.

Outside in the courtyard, five or six of his pursuers were already searching the overflowing skips that skirted the concrete area, apparently desperate to find the fugitive. Others moved on towards an alleyway that opened out into a deserted street.

'Stop the film,' Chapman said suddenly, getting to his feet.

Bradley hit the pause button.

'It didn't rain in London last night, did it?' the DI asked.

'We haven't had a drop of rain for over a week,' Maggie told him.

'Then this wasn't shot in London,' Chapman said. 'Look, the street's wet. You can see the puddles.' He pointed at the screen. Street lights were indeed reflecting in the small pools of water on the tarmac. 'Check and see which parts of the country had rain last night.'

Mackenzie scribbled something on a notepad.

Bradley started the film running once again.

The next shot showed the fugitive still alone in the darkened room. Moving stiffly because of the wound in his shoulder, he reached around on the dusty floor, his hand closing on a house brick. He hefted it before him, apparently satisfied with the weight.

He'd barely had time to appreciate his newly found weapon when the door of the room inched open a fraction.

One of his pursuers edged slowly into the room, the floorboards creaking beneath his weight. He was carrying a large double-edged knife. He squinted into the darkness, moving closer to the centre of the room, and then, as the detectives watched, he stuffed the knife into his belt, grunted, unzipped his flies and began urinating.

Bradley grinned.

The fugitive, realising that his pursuer's back was to him, took his chance. He advanced quickly towards the urinating man and struck him with immense force on the back of the head.

The man went down heavily, the first blow having rendered him unconscious.

The fugitive struck him three more times, the final blow caving in the skull. Blood and brain matter sprayed up from the gaping wound, some of it splattering the fugitive.

'He's dead,' Mackenzie said with an air of finality. 'You can see where he's shit himself.' He indicated the dark stain on the rear of the pursuer's jeans.

'So is this officially a snuff movie now?' Bradley wanted to know, looking at Chapman.

The DI ignored the question, watching instead as the fugitive rolled the body over and pulled the knife from the belt. He gripped it in his fist for a moment and then left the room, descending the stone steps cautiously before pausing at the bottom. The courtyard was empty. He touched his right ear, hesitated a second, then turned to his left.

The narrow alley the detectives had seen before led him into the empty street. He hesitated by a doorway, then pushed it open and went through into a corridor lit by one unshaded bulb hanging from the ceiling on bare wire. The corridor turned at right angles and he followed it round until he came to more steps. He climbed those and emerged on what appeared to be the landing of a house. There were large holes in each of the walls. Up ahead of him there was a light and he moved towards it.

'How does he know which way to go?' Maggie wondered. 'We haven't seen any more of those direction arrows.'

57

'Could he have been there before?' Mackenzie offered.

On screen, the fugitive paused, looking down about ten feet into a public toilet. It seemed to be empty. He waited a moment, then dropped down on to the cold white tiles. The sound of footsteps close by sent him spinning round in panic.

'He needs to find some cover,' Chapman said. 'It's too bright in there.'

The footsteps drew nearer.

The fugitive moved to his left, towards a row of cubicles. He ducked inside the nearest one, the knife gripped in his fist.

One of his pursuers moved into view.

He was carrying an axe.

He moved towards the first of the cubicle doors and pushed it open using the axe blade.

Three cubicles away, the fugitive gripped his knife and waited.

13

Chapman watched the screen impassively as the pursuer checked the second cubicle and found it empty.

'Knife against axe,' Bradley mused. 'My money's on the axe.'

'Unless the guy with the knife can take the other geezer by surprise,' Mackenzie said, sitting forward in his seat.

'For Christ's sake, you'll be taking bets on it next,' Maggie said disapprovingly.

'Just shut up, all of you,' Chapman hissed, eyes still fixed on the screen.

The pursuer was about to look into the next cubicle. He pushed the door with his foot, satisfied when it swung open to reveal just the lavatory within.

He moved to the fourth one.

The fugitive struck quickly and without warning.

As soon as the fourth door was pushed open, he propelled himself from inside the cubicle, rushing at his pursuer, slamming into him.

Both men crashed to the ground, the impact knocking the axe from the pursuer's hand. It skittered across the tiled floor into the trough beneath the urinals.

Its owner rolled over, trying to reach it, but the fugitive reacted faster, pinning the man with his weight and swinging the knife round in a wide arc.

He drove it into the pursuer's left shoulder, tore it free again and struck at the man's head. The point of the blade dug easily into the base of the skull and the fugitive struck again, burying the double-edged metal in the flesh there and using both hands to wrench it upwards. It split two of the pursuer's vertebrae and severed the spinal cord. The man's body jerked uncontrollably for a second then lay still in the middle of a widening pool of blood.

The fugitive rolled off, pulling the knife free with one hand and reaching for the dropped axe with the other. The knife he pushed into his belt. Gasping for breath, he staggered to his feet, anxious to be away from the dead body but aware also that there were others still searching for him. Some of them were ahead of him.

He moved quickly out of the toilet and found himself in what looked like a hallway. There was a flight of steps leading upwards and he took them, stopping once to get his breath.

He emerged moments later on to another deserted street.

'What the fuck is going on here?' Chapman said under his breath. 'Look at the street. The road.'

The other detectives squinted at the scene before them.

'The fucking tarmac's bone dry,' Chapman pointed out. 'So is the pavement.'

Maggie peered more closely at the screen.

'He can't have gone more than a hundred yards,' she said, a note of bewilderment in her voice.

'So we're looking for a location where it rains in one fucking street while the next one stays bone dry,' Chapman snapped. He shook his head. 'Those streets can't be more than a hundred yards apart. It doesn't make sense.'

On screen, the fugitive was approaching an abandoned house.

The windows had been boarded up and the front door had been removed. He entered the building warily, then, satisfied that he hadn't been seen, moved to his left, down a flight of steps. He was faced by a metal gate.

It was padlocked.

He glanced behind him, presumably wondering if his pursuers were close by.

Again he looked at the padlock. Then, after a moment's hesitation, he brought the axe down hard on it.

'They'll hear him,' Maggie said.

'What choice has he got?' Bradley asked. 'By the look of it, there's no other way off that street.'

The fugitive struck the padlock three times before it finally shattered. He tugged the chain away and pushed the metal door, advancing into another subterranean room lit only by a single unshaded bulb.

Beyond it was a long corridor. There was light at the far end.

The fugitive hesitated, looking behind him.

'He can't go back,' Maggie said. 'The ones following will get him.'

He moved into the corridor, sticking to the shadows, his body pressed against one wall. As he walked, he pulled the knife from his belt and held that in his other hand.

He was halfway along it when a figure appeared at the far end.

The fugitive froze.

For interminable seconds the distant figure remained silhouetted against the light at the end of the corridor. Then he pointed down the darkened walkway with the knife he held.

Immediately, half a dozen other figures joined him in the corridor.

They all made for the fugitive, who bolted back towards the subterranean room from which he'd come. Then he tripped on some fallen roof beams and they were on him like hounds on a fox.

Knives, machetes and crowbars flailed, all striking madly at the downed man, puncturing, cutting and shattering bones, flesh and muscle. Blood burst from his wounds and he struck out helplessly as they swarmed around him.

The fugitive struck one of his attackers on the knee with the axe, a final defiant gesture that split the man's patella and shattered the upper part of his shin bone, but it was a futile act. The doomed man rolled despairingly over on to his back as more and more blows rained down upon him.

A machete split open overalls and flesh to expose his intestines.

Entrails seemed to boil up out of the massive cut and the dying man thrust his hands into the bloody mass as if trying to push it back inside himself.

Another blow from a crowbar shattered his nose and loosened his mask. Portions of it came away along with pieces of bone.

'Wait a minute,' Chapman snapped, moving closer to the screen. 'Freeze it. Bradley did as he was instructed.

The DI could see a tattoo on the dying man's neck, exposed as part of the mask was torn away.

'This one's real,' he announced flatly.

'The first four were fakes but you think this one's genuine?' Bradly said disdainfully.

'How can you be sure, Joe?' Maggie asked.

'I recognise the tattoo on that guy's neck,' Chapman said quietly. 'I know the victim.'

14

'Craig Gibson. I arrested him three years ago for assault.'
Chapman was still staring at the frozen film.
'Enlarge that frame,' he said to Bradley, who nodded
and obeyed. 'Zoom in on the tattoo.'
'Assault on who?' Maggie wanted to know.
'His missus,' Chapman told her. 'He'd just done a two
stretch for GBH. She got pregnant while he was inside.
One of his old mates. He left the Scrubs and, first day
out, he broke her jaw in two places and drove a car into
the geezer who knocked her up.'
'Welcome home,' Mackenzie intoned, looking at the
maximised image on the screen.
'And you're sure it's him?' Maggie pressed, also
inspecting the enlarged frame.
'You can read the tattoo,' Chapman said, tracing the
outline of the letters with one index finger. *Don't tread
on me.* He nodded. 'That's Gibson. No question.'
'So he was the only person who ever had that tattoo?'
Bradley said scathingly.
'It's him,' Chapman snapped, rounding on the DS. 'I'd
bet my fucking life on it.'

'How long's he been out this time?' Maggie asked.

'About six months. He got time off for good behaviour.'

'It doesn't look like it's done him much good,' Bradley commented.

'Right,' Chapman said. 'I want to know Gibson's whereabouts during the time leading up to his death. Where he was going. Who he talked to. Everything he was doing.'

'Why are you suddenly convinced that Gibson's death is real but the other four aren't?' Bradley asked. 'Just because you arrested him doesn't make this any more credible as a snuff movie, does it?'

'It does because now we've got a face and a name and when we've got those we can find a motive,' Chapman insisted. 'Re-check the other four dead men too. Go back through those fucking films frame by frame and check everything. Gibson might be the key to all this.'

'How?' Bradley demanded.

'That's what we're going to find out, dummy,' Chapman snapped.

Bradley glared at him for a second. 'What if there's no link?' he said.

'Find one,' Chapman told him, heading for the door.

'Where are you going?' Maggie asked.

'I'm going to talk to Gibson's missus,' the DI told her. 'See what she can tell us. Maggie, you check with Wandsworth – that's where he did his last stretch – see if he made any enemies while he was inside. Bradley, you and Mackenzie go over this film and the others again. I want something to go on when I get back.'

'We haven't even been able to find the source of the website yet and you want details on the other victims?' Bradley exclaimed.

'I told you, go through the films again. Look at them more closely.'

'Fuck me,' Bradley grunted. 'We've already looked at them a hundred times.'

'Well look again,' Chapman rasped.

He slammed the office door behind him as he left, heading towards the lift that would take him to the ground floor. He glanced at his watch.

The drive to Clapham shouldn't take more than twenty minutes.

He hoped Mrs Gibson would be in.

15

Anthony Seymour could smell the delicate scent of the dahlias he held as he stood at the graveside.

He waited a moment then carefully knelt, extending the small bouquet towards the marble headstone.

He heard the joint of his left knee crack loudly as he lowered himself. The grass around the grave was still a little damp after the shower that had fallen early that morning but Seymour ignored the fact that moisture was seeping through the material of his trousers.

A breeze rustled the cellophane around the dahlias and Seymour shivered involuntarily, his head still bowed reverentially. The grave itself was inside a larger plot of land enclosed by a low, wooden fence, which was entered via a gate. In the corners small topiary bushes, each one immaculately tended, stood sentinel. There wasn't another grave within fifty feet of the plot in any direction. Seymour had insisted on that when he'd purchased it. In time, the topiary bushes would grow larger until they formed a barrier around the plot, hiding it from prying eyes.

Privacy was important to Anthony Seymour. It always

had been. Fortunately, it was a commodity that could be bought. He'd found, over the years, that with the kind of fortune he possessed, there was very little that couldn't be.

He adjusted his position at the graveside, removing some leaves from the marble plinth and pushing them into the plastic bag he had withdrawn from his jacket pocket. They would be disposed of on the way out of the cemetery.

Pauline Seymour, the inscription on the gravestone read. *Beloved Wife and Mother. At peace in the arms of angels.*

He glanced at her birth and death dates and shook his head.

She'd been fifty-two when she died, seven years younger than he was now.

Seymour felt he wanted to say something but he couldn't find the words. He merely stared at the gravestone as if hoping that his thoughts could somehow penetrate the shining black marble.

He got to his feet, kissed the tips of his index and middle fingers and pressed them to the cold stone, murmuring something under his breath.

It was just over eighteen months since her death but the memories of that terrible time were still so vivid in his mind that it only seemed like yesterday. He could remember every sight, sound and smell. It was carved on his soul. Scar tissue on his being.

Seymour turned towards the gate in the wooden fence and walked out of the plot, his slow deliberate steps taking him towards the tarmac driveway that ran through the cemetery. The Rolls-Royce was parked there waiting, the uniformed driver standing beside the rear door holding it open for him. He thanked the man and climbed in as some watery sunlight glinted off the tinted windows.

'You could send somebody to put flowers on her grave,' another voice in the back of the car told him. 'You don't have to come yourself.'

Seymour eyed the source of the comment blankly.

Stella Crane was twenty-six. Shoulder-length straight blonde hair. Bone structure a supermodel would have killed for and a stunning figure encased in a navy Dolce and Gabbana two-piece. She crossed her slender legs and sniffed loudly.

Seymour pointed to her left nostril.

There were still some grains of cocaine visible on her flawless skin.

Stella brushed them away with one finger.

'Show a little respect,' Seymour said, gazing out of the window at his wife's grave. 'If you want to take that stuff then don't do it here.'

She eyed him warily for a second then nodded. 'I'm sorry,' she told him quietly.

Seymour didn't answer.

The car pulled away.

16

Chapman slumped wearily behind the steering wheel of his car and glanced at the house he'd just left.

The sound of trains entering and leaving Clapham Junction station filled the air. The house was within spitting distance of one of its entrances. A goods yard was clearly visible off to his right. Chapman wondered how anyone round here ever managed to sleep with the constant coming and going of trains day and night.

The detective pulled his mobile from his jacket pocket, punched in the number he wanted and waited.

He recognised the voice that finally answered.

'Maggie, it's me,' he said. 'I spoke to Gibson's wife. She says she hasn't seen him for over a week. He moved back in with her after he got out of the Scrubs.'

'Did you tell her he was dead?' Maggie asked.

'No. It was difficult enough getting her to talk anyway; if she thinks he's dead then she'll shut down completely. I left her my number, told her to phone if she hears anything. Who he was working with. Whether any of his old firm might have wanted him dead. That sort of shit.' He took a drag on his cigarette. 'What about you? Anything worth telling me?'

'We think we've identified the victim from the second film,' she said.

'Who is he?'

'Matthew Webber. Thirty-four years old. He went missing nearly a fortnight ago.'

'Who identified him?'

'A desk sergeant from Lewisham. We e-mailed stills of the victims to all the nicks in the country. This guy is convinced that Webber's the second victim.'

'How can he be so sure?'

'It's his brother. Webber's the black sheep of the family apparently. He's been in and out of prison all his life. Not something you'd want to broadcast if you're on the force, is it? He said that Webber had a portion of one finger missing from his left hand. He saw that in the picture we sent, and got in touch.'

'So Webber had form? What kind of jobs?'

'Burglary. Car theft. Small-time stuff.'

'But he was a villain. Just like Gibson. That could be a link. Check out anyone with form who's gone missing in the past month.'

'You think all the victims are villains?'

'It's possible. This might be the break we've been looking for.'

'Are you coming back to the Yard now?'

'I'll be there in an hour or so. I want something by the time I get back, Maggie. Get Bradley to run it through the computer.'

'He's checking the other films.'

'As long as he's doing something.'

He terminated the call, started the car and guided

it towards the end of the road, waiting at the junction until passing traffic permitted him to swing out.

He was about to turn when he saw the girl.

She was walking briskly in the direction of Clapham Junction station. Short blonde hair that the dye was beginning to wash out of. Tight jeans. A black fleece. Grubby trainers.

'Carla,' he murmured under his breath.

He slammed on the brakes, left the engine running and jumped out of the car, dashing into the middle of the road.

'Carla,' he called after her.

The girl didn't look at him, but merely kept walking.

Chapman hesitated a moment then set off after her. 'Carla,' he shouted again and, this time, the girl glanced briefly over her shoulder and saw him hurrying after her.

She began to run.

'Wait,' Chapman called, increasing his own pace.

He dodged to his left and ran on to the pavement, pushing past some pedestrians in his haste to reach the girl. By now she was hurtling along the street, anxious only to put as much distance between herself and Chapman as possible. She turned a corner and he rushed after her.

'Wait,' he bellowed.

She ran on.

He caught her thirty yards further on, grabbing at her shoulder, spinning her round to face him.

'Carla,' he panted.

The girl looked at his sweat-slicked face with a combination of apprehension and bewilderment. 'What are you doing?' she demanded, taking a step away from him.

'I'm sorry,' he said breathlessly. 'I thought you were someone else.'

She continued to back away from him. 'Fucking weirdo,' she hissed.

'I'm sorry,' he said again, watching her as she turned and hurried away.

'What's your game, mate?' a passing motorist called angrily.

Chapman didn't answer. He stood on the pavement, aware of the stares of passers-by, conscious of his heart hammering inside his chest.

Get a grip. So, she looked like Carla. Thousands of girls in London look like that. Do you really think it's going to be that easy to find her? No chance.

He nodded to himself, then turned and headed slowly back to his car.

17

Anthony Seymour dug his slender fingers into the tub of food and scooped out some more of the dried pellets. He held them for a second longer then threw them into the pond, watching the large koi carp jostling in the water as they fed.

Seymour dropped two more pellets close to a large white fish with red markings and smiled as it devoured them. The fish was his favourite and, at such a stupendous size, it was also the most expensive of the lot.

He stood up, brushing his hands together to remove the flecks of dried food. The midday sunshine was bright and it sparkled pleasingly on the surface of the large pond, warming the back of Seymour's neck as he turned away from the water and headed towards the entrance of the maze.

Within the confines of the privet hedges he strolled slowly, his feet crunching gravel as he walked. He knew exactly which route would take him to the centre of the puzzle and he moved faultlessly to left or right, avoiding the dead ends that so maddened other visitors. Not that many others entered the maze any more.

Very few people even visited the house, let alone enjoyed the vagaries of the grounds. But that was the way Seymour wanted it. He didn't want people around him. Not any more.

When he reached the centre of the maze he seated himself on one of the wooden benches there and pulled his mobile phone from a pocket of his trousers. He found the number he wanted and called it.

A familiar voice answered.

'I need another five units,' he said flatly. 'As soon as possible.'

The voice at the other end asked him if the end of the week was acceptable.

'Just take care of it,' Seymour told the voice. 'And make sure the quality is better than last time.'

The voice apologised.

'I'll contact you again when I need to,' Seymour snapped and terminated the call. He slid the phone back into his pocket and stretched his legs out in front of him, head tilted back to enjoy the sunshine.

He closed his eyes for a moment but snapped them open again when he heard footsteps on the gravel path. He looked up to see who had managed to join him in the centre of the maze.

There was no one there.

'Anthony.'

He heard his name being called from the other side of one of the high privet hedges.

'What do you want, Stella?' he called back.

'I wanted to talk to you,' she answered. 'I tried to find you but I got lost in here.'

'That's the idea,' he told her, a slight smile touching his lips.

'How do I reach you?' she persisted.

Seymour looked in the direction of her voice but didn't get to his feet.

'Take the path to your left, then turn right and then right again,' he instructed, sighing wearily.

He closed his eyes once more, listening to her footfalls on the pathway as she followed his directions. She finally emerged a few feet away to his left. Seymour looked evenly at her as she walked across and seated herself on the bench beside him.

'I wondered where you were,' she said. 'I was going to have some lunch, and I wondered if you were going to join me.'

'You don't usually eat much after you've been taking that shit,' he told her disdainfully, flicking her nose with his index finger.

'I just wanted to be with you.'

'How touching,' he said sardonically.

'Did you use to sit in here with your wife?' Stella asked. He nodded.

'It's not your fault she killed herself.'

Seymour shot her a furious glance.

'I know I can't replace her, Anthony, but—'

'No,' he snapped. 'You can't.'

There was a long silence between them, finally broken by Seymour.

'Tell me again why you came in here.'

'It's Thomas,' she told him. 'He's been asking for you.'

Seymour got to his feet immediately and strode towards the path leading out of the centre of the maze.

'Wait for me,' Stella protested.

He walked on.

18

Detective Inspector Joe Chapman looked at the frozen images on his computer screen and shook his head.

Each one showed a man dressed in overalls and a mask. In each shot, the man was either dead or in the process of being killed.

He glanced down at the notepad before him, at his own spidery scrawl.

Victim one: name unknown. Killed with a knife.
Victim two: Matthew Webber. Killed with a pitchfork.
Victim three: name unknown. Throat cut.
Victim four: name unknown. Shot and beheaded.
Victim five: Craig Gibson. Multiple stab wounds and blunt trauma.

Beneath that:

Two victims known to have criminal records.
Is there a link?
Are other victims also villains?

All killed in same location? By same people?
MOTIVE?

Too many fucking questions and not nearly enough answers. Chapman ran a hand through his hair. He could feel the beginnings of a headache gnawing at the base of his skull. He felt as if he'd been staring at the computer screen ever since he'd walked back into his office earlier that afternoon, and the more he looked at it, the less anything made sense to him.

He reached for the plastic cup on his desk, wincing when he tasted the cold coffee on his tongue.

Get a fresh one out of the machine down the corridor. You need a caffeine rush. Might help you think.

Chapman was about to get up when the door of his office opened.

'The computer checks you requested,' Maggie told him.

'Come in, Maggie,' he said wearily. 'Sit down.'

She did as he instructed, handing him the printed sheets.

'Fuck it,' he grunted, surveying the wealth of material before him. 'For now, just give me the short version.'

'We started by checking the names of all known villains who've disappeared around the country in the past month,' Maggie began.

'How many?'

'Three hundred and seventy-two.'

'Great,' he murmured.

'So, we narrowed the search to known villains who've disappeared in the past month in London,' she told him. 'Just to make it a bit easier. On the assumption that the snuff films were actually shot here.'

'And?'

'Twelve. And that includes Gibson and Webber. Of the other ten, we managed to eliminate three more names. A couple of old lags who died and another guy who was killed in a car crash last week.'

'Just seven. Why the fuck didn't someone run a check before?'

'Bradley wanted to but you wouldn't let him until you were sure the snuff movies were kosher.' Maggie raised her eyebrows.

'Right.' The DI nodded. 'What about the seven who are left?'

'We've got addresses for where they were last resident. Bradley and Mackenzie are checking them out now.'

A slight smile creased Chapman's face.

'We're going to nail these bastards, Maggie,' he said.

'I don't doubt it,' she told him, getting to her feet.

'Maggie,' he called as she reached the door. 'Do you fancy a drink later? When we've finished here?'

'Joe, I can't,' she said, almost apologetically. 'Jason's cooking a meal tonight, and . . .' The sentence tailed away.

'Oh, well, don't mess him about then. God forbid his soufflé should drop.'

There was an edge to Chapman's words that Maggie wasn't slow to pick up. She paused in the doorway, her lips parted, as if preparing to say something else. Finally, she turned away, closing the door behind her.

Chapman heard her footsteps die away in the corridor beyond.

19

'Hello, Thomas.'

Stella carefully closed the bedroom door behind her, her heart thudding hard against her ribs.

He had his back to her as she entered and, when he didn't turn, she wondered if he'd heard her.

'Thomas,' she repeated.

She stood where she was, teetering on three-inch heels, her legs quivering slightly. The skirt she wore was very short. Soft leather. It showed off her tanned, shapely legs to perfection. The white shirt that was loosely tucked into it was also designed to show off her pert breasts to their best effect. Her hair was freshly washed, cascading like a silvery yellow mane over her shoulders.

Stella licked her lips, aware of how dry her mouth was.

She took another step towards his turned back.

Thomas Seymour spun round on his seat and looked blankly at her.

He was a big man. Almost six feet tall, weighing close to thirteen stone. He had thick, lustrous black hair (it had grown back well, even over the area where the surgeons had entered his skull during one of the operations) and large grey-green eyes. He was twenty-eight years old. Under other circumstances, Stella might well have found him attractive.

Of course, the scars on his face didn't help, but she imagined that, before he acquired those disfiguring marks, he must have been popular with the women. She attempted to fix her attention on his eyes, not to gaze too intently at the scars that criss-crossed his features, but however hard she tried she couldn't help herself.

The most prominent of the blemishes was a deep V-shaped crevice in the skin of his lower jaw that reached from just below his ear to the point of his chin. There were other bad ones on his cheeks but none as deep as that one. Another, close to his right eye, had gouged the flesh as far down as his lower lip.

It was from that same lower lip that she now saw spittle hanging like a thick, translucent pendulum.

Stella tried to swallow but her throat was too dry. When he got to his feet and took a couple of faltering steps towards her, she only just managed not to back away.

Thomas muttered something unintelligible under his breath, the words lost in the mucoid gurgling he uttered deep in his throat. The spittle on his lip dropped to the carpet with a splat.

He looked her up and down hungrily and something approximating a smile spread across his features.

Stella moved towards him, forcing herself to return the smile even though she knew he wasn't looking at her face. She could see that his eyes were now fixed on her legs. He watched the perfectly defined muscles in her calves and thighs tighten as she walked.

He held out one large hand towards her while with

his other he rubbed the front of his trousers, squeezing occasionally. Stella could see that he had an erection.

She climbed on to his bed and sat on the edge, unbuttoning her shirt to reveal a black bra beneath. Her fingers were quivering as she performed the task but Thomas neither noticed nor cared.

'Come here,' she breathed, as evenly as she could.

He grunted loudly and shuffled nearer to her, his eyes now drawn to her bosom. She saw his interest and pulled her shirt off, cupping both her firm breasts and pushing them upwards to accentuate her cleavage.

'Is this what you want?' she purred, closing her eyes.

At least with her eyes shut, she didn't have to look at his scars.

Thomas made a sound deep in his throat, his breathing becoming ragged. Stella looked at him long enough to see that he was rubbing more frenziedly at his erection. She reached out and touched his hand.

'I'll do that,' she told him.

He pulled his hand away and raised it into the air. For a split second she thought he was going to strike her and flinched, but that large hand slowly dropped to his side.

Kneeling before him, Stella began to unfasten his trousers.

'It's all right,' she told him softly. 'It's all right.'

She slid his trousers gently over his hips, then quickly removed his underpants to reveal his erection. Focusing on his stiffness, she closed her slender fingers around it and began to move them gently back and forth. He grunted loudly and she felt his penis stiffen even more under her expert ministrations. She licked her lips, preparing to take him into her mouth, noticing that his large, swollen testicles were already tight to his body.

With any luck, she told herself, at least this wouldn't take long.

When he gripped her hair she almost screamed. He pulled her upright with ease until she was facing him. He licked his lips with his lolling, spittle-flecked tongue and, again, she saw mucus hanging from his lips.

He kissed her.

She felt his thick, warm spit spread across her lips and chin; then his tongue licked over her teeth.

Stella closed her eyes tightly and, for one fleeting second, feared she was going to be sick as she felt his glutinous sputum dribble down her throat.

He laughed throatily and nodded and she managed to smile back through her distress.

Thomas grabbed at her left breast with one large hand, pulling at her bra, anxious to feel the soft, firm warmth of her against his palm and fingers. Still kneeling, she reached back and unhooked her bra, pulling it off, allowing him to grab wantonly at her breasts. He squeezed so hard she felt red-hot pain lance through her and she tried to pull away.

He released her, watching as she lay back on the bed to pull off her shoes then slip off her skirt and thong. She lay naked before him, her body shuddering, red marks already beginning to stand out vividly on her breasts from the force of his attention.

He shuffled closer to the bed, almost tripping over his trousers and pants, but Stella hurriedly sat up and leaned forward again, towards his jutting penis.

Again Thomas grunted throatily, the sound dissolving into an exhalation of pleasure as she finally closed her mouth over his erection.

He thrust his hips towards her, his penis butting hard against the back of her throat, making her momentarily gag. Her heart jumped as she felt him clamp both powerful hands on to the back of her head and, for a few moments, she thought he might choke her. Then, to the accompaniment of his low moaning, she felt and tasted his oily fluid in her mouth and throat and swallowed as best she could, given the volume of his outpouring.

Some of the semen dribbled over her lips and down her chin, and as he stepped back from her he saw the ejaculate there and laughed happily, his whole body shaking.

Stella fell back on to the bed, hastily wiping her mouth with the back of her hand. Thomas stood over her, still laughing.

In his room on the floor above, seated before one of the four television screens that carried pictures from his son's bedroom, Anthony Seymour smiled softly.

'Good boy,' he said quietly.

And a single tear rolled down his cheek.

20

Chapman closed the front door gently behind him, then locked it and slid the bolts into place.

He wasn't even sure of the time. He hadn't looked at his watch since he'd got on the tube at Charing Cross and that had been around half past midnight as far as he could remember.

It had been another fruitless night. Roaming the streets more in hope than expectation, looking for Carla. Showing the same photograph in places where he thought she might have been. Hearing the same answers when he asked if she'd been spotted.

Never seen her.

Don't know her.

He exhaled deeply and glanced up the stairs, knowing that even if he went straight up and got into bed, sleep would elude him as surely as the whereabouts of his daughter. Instead, he pushed open the sitting-room door and walked in.

'I thought you weren't coming back.'

The voice startled him.

'Jesus, Laura,' he exclaimed. 'What are you doing sitting here in the dark?'

He clicked on the lamp near the sitting-room door and a small puddle of dull yellow light illuminated his wife, who was seated at the far end of the sofa. She was wearing a long, dark blue dressing gown. Wrapped in it as if it was a shroud.

'I was waiting for you,' she told him, watching as he crossed to the drinks cabinet on the far side of the room. 'I couldn't sleep. I was worried about you. I thought I might as well sit up and wait.'

Chapman poured himself a large measure of brandy and took a swig, the alcohol burning its way to his stomach.

'You could have rung, let me know what time you were going to be home,' Laura continued.

'Want one?' he asked, holding the bottle of Hennessey up before him.

She nodded. 'Why not?'

He poured her a measure, handed her the glass, then refilled his own and sat down at the opposite end of the sofa.

'So.' He smiled, humourlessly. 'How was your day?'

'Don't make small talk with me, Joe,' she said, sipping at her brandy.

'What do you want to talk about?'

'You've been out looking for Carla again, haven't you?'

'You should have been the detective.'

'I told you before, she'll come home—'

'When she's ready,' he interrupted irritably. 'I know, I remember you saying it. Well fuck that. I want her home now. I don't want her flouncing back here when she feels like it. I want her here because I found her. Because I told her to come home.' He rolled the glass between his palms, his anger dissipating a little. 'I thought I saw her today. In Clapham. A girl who looked just like her.'

'What did you do?'

'I chased her. I felt like a right cunt when I caught her and found out it wasn't Carla.' He downed some more of the alcohol.

'What were you doing in Clapham?'

'Interviewing the wife of a possible murder victim.' He got to his feet. 'Does it matter?' He crossed to the drinks cabinet and refilled his glass again.

'You can talk about it if you want to, Joe. If it helps.'

'Don't pretend to be interested in my work now, Laura. Not after all these years.'

'You always said you didn't like talking about it, that you didn't want me to know about the cases you worked on because of the horrible things you saw.'

'I didn't. But sometimes I bottled things up, didn't get the bad cases off my chest because I knew you couldn't do anything to help.'

'I would have tried,' she said, her voice catching. 'If you'd wanted to talk I would have listened.'

'You wouldn't have been able to take it, Laura. You wouldn't have understood what I was feeling.' He downed more brandy.

'And who would?'

He shrugged.

'Another detective?' she persisted. 'Another woman?'

'What's that supposed to mean?'

'Come on, Joe, don't tell me you've never been tempted. There must have been other women you've fancied. Especially in the last couple of years. I mean, our sex life's not exactly going to set the world alight,

87

is it? I can't even remember the last time you came near me.' She undid her dressing gown and pulled it open slightly. 'Am I that repulsive?' She opened it further, revealing the black vest top and shorts beneath.

'Of course not. It's not that,' he said dismissively.

'Well what is it? What am I supposed to think? You don't want to have sex with me. Why not? I want to know what's wrong with me. Perhaps I can do something about it. Make you fancy me again.'

'It's not you,' he said more forcefully. 'It's my work and everything to do with it.'

'It hasn't been your work for the last two years, Joe. Don't use that as an excuse. Just be honest with me.'

'How do I know you haven't been getting shafted by someone else? I wouldn't blame you if you had.'

'I wouldn't do that to you. I wouldn't hurt you like that.'

'If I didn't know about it, it wouldn't hurt me.'

'I'd know and I wouldn't do it. I don't care what you think of me, Joe, I still love you.'

He nodded slowly. 'I know,' he murmured.

'Do you still love me?'

'Of course I do.'

'Then tell me.' She got to her feet and crossed to him. 'Tell me you love me.'

He held her questioning gaze. 'I love you,' he told her.

She leaned forward and kissed him lightly on the lips. Chapman touched her cheek tentatively as she stepped back.

'Are you coming to bed now?' she wanted to know.

'Soon,' he told her.

'I meant what I said, Joe. If you want to talk about work, about anything, I'll listen. I'll always be here for you.'

He smiled gratefully. 'I know that,' he said.

She walked out into the hall, closing the door behind her. As Chapman sat down on the end of the sofa again he heard her footfalls on the stairs.

It was more than an hour and another four glasses of brandy before he followed her.

Acquisition

Harry Copeland scooped the remains of the hamburger out of the dustbin, delighted not only that barely one mouthful had been taken but also that it was still warm.

He had no idea why the man who'd bought it, now barrelling off down Shaftesbury Avenue in the direction of Piccadilly, had dumped it but he didn't care either. It was the first hot food he'd had for two days and Harry was determined to enjoy it. He lifted a discarded newspaper and found a milkshake carton beneath. Harry took off the top and looked inside.

Even before he saw the contents, the stench of rancid milk told him that he wasn't going to have a beverage to go with his newly found meal.

He dropped the container back into the bin and wheeled round, heading back towards Cambridge Circus.

Despite the fact that it was almost two in the morning, there were still a few people on the streets. Cars were still moving up and down the thoroughfare. Across the road to his right, he saw the gaudy sign that marked the entrance to Chinatown. He wondered for a moment if he should wander through that area. The many restaurants there put out their rubbish about this time, and more than once he'd picked up some tasty morsels from their bins. For the time being, however, he contented himself with continuing up the street.

He passed a man in his early twenties lying on the pavement outside the Prince's Theatre. He was wrapped in a dirty sleeping bag, his head resting on a Marks and Spencer bag stuffed full of newspaper. The makeshift pillow must have been effective, Harry guessed, as the man was fast asleep, oblivious to the traffic and passers-by in Shaftesbury Avenue.

Harry himself would soon have to settle down for the night. Which doorway or stretch of pavement would be his bed he hadn't decided yet.

Since arriving in London three days before he'd been reduced to those kinds of sleeping arrangements. One of the girls he'd spoken to outside King's Cross last night had told him there were some empty houses off Pentonville Road where he could squat if he wanted but Harry hadn't bothered investigating them yet.

When he'd left his home in Leeds he'd known that it wouldn't be easy in the capital but anything was preferable to his fucking stepfather's coming into his room pissed while his mum was on night shift. Dirty bastard. Harry had tried telling his mother what had been happening but she hadn't believed him and his stepdad had merely belted him by way of reprisal. The cunt.

Harry didn't know how his sister put up with it. She was thirteen. Four years younger than Harry. He'd tried to persuade her to come with him. He'd told her she had to get away from the bastard who kept touching them both between the legs when he was pissed. And if he wasn't touching them, he got them to touch him. Twat. Fat, fucking twat.

Harry had even rung Childline but the stupid cow on the other end of the line had just told him to tell his mother and then the police. Yeah, right, like they were going to believe him. When his stepdad had checked the itemised bill and seen the Childline number, he'd belted Harry again. The shithouse.

He took the last bite of the hamburger and wiped his hand on his jeans, deciding he'd head for the big building at the top of the next street. Centre Point he remembered it was called. Others like him slept on the pavement beneath one of the massive concrete pillars. It was warm and at least he would have company. He walked past a café, gazing in longingly at two people sitting drinking coffee. Harry dug in his pocket but pulled out just fifteen pence. All the money he'd brought with him had gone now. He'd go back to see that girl outside King's Cross tomorrow; she'd told him there was a bloke he could see who'd find him work. She hadn't said what kind of work. Just mentioned something about punters. Whatever the fuck they were.

Harry was outside Foyle's when the black Transit pulled up beside him. He hadn't even noticed it follow him up Shaftesbury Avenue and Charing Cross Road. Why should he?

The man who got out was dressed in black jeans, a T-shirt and a leather jacket.

'You looking for somewhere to stay?' he asked.

Harry didn't answer.

The man dug in his pocket and produced a ten-pound note.

'Here, take that,' he told Harry. 'That should help you.' Then he turned back towards the Transit.

'What's that for?' Harry asked, looking at the note in his hand.

'I work with the council,' the man told him. 'We run a hostel for runaways like you. If you want somewhere to sleep for the night I can give you a number to ring.'

'How do you know I'm a fucking runaway?' Harry enquired.

'It's my job to know,' the man told him, smiling. 'Do you want that number or can I give you a lift there now?'

'Somewhere to sleep?' Harry repeated.

'There's food there too,' the man told him.

'And you're with the council?'

'I can show you ID if you like,' the man offered. 'Or will you trust me? I only want to help.'

Harry nodded.

The man smiled. 'Get in the back,' he said, opening the doors of the Transit.

Harry walked to the rear of the vehicle as the man pulled the doors wide.

Harry climbed in.

Then he saw that there were already four other youths inside. The oldest was a girl who looked about nineteen.

Each one was bound and gagged.

Harry felt a crushing blow on the back of his head, and blacked out.

The doors slammed behind him.

21

'Luke Johnson, age thirty-one. Six months for car theft. Another two years for driving while disqualified, and failing to stop. He hit a guy of twenty-two who was in a coma for three weeks.'

Chapman nodded as the DS continued, looking at his superior to ensure he was still listening.

'He disappeared two weeks ago,' Mackenzie finished. 'No one's seen hide nor hair of him.'

'No one reported him missing?' Chapman enquired.

'He was on parole when he disappeared,' Bradley explained. 'He was supposed to report in to his local nick once a week. He didn't.'

'What about the other two?' Chapman asked.

'Gordon Tatum, aged twenty-seven, and John Buckman, aged thirty-four. Both did stretches for burglary and aggravated assault.'

'So,' Chapman mused. 'They could quite possibly be the other three men in the other three snuff movies.'

'But we've got no way of confirming that until we find their bodies,' Maggie interjected. 'We can't identify them as the victims until we find them.'

'I realise that,' Chapman said. 'Just humour me and let's say that the three guys here and the two we've already got are beyond question the victims in these snuff movies. What we now need to know is why.'

'Some kind of revenge thing?' Bradley offered.

'It's an elaborate one if it is,' Chapman said.

'Someone with the muscle not only to snatch them but also to keep them prisoner somewhere and then to hire other people to kill them,' Maggie said.

'Somebody they've crossed?' Bradley wondered. 'Some other firm?'

'I doubt it. They didn't work together, did they?' Chapman asked.

'Even if they did and it is some kind of revenge thing, that still doesn't help us find out who the actual killers are,' Maggie reminded them. 'These victims have all done their time. They've been punished by the law. If it was a vigilante operation we should be looking at guys who escaped sentencing and are still working. These five weren't active when they were taken.'

'We don't know they were taken,' Bradley said disdainfully.

'They went missing,' Chapman snapped. 'That qualifies as being taken.'

'We don't know they were kidnapped,' Bradley countered.

'Well, my guess is they didn't end up on the sets of those snuff movies out of fucking choice,' Chapman told him. 'Someone wanted them there so that's where they finished up.'

'So, again we're left with the problem of who'd have the pull to engineer something like this,' Maggie said.

'And for no visible profit either,' Bradley added. 'As

95

we've said before, whoever set up that website isn't making any profit out of it.'

'So the reward for the maker of the films is purely and simply the deaths of the men involved,' Chapman said quietly.

'It might be a coincidence that they're all villains,' Mackenzie offered.

'It's a big coincidence though, isn't it?' Chapman said. 'Five guys, all with criminal records. I'm willing to bet that's the link.'

The four detectives fell silent, as if a switch had been thrown. It was as if they were simply talked out. Empty of words and ideas for the time being. Maggie looked at each of her colleagues in turn. Mackenzie gently tapped his lower lip with the end of a biro. Bradley was chewing a piece of bitten-off fingernail.

The silence was finally broken by Chapman.

'What if someone paid them to be there?' he mused.

'Then they're more stupid than we originally thought,' Bradley grunted. 'Who the hell is going to get involved in something like that? Even for money?'

'Everyone's got a price,' Maggie said. 'But I can't understand why anyone would volunteer to be involved in something that might cause their deaths. No matter how much money they were being offered.'

'People do things that might cause their deaths every day,' Mackenzie said. 'And most of the time they're the ones who pay. What about mountaineers? Bungee jumpers? Base jumpers?'

'No one's going to knowingly get involved in a snuff movie, are they? Especially if they're the victim,' Bradley said with an air of finality.

'Perhaps they were told they had a chance of getting through it,' Maggie suggested 'Of not being hurt.'

'Remember those kids in the States a few years back?' Chapman interjected. 'They made some videos called *Bumfight*. They went on to the streets and paid drunks or down and outs to fight so they could film it. Then they put the fights on the Internet. They made a fortune out of it.'

'Except whoever's putting these snuff movies on the Net isn't making a penny,' Bradley pointed out.

'I know that,' Chapman said. 'But it's the same principle. Someone could have paid Johnson, Tatum, Buckman, Gibson and Webber. Offered them money. I doubt if whoever did it told them they were going to be appearing in a fucking snuff movie.'

'In some ways it makes more sense than the possibility of their having been kidnapped,' Maggie added.

'Does it?' said Bradley. 'Is it easier to buy someone than to kidnap them?'

'It's a possibility,' Chapman snapped. 'And at the moment, that's all we've got. Five men, all with criminal records, have become the victims in five different snuff movies. We don't know how and we don't know why.'

'Whether they were paid or snatched it would still have to be by someone with the resources to stage this kind of thing,' Mackenzie said.

'I agree.' Chapman nodded. 'I'm also willing to bet that there'll be more deaths. If the killings stop with these five I'll be very surprised.'

22

Night had brought rain with it: showers punctuated by the odd rumble of thunder that threatened a downpour later. The pavements in and around Leicester Square, already slick with moisture, reflected the different-coloured neon that glowed from the front of countless cinemas, shops and restaurants.

Detective Inspector Joe Chapman stood before the entrance to the Crystal Rooms in Cranbourn Street, glancing into the amusement arcade, his eyes scanning the faces within.

He ran a hand through his hair as he entered, wiped some of the rain on his jeans, then dug his hands into the pockets of his leather jacket.

There was loud music blaring out, mingling with the sound of slots and video games to create a deafening cacophony. To his right, Chapman heard the metallic clatter of coins from a fruit machine. He looked round to see two lads in their teens scooping out the winnings.

Might be enough to buy you some smack, Chapman thought, looking at the second of the youths, a tall, gaunt, pale-looking individual with black hair and several piercings in his bottom lip.

To his left, another lad was firing a plastic gun at a video screen, cheering as each shot blasted more bloodied fragments from the zombie that was advancing towards him.

Chapman moved quickly towards the back of the building, walking swiftly over the threadbare carpet. He looked at the assistant in the change booth. She was reading one of the celebrity magazines, gazing at pictures of the latest nonentity to achieve notoriety. She didn't even look up when she pushed a pile of fifty-pence pieces towards a youth dressed in a Slipknot sweatshirt and a pair of ripped jeans.

The detective reached a set of wide stairs and descended.

Halfway down he heard the crack of pool balls slamming against each other. Seconds later he emerged into the subterranean depths of the building and surveyed the room he had entered.

There were eight pool tables in this basement, each one of them in use. Around the periphery of the playing area were more fruit machines and video games, designed to keep those waiting to play amused until it was their turn.

It was towards one of these video games that Chapman now walked, his attention focused on the youth leaning against the machine.

'You were supposed to call me,' Chapman said, pushing the lad with the flat of his hand.

Rio Richardson spun round, angry at the interference.

'Fuck off, man,' he hissed when his gaze alighted on Chapman.

'Remember me?' Chapman snapped, stepping closer to him.

'How did you find me?'

'I'm a detective,' Chapman reminded him. 'Now, what have you got to tell me?'

'I ain't got nothing to tell you, man.'

'Then you're under arrest, you little ponce,' growled the DI, gripping Richardson's arm and pulling him towards the stairs.

Many other eyes were now turning in the direction of the two men. Pool and video games suddenly seemed to have become less interesting to the denizens of the room. The fracas building before them seemed more entertaining.

'I told you I'd find you,' Chapman rasped. 'And I told you I wanted information. Now you tell me something worth hearing.'

'All right,' Richardson protested. 'Just let go of my fucking arm.'

He tried to break free, but Chapman held him like a terrier holding a rat. Suddenly, the detective dragged Richardson towards him, his face inches from the younger man's.

'I don't care how I have to take you in,' he said through clenched teeth. 'You can walk or they can wheel you in on a fucking trolley. Because if you don't stop trying to get away I'm going to break both your fucking legs. Got that?'

From a nearby pool table a tall man took a step towards the struggling duo.

'Is something wrong?' he wanted to know, his cue cradled in his hands.

'Yeah, you're sticking your nose in where it's not wanted,' Chapman told him. 'Get on with your game.'

The man hesitated a moment then nodded.

Chapman continued to drag Richardson in the direction of the stairs.

'Just stop, will you?' the younger man protested, stumbling on the first step.

'You should have called me,' Chapman told him.

'I forgot, man. Listen, I fucking forgot, right?'

'Move,' Chapman rasped.

'It's about that girl, right?' Richardson said. 'The one in the picture you showed me.'

Chapman eyed him malevolently.

'The blonde girl,' Richardson continued. 'The one with the short hair.'

Chapman pushed him up another couple of steps.

'I've seen her,' Richardson blurted out. 'Hear what I'm saying? I've fucking seen her.'

23

They sat at a window table in the Burger King on the corner of Leicester Square.

Richardson sat on one side, occasionally glancing at the other occupants of the eatery, sometimes watching the people outside, or just looking at the spots of rain on the glass.

Opposite him, Chapman kept his gaze fixed on the youth. Every now and then he'd take a sip of his strong coffee but, other than that, his attention was focused on Richardson.

'Where did you see her?' he demanded.

'I'm pretty sure it was her,' Richardson said.

'You'd better not be bullshitting me, you little bastard,' Chapman breathed, leaning towards him.

'No, I'm sure it was her, man. I remembered the photo. She was a good-looking girl, know what I mean? I always remember good-looking girls.' He grinned.

Chapman didn't return the smile. 'Where?' he repeated.

'Just off Oxford Street. In a café.'

'When?'

'Day after I first saw you. About ten at night. She was with a girl I know. That's why I remembered her.'

'And this other girl? Was she out of your stable?'

'No, but she owed me some money for some gear that I got her. About forty quid. I wanted that money. I told her I wanted it by the next night or she was in trouble.'

'What were you going to do, hard man? Slap her around?'

'Some of these bitches need that, man. They take the piss, you know?'

'Did you speak to Carla that night?'

'No. She just sat there while I was talking to this other bitch, innit?'

Chapman regarded the youth evenly for a moment then shook his head.

'You're lying,' he said flatly.

'I ain't lying, man,' Richardson protested.

'Why would you remember one little conversation like that? What made it so fucking memorable?'

'I told you, this other bitch owed me money. I always remember when people owe me money, innit?'

'Bullshit.'

'It ain't bullshit, man. I told her to bring me the money she owed me the next night, right? But she never brought it. I went to the place where she squats but she weren't there.'

'Was Carla there?'

'No. I don't know where she was. I don't even know if she was staying at that squat.'

Chapman shook his head dismissively.

'No, listen, you don't understand,' Richardson went on. 'The other reason I remembered this bitch who owed me money is because she ain't the first one who's gone missing in the last month.'

'Missing. What the fuck are you talking about?'

'People been going missing off the streets, man. People I know.'

'Of course they go missing, dickhead. They're runaways. Most of them probably went back where they came from in the first place.'

'No. I heard that some of them have been taken.'

Chapman sat bolt upright in his seat. 'Taken by who?' he said quietly.

'No one knows. One day they're there, the next day they ain't.'

'Who told you this?'

'Other people I know. Other people in my line of work.'

'Pimps and pushers,' Chapman sneered.

'All you coppers reckon you hate us but you need us to tell you what's happening on the streets.'

'All I need you to tell me, you little cunt, is where my daughter is.'

Richardson raised his eyebrows. 'So, that blonde bitch is your daughter?' He smiled. 'Fuck me. She is fine. She don't get her looks from you, man.'

Even if Richardson had seen what was coming, there was no way he could have avoided it.

With lightning speed, Chapman reached across the table and seized the younger man's head. In one fluid movement he slammed it down hard on to the table top.

Richardson shouted in pain, the noise barely drowning out the crack of breaking bone.

Chapman pushed him back in his seat, blood now pouring from his broken nose. Some of the red fluid had spilled across the table, mingling with the DI's spilled coffee.

Someone inside the Burger King screamed. Two people

got up and quickly walked out. Those remaining gazed at the detective and his companion but no one else moved or spoke.

Richardson touched his blood–spattered face, aware that red clots were now staining his shirt and jeans. He coughed, thought he was going to pass out.

'I want names,' Chapman rasped. 'Names of the people who've gone missing.'

'I don't know them,' Richardson groaned, moving his fingers to his pulverised nose.

'Well find out,' the detective snapped, getting to his feet. He walked behind the swaying figure of the younger man and leaned close to him.

'You tell me who's gone missing,' he demanded. 'Find out. Then ring me. And you find out where my daughter is. Or next time it won't be your nose I break, it'll be your fucking neck.'

24

'Richardson said that people had been disappearing off the streets. People he knew.'

Chapman sat back in the passenger seat of the Ford, the hand holding his cigarette poking out of the open window.

Maggie brought the vehicle to a halt at red traffic lights and glanced at her superior. 'Do you believe him?' she asked.

Chapman shrugged. 'There'd be no reason for him to lie. And if he's right I'd like to know where these people are disappearing to.'

'Runaways.'

'Runaways. Pimps. Pushers.'

'Perhaps someone's cleaning up the city for us. First criminals, now the street life.'

They both looked at each other.

'Do you think there's a link, Joe?' Maggie asked.

'It could just be a coincidence,' he said. 'We'll have more to go on when Richardson gives me some names.'

'What if he goes missing too?'

Chapman grinned. 'That would be a real loss to fucking humanity.'

Maggie laughed and drove on as the lights changed. 'If you don't mind my asking, Joe, what were you doing out and about in the West End with Rio Richardson last night?'

Tell her about Carla.

He took a drag on his cigarette.

What's the point? Besides, it's nobody's business but yours. She doesn't need to know.

'Just following leads, Maggie,' he told her. 'That's what we get paid for, isn't it?'

She nodded.

'What about you?' he asked. 'How did your meal go? What did lover boy cook for you?'

She glanced at him briefly and saw that he was staring disinterestedly out of the windscreen.

'Jason made a Thai curry for us,' she said. 'It was very nice.'

Chapman merely raised his eyebrows. 'And afterwards?' he asked. 'Off to bed?'

This time she didn't look at him. She could hear the scorn in his voice. And something else.

Jealousy? Anger?

'Drop it, will you, Joe?' she said wearily.

'I was just curious,' he said, still through the windscreen. 'Just trying to show a little interest in your new life.'

'Thanks all the same, but you don't have to.'

Chapman shrugged.

The police radio crackled loudly in the awkward silence and both of them heard the transmission.

'Puma Three requesting support,' the voice said quickly. 'Support needed immediately.'

'Puma Three, this is control, what is your position?' a female voice enquired.

'We're at the Corsica Street flats in Highbury,' the first voice said urgently. 'Corner of Corsica Street and Calabria Road. Repeat, support needed urgently. Suspect is believed to be armed. We have a possible hostage situation.'

'We're about five minutes from there,' Chapman snapped. 'Take the next right.'

Maggie nodded and swerved the Ford across the road, narrowly missing an oncoming van. The driver hit his horn angrily, gesturing at her as she cut past him. Maggie gripped the wheel more tightly and threw the car round a tight bend. It hit the pavement, mounted it, then skidded back into the road.

Chapman didn't speak. They drove on.

25

Chapman looked up towards the fifth floor of the building towering above him. Each of the flats had a small balcony complete with a metal guard rail. Some had washing draped over the rails, drying in the warm light breeze of the morning. The smell of drying laundry mingled with the odour of warm rubber and hot engines from the other police cars parked around him.

There were at least a dozen uniformed men moving about, some inside the building, some taking up positions in the small gardens that surrounded the block of flats. Some of the residents of the adjacent block were on their own balconies, peering at the comings and goings, intrigued by the presence of so many policemen.

'How long's he been in there?' Chapman asked the constable standing beside him.

'About ten minutes,' the man told him. 'A neighbour heard shouting coming from the flat and called us. Apparently the bloke's been having emotional problems for a while now.'

'What kind of emotional problems?' Maggie enquired.

'His wife left him two weeks ago.'

'Was it the neighbour who told you he was armed?' Chapman wanted to know.

The constable nodded. 'She thinks he's got a knife.'

'Are you sure that's all he's got?' Chapman said.

'As far as we know.'

'What's his name?' Maggie asked.

'Giles Allen.'

'Any previous?' Chapman asked.

'He's on the sex offenders' register,' the constable said slowly.

Chapman looked at the man then back up to the fifth floor. 'Who's in there with him?'

'His daughter. She's fourteen.'

'So, are we looking at a hostage situation here?' Maggie asked. 'That's what was said on the police radio.'

'He's locked himself in the flat and he won't let his daughter out but it's not the girl he's threatening to kill, it's himself,' the constable told them. 'That's why we didn't ask for a negotiator.'

'So who the fuck's going to talk him out of there?' Chapman said, still looking up.

The constable looked at the detective. 'He says that if anyone goes in, he'll kill himself in front of the girl.'

'Any idea why he wants to kill himself?' Maggie asked.

'He says he's ashamed of himself.'

'Hold on,' Chapman interjected. 'If no one's spoken to him, how the fuck do you know all this?'

'The neighbour told us when she called for help,' the constable said.

'Jesus Christ,' grunted Chapman, looking towards the front entrance of the flats. 'Give me a radio.' He held out his hand, waiting while the constable hurried to his car and returned carrying a two-way. Chapman took it from

110

him and set off for the main entrance. 'Which flat's he in? What number?'

'Twenty-four.'

'Do you want me to come with you?' Maggie called.

'Please yourself,' Chapman said, over his shoulder.

'Should we evacuate the other residents?' the constable asked.

'Let me talk to him first,' Chapman told the uniformed man. He paused at the doorway and looked at Maggie. 'Are you coming or not?'

She hurried across to join him. Together they headed for the lift that would take them to the fifth floor.

The lift bumped to a halt at the fifth floor and the doors slid open.

Chapman and Maggie stepped out on to the concrete landing, both of them looking around. There were four flats on each level and Chapman headed straight for the door of the dwelling before him.

'Shall I check the others?' Maggie asked.

'No need,' Chapman told her. 'Not yet.'

The door to number twenty-three opened slightly and an old woman peered inquisitively out.

'Can you step back inside, madam?' Chapman said.

'Who are you?'

'Police,' Maggie replied. 'Now please go back inside until it's safe.'

'I called the police,' the woman informed them. 'I don't like him.' She jabbed a finger towards the door of number twenty-four. 'You can't trust people like him.'

'You called because you heard shouting,' Chapman stated.

'Him. That Allen,' the woman said. 'He was shouting

and crying. I mean, what kind of man cries like that? And in front of his daughter too. Bloody poof.'

'Have you heard anything since you called the police?' Maggie enquired. 'Any sounds? Any talking or raised voices?'

'I heard him crying again.'

'Has anyone left the flat?' Chapman asked.

'Not that I know of. He's still in there, with his daughter,' said the woman sniffily. 'Bloody lunatic.'

'You told the police he was armed with a knife,' Chapman reminded her. 'Are you sure? Did you actually see any weapons?'

'I thought I heard him say he had a knife.'

Chapman glanced briefly at Maggie and raised his eyebrows.

'Can you step back inside, please,' Maggie said, ushering the woman back behind her front door.

'His wife left him, you know,' the woman went on. 'Can't say I blame her. I heard he's a kiddy fiddler. Dirty sod. And them with a daughter too. You never know who to trust these days, do you?'

'Inside,' Chapman snapped, jabbing a finger at her front door.

The door of number twenty-three was closed, albeit reluctantly.

Chapman shook his head, then moved closer to the entrance to number twenty-four. He banged three times, hard, and waited.

'Mr Allen,' he called. 'Can I speak to you, please? My name's Chapman. I'm a police officer.'

Silence.

Chapman banged again and pushed against the door. It wouldn't budge.

'Leave me alone.' The words came from behind the door. 'I haven't hurt anyone.'

'We know that,' Chapman called. 'We don't want you to hurt yourself, Mr Allen. We were told you'd threatened to kill yourself.'

Silence.

'Is your daughter in there with you, Mr Allen?' the DI persisted.

A moment's hesitation. Then: 'Yes,' the voice called back.

'Why don't you send her out?' Chapman said. 'Then you and I can talk. No one wants to hurt you. I just want to help.'

'You can't help me.'

'Until we talk you don't know that,' Chapman told him. 'Let me come in. I'll stand at the door if you want me to. I just want to hear what you've got to say.' He glanced briefly at Maggie. 'Send your daughter out and I'll come in and we'll talk.'

'No tricks?' Allen said.

'I told you, I'm only concerned that you don't hurt yourself, Mr Allen. Whatever you want to talk about I'll listen.'

There was a moment's silence and then the sound of movement from behind the door. Chapman heard the scrape of a bolt being slipped. He stepped back a couple of paces, looked at Maggie and nodded.

The door of number twenty-four swung open.

The girl standing on the threshold was about fourteen, dressed in a pair of combat trousers, trainers and a T-shirt. Pretty kid. Short blonde hair and green eyes.

Jesus, she's the dead spit of Carla. The way she's dressed. The hair, everything.

Chapman could see that she'd been crying.

But she's not Carla, is she? Now get a fucking grip.

The girl hesitated in the doorway of the flat for a moment, looking back.

114

'You go,' Allen called.

'Come on, sweetheart,' Chapman said warmly. 'It's all right.' He beckoned to Maggie. 'Take her downstairs. I'll talk to him.'

Maggie nodded and ushered the girl off in the direction of the lift. Chapman stepped across the threshold of number twenty-four. Giles Allen was standing at the end of the narrow hallway, close to the door of the small kitchen. He was a slim man in his early forties with pinched features and black hair.

He had a large kitchen knife clutched in one hand.

Chapman closed the door behind him.

'You made the right decision, Mr Allen,' he said quietly. 'Letting your daughter go. You wouldn't have wanted to hurt her, would you?'

'I'd never hurt her,' Allen stated, still holding the knife.

'She's a beautiful girl.'

'Have you got kids?'

'A daughter. Only a few years older than yours, as a matter of fact. They look alike, too.' Chapman managed a smile.

'How old is she?'

'Seventeen.'

Allen nodded. 'Mine's fourteen,' he said, his mouth twitching. 'A bit old for me now.'

Chapman frowned slightly, aware of the change in Allen's voice. His words were growing stronger.

'Not my taste any more,' Allen went on, licking his lips. 'When she was younger it was different but I haven't touched her since she was twelve.' He smiled. 'Do you still want to talk, detective?'

115

27

'You came in here to talk to me, didn't you?' Allen continued. 'Don't you want to hear what I've got to say?'

Chapman regarded the other man warily for a moment then took a step closer to him. Allen raised the knife a little higher.

'Are you going to try to use that on me?' the detective asked, nodding in the direction of the gleaming blade.

'No. I said I didn't want to hurt anyone and I meant it. The only person I was ever going to hurt is myself.'

'Why would you want to do that?'

'Because I'm ashamed of myself. Ashamed of what I am.'

'A paedophile.'

'That's a convenient label.'

'What would you call yourself?'

'Misunderstood.' Allen smiled crookedly. 'But no one ever wants to understand people like me, do they? It's easier to label us. To hate us.'

'What do you expect?'

'I don't expect anything, detective, but people who don't understand what I'm feeling should keep their opinions to themselves.'

'I know you're on the sex offenders' register. Is it for what you did to your daughter?'

'No one ever found out about that. She never told. She was a good girl. It was the others who told.' He took a deep breath. 'I'm not proud of what I did but I couldn't help myself. I have needs, and because they're different from the average person's I'm ostracised. Men have sex with women because they have needs. Women have sex because they like it, but because I indulged in my . . . how can I put it . . . in my desires, I was labelled a pervert.'

'Having sex with kids isn't exactly normal, is it?'

'Not in your world, detective,' Allen snapped. 'But I couldn't help myself.'

'Why abuse your own daughter?'

'It wasn't abuse,' Allen said softly. 'It was my way of showing how much I loved her.'

Chapman felt the knot of muscles at the side of his jaw pulsing angrily. He held Allen's gaze, trying not to reveal the seething anger building steadily inside him.

You fucking sick cunt.

'When I used to bath her, I touched her,' Allen said, tapping between his own legs. 'And when she got older, I taught her how to touch me.'

You twisted, sub-human piece of shit.

By his sides, Chapman clenched his fists until his fingernails dug into his palms.

'I was always gentle with her,' Allen continued. 'I never hurt her.' He looked at the detective. 'Your daughter's seventeen, you say.' He smiled. 'She's a young woman. Firm breasts. Tight little arse. Slim legs.' He grinned more

117

broadly. 'Soft lips. Don't tell me you've never looked at her and thought what it would feel like to touch her.'

Chapman could feel himself shaking with fury. 'She's my daughter,' he said, as evenly as he could.

'She's still a young woman with a woman's body,' Allen persisted. 'She'd be too much for me, though. As I said, I like it when they're younger. Not so developed. I like how it feels between their legs. Soft. Hairless. So smooth. Like silk.' He smiled. 'Why do you think so many women shave themselves down there?' Again he touched between his legs. 'Perhaps it's because men like to be reminded of when all women were just girls. Just little girls.' He smiled again.

'You're not ashamed of what you did,' Chapman said through clenched teeth. 'You *like* talking about it.'

'I wanted to be normal,' Allen rasped. 'I didn't ask to be made this way, to feel the way I do. I wanted to kill myself. It's been two years since I touched a child but I know that I'll do it again. I can't help it.'

'So your answer is to kill yourself ?'

'What else is there? No one wants to help me. All people want to do is hate and ridicule and condemn.'

'So kill yourself,' Chapman told him. 'Do it now.'

Allen pressed the blade to his left wrist, gazing down at the gleaming edge that was digging into his flesh.

'You think I won't,' he chided.

'I know you won't,' Chapman sneered.

Allen pressed harder on the blade and looked at Chapman but the detective merely shook his head.

'You gutless bastard,' he hissed. 'You don't want to kill yourself. If you did you'd cut yourself properly.'

Allen drew the blade quickly across his left wrist.

Blood spurted violently from the gash as the wound opened like a yawning mouth, one of the severed veins clearly visible. More red fluid pumped from the gash and Allen dropped to his knees, tears beginning to flow down his cheeks.

Chapman took a step towards him and knelt beside him, ignoring the blood that spattered him.

'I told you you didn't want to die, you cowardly little shit,' the detective snarled.

'I did it,' Allen wailed. 'I cut myself. I'm going to die for what I've done.'

'You won't fucking die, because you cut *across* the wrist. You severed a couple of veins. They'll tourniquet it, give you a transfusion and you'll be out of hospital by the end of the week.'

'You're going to let me die.'

'That's what you said you wanted but you don't, do you? If you wanted to die, you'd have done it properly.'

Chapman clasped one fist round Allen's right hand, which was still holding the knife, and grabbed the man's left wrist with the other, pulling it towards him, straightening the arm. Blood was still pouring from the cut, spraying the floor and the two men as they knelt there.

'If you want to die then do it properly,' Chapman snarled.

Still holding Allen's right hand, the detective forced the other man to raise the blood-stained knife and bring it down into the crook of his own left arm, still clamped in Chapman's vice-like grip.

The point punctured the flesh easily. Allen screamed in pain.

'Do it, you gutless fuck,' Chapman spat, saliva spraying the side of Allen's face. 'Do it.'

Gripping Allen's right hand in an unbreakable hold, Chapman dragged the knife from his elbow all the way down to his wrist.

The blade sliced effortlessly through flesh and muscle and the detective felt it scrape bone as it tore open the radial artery.

Blood spouted. A great gout of it that erupted into the air.

'No,' screamed Allen, but already, guided by Chapman, the knife was digging into his left arm again.

It hacked deeply from the bicep all the way to the base of his thumb, severing the ulnar artery.

More blood burst into the air and Chapman held the other man before him, feeling his body shuddering violently. Allen dropped the knife.

'This way, they can't tourniquet it,' the DI hissed. 'This way they can't stop the bleeding.'

Allen was sobbing uncontrollably now, his left arm hanging uselessly, pumping blood. The flesh and muscles were shredded, the ruined arteries poked through the pulped crimson mess like two headless worms vomiting his life fluid into the air.

'This is what you really wanted, isn't it?' Chapman gasped, still clinging to Allen. 'Do the other arm too. Make sure.'

Holding Allen's blood-soaked left hand, Chapman closed the other man's fingers around the discarded blade. He forced Allen to lift it, and guided the point towards the dying man's right arm.

'Finish it, you sick fucking bastard,' Chapman grunted, pushing the point of the knife into the soft flesh inside the elbow. 'You'll be dead before they get you to the fucking hospital.'

He felt Allen bucking wildly against him but the man hadn't the strength to resist and the knife tore savagely into his right arm, slicing through the arteries there.

More blood erupted from the wound.

'Happy now?' Chapman shouted with something like triumph in his voice.

He was about to step back when the flat door swung open.

'Oh, my God,' muttered the constable who stood there.

Beside him, Maggie looked on, her features twisted somewhere between revulsion and horror.

Chapman, his face and clothes drenched with blood, stared blankly at them. Finally, he let the body of Giles Allen slip forward from his grasp. The man lay still at his feet in a pool of his own blood.

Chapman didn't move.

28

The interview room at Hornsey Road police station was about ten feet square. The walls were painted a plain cream colour and, Chapman thought as he looked around at them, they could do with a fresh coat of paint. It was peeling off in a number of places, not least close to where he sat. He wondered if all suspects entertained the same thoughts and observations when they were waiting to be questioned. After all, over the years, he'd been in rooms like this often enough. He reached behind him and patted the pockets of his jacket, searching for his cigarettes, forgetting that they'd been taken when he'd first been brought in.

Christ, he needed one now.

Apart from a small table, upon which rested a tape recorder, and three plastic chairs, the room was empty. The detective was more used to being on the other side of the table, though. He ran a hand through his hair then picked off another scabrous piece of peeling paint from the wall. He dropped it beneath the table with the other fragments he'd already pulled off.

Tiring of this, he reached for the styrofoam cup

before him on the table and sipped at the contents. Surprisingly, the tea was still warm, so he downed what was left and then sat back in his seat, his fingers spread wide on the table before him.

He'd been allowed to wash his hands when he got to the station but there was still blood on the skin, mainly in the cracks between his fingers and under his nails. It had dried to a rusty colour by now. Chapman began picking beneath his left index finger nail, pausing only when he heard movement outside the interview room.

The door opened and two familiar faces appeared.

'Is this usual procedure?' Chapman asked as DS Maggie Grant and DS Michael Bradley walked in.

They said nothing, merely seating themselves opposite their superior.

'I bet you're loving this, aren't you, Bradley?' Chapman commented.

'If you hadn't killed Giles Allen it wouldn't be happening, would it?' Bradley said coldly.

Maggie looked across the table at him, her lips opening as if she was about to say something, but in the end she remained silent.

'What else do you want to hear?' Chapman enquired, sitting back. 'I'm not going say anything different now from what I said half an hour ago.' He nodded in the direction of the tape recorder.

'Are you sure you don't want a brief?' Maggie asked.

Chapman shook his head.

'Why don't you help yourself, Joe?' Bradley said. 'No one wants to see you go down.'

'Except you?' Chapman countered. 'Don't try to pretend you're not fucking delighted with this situation, Bradley. If I go down, that opens the door for you, doesn't it?

123

Detective Inspector Bradley. Got a ring to it, don't you think?'

'Whichever way you look at it, Giles Allen is dead because of you,' Bradley said.

'One less nonce case on the planet,' Chapman grunted. 'Excuse me if I don't burst into tears.'

'You said that Allen was going to kill himself,' Maggie interjected.

'That's what he told me. He said he wanted to die. I helped him. Simple as that.'

'You murdered him,' Bradley stated.

'You'll find some of my prints on the knife, but who's to say I wasn't trying to get it off him? Trying to stop him cutting his wrists?'

'There were witnesses.'

'Witnesses have been known to be wrong,' Chapman reminded him. 'You should know that.'

'Are you denying you killed him?'

'He was holding the knife himself,' Chapman said flatly.

'And you were holding him,' Bradley snapped. 'Forcing him to cut himself to fucking shreds. He'd lost so much blood he was dead before they even got him to the ambulance.'

Chapman merely shrugged. He looked at Maggie. 'Any chance of a cigarette?' he asked.

'Don't you want to get out of here, Joe?' she protested. 'Let us get you a brief, for Christ's sake. You're being transferred to Wandsworth in the morning.'

'I just need time to think,' Chapman told her.

'About what?' Bradley hissed. 'How long a stretch you're going to do for murdering Giles Allen? You're finished, Chapman.' He got to his feet and looked at Maggie. 'Come on,' he said. 'We're wasting our time.' He turned towards the door.

Maggie hesitated a moment longer, then joined him.

'So that cigarette's out of the question then?' Chapman called, a thin smile on his lips.

Moments later, two uniformed constables appeared. Both eyed him warily but the detective merely got to his feet and joined them.

'Back to the cell,' he said flatly.

The first man nodded and all three of them headed down the corridor towards the four cells the police station boasted.

The constables hesitated a moment then stepped back, allowing Chapman to walk into the cell.

The metal door clanged shut behind him.

29

Chapman had no idea what time it was when he woke.

What had surprised him initially was how easily and how quickly he'd been able to fall asleep on the single bed in the cell.

Now he sat bolt upright and rubbed his eyes, aware only that the light spilling through the narrow window high in the was a dull grey.

Early evening, he guessed, and he glanced at his watch to confirm it.

7.06 p.m.

And now he heard the sound again. The sound that he realised had woken him.

Movement outside his cell (outside his cell, how fucking crazy did that sound?), first footsteps, then the sound of keys and voices.

The detective turned to look in the direction of the sounds, wondering if he'd been dreaming. Then he saw the door open.

One of the constables who had walked him back from the interview room earlier peered in at him.

'Detective Inspector,' the man said quietly.

'What's going on?'

'Someone to see you, sir,' the constable went on. 'I know it's not usual in these circumstances but, well, me and some of the other men were talking.' He took a step inside the cell. 'We know what happened. With you and that Allen bloke. That bloody nonce.' The constable paused, as if to check that Chapman was still listening to him. 'We want you to know we're all on your side, sir.'

'My side?' Chapman said, sounding a little bewildered.

The constable nodded. 'You can only have five minutes, I'm afraid,' he said. He motioned over his shoulder and Chapman saw a second person join him.

'Laura,' the detective breathed.

She walked in tentatively, looking around at the inside of the cell and then straight at her husband.

'Five minutes,' the constable said and slid the door shut behind her.

Chapman crossed to his wife and embraced her.

'You shouldn't have come here,' he said, holding her tightly to him.

'I had to see you,' she told him. 'I had to know what happened.'

'I'd have thought they would have told you that.'

'I mean why you did it.'

'Who told you I was here?'

'Maggie Grant,' she said. 'She's a nice woman.'

'Yeah,' Chapman breathed, looking down at his hands.

He sat down on the bed and patted the blanket, indicating that Laura too should sit. She did so, taking his hand and sniffing back tears.

'Why, Joe?' she asked. 'Why did you kill that man?'

'She looked just like Carla,' Chapman said flatly. 'The girl. Allen's daughter. He'd abused her until she was twelve.'

A single tear ran down Laura's cheek.

'He had it coming, Laura. I'm not going to run from this. Let them put me on trial. Let them hear what happened. I don't care.'

'And if you go down?'

'I won't.'

'You killed him, Joe.'

Chapman didn't answer.

'You didn't do it for Carla, did you?' she breathed. 'You did it for yourself. You were trying to make it up to her, weren't you? In your head. You thought that by killing a child molester you were somehow killing all the men out there who could hurt Carla.'

'Very profound.' He smiled humourlessly.

'It's true. I know how your mind works.' She glared at him. 'What good are you to me in prison? What good are you to Carla? Did you think of that?'

'I won't go down for it,' he said defiantly. 'There isn't a court in the country that will convict me.'

'You sound very sure of that, Joe.'

He reached out and squeezed her hand gently. 'Trust me,' he murmured.

'That's asking a lot,' she told him.

For what seemed an eternity they sat in silence. Chapman reached across and tenderly wiped a tear from her cheek.

'I'm sorry,' he whispered.

The cell door opened and the constable peered in almost apologetically. 'Time's up.'

Laura got to her feet. She walked to the cell door, then hesitated, looking back at Chapman, both of them wanting to speak but not knowing what to say. Then she was gone.

The cell door closed once more.

30

Anthony Seymour glanced over the top of the book he was reading, his attention caught by the large television screen mounted on the wall across the spacious bedroom.

The news was on. A story about a kidnapping in Spain. Some child on a school trip had been abducted. Seymour fumbled for his bookmark, slid it into place and put the heavy tome down on his bedside table. With his other hand he reached for the remote and pushed up the volume on the TV.

The story finished and was replaced by one about a bomb blast in Israel. Seymour watched impassively as the pictures of the victims spread across the screen.

'What's that?'

He heard Stella Crane's voice but it didn't distract him from what was happening on the television.

She walked from the en suite bathroom towards the bed, padding barefoot across the luxuriously thick carpet and the expensive rugs, allowing Seymour to look at her. She was wearing just a pair of skimpy white knickers and a short white top that barely covered her breasts, but Seymour seemed unmoved by her presence.

'I asked what was on,' she repeated, climbing into bed beside him.

'Nothing to interest you,' he said, without looking at her.

She reached for the glass of Bacardi and Coke on her own bedside table and took a sip.

'I want to go shopping tomorrow,' she told him.

'Fine. You go. I'll get the driver to take you.'

'Can't you come with me?'

'I've got things to do here,' he said. 'Besides, you don't need me to tell you how to spend money.'

'I just thought we could have lunch out, that it might be nice for us to spend some time together.'

Seymour held up a hand to silence her as he suddenly sat upright in bed, his attention riveted to the screen. He pushed up the volume once more, listening intently as the newsreader spoke. However, it wasn't so much the words he heard that held his attention as the photograph behind the newsreader.

Seymour was gazing intently at a picture of Detective Inspector Joe Chapman.

'. . . in London earlier today. The man, Detective Inspector Joseph Chapman, was placed in custody immediately by colleagues, some of whom witnessed the incident. Detective Inspector Chapman was taken to Hornsey Road police station where he was detained for questioning.'

'Who is that?' Stella asked.

'A man I know,' Seymour said quietly, still gazing at Chapman's photo.

'How do you know him?'

'He was the detective in charge of the investigation when Thomas was attacked.'

'But they never caught the men who attacked him, did they?'

131

Seymour shook his head. 'No,' he said through clenched teeth. 'They didn't have enough evidence. No witnesses. That's what we were told. That's why the case was closed. They said there was nothing more they could do.' He dropped the remote on the bed and swung himself round until his feet touched the floor. 'My son was beaten almost to death. Brain-damaged. And that detective couldn't even find anyone to prosecute for it.' He got to his feet and walked across to the bedroom window, where he stood gazing out into the darkness. 'And because of that my wife killed herself. She couldn't bear to see him the way he is now. That detective was responsible for me losing my son and my wife.'

Stella looked helplessly at Seymour's back.

He stood there a moment longer, then returned to the bed and reached for the phone on his bedside table. He picked it up and jabbed the number he wanted, his face set in hard lines.

Finally it was answered.

'I've just seen the news,' Seymour snapped into the receiver. 'Why the hell didn't you tell me?'

The voice on the other end tried to say something but Seymour cut across it.

'Never mind that,' he rasped. 'We need to talk.'

31

'I'm sorry about this, Joe.'

DS Maggie Grant fastened the handcuffs round Chapman's wrists and stepped back.

'Don't be,' the DI told her. 'You're only doing your job.' He nodded curtly at her, then walked out into the walled car park at the rear of Hornsey Road police station.

The police van was waiting there, its rear doors held open by a uniformed constable. Chapman walked briskly to it and climbed in, seating himself on one of the benches there. The uniformed man clambered in behind him, closing the doors in the process.

Led by a single police car, the van pulled out of the car park and turned towards the road. Maggie slid behind the steering wheel of the Ford and followed.

An oncoming car slowed down then stopped, the driver waving the vehicles on. The driver of the police car raised his hand in acknowledgement. The little convoy turned left into Hornsey Road.

'I meant what I said last night, sir,' the uniformed man in the back of the police van with Chapman said. He was seated opposite the detective, broad arms folded across his chest.

Chapman looked at him and shook his head. 'What was that? I heard a lot of things last night.'

'About everyone being on your side.'

'Thanks.'

'I bet the jury will be too when it comes to it. On your side, I mean.'

'I hope you're right.'

'Bastards like Allen don't deserve to live,' said the constable, steadying himself as the van took a corner a little sharply. 'They're scum. I've got a couple of kids myself. If I thought anyone was ever going to do anything to them . . .' He allowed the sentence to tail off.

'Seeing as you sympathise so much,' Chapman said, 'you wouldn't have a cigarette, would you?'

'Don't smoke,' the constable told him.

Chapman nodded.

Maggie made sure that she kept a reasonable distance from the police van in front of her. Far enough for safety but not so far that another car on the road slipped into the gap.

She wondered what was going through Chapman's mind. Pondered on how bizarre a situation this must be for him. A man who'd spent his whole career putting criminals behind bars now treated the same as the men he'd always hunted. Had circumstances been different, she might, she told herself, have enjoyed the irony. She stepped gently on the brake as the little convoy came to a halt at traffic lights.

She never even noticed the black Audi pull in close behind her, and even if she had she would have thought nothing of it. Why should she? There was nothing in the appearance of the driver or his passenger to cause her alarm or undue interest.

'Why Wandsworth?' Chapman asked as the van continued along the road. 'The Scrubs is nearer.'

'That's just what we were told,' the constable said.

'Just obeying orders.' Chapman smiled to himself.

He wondered how many men he'd put away there were inside Wandsworth. How many he personally had been responsible for bringing to justice now residing there. Five? Ten? Twenty?

And all of them will be waiting for you when you get there.

He drew in a deep breath and sat back, wondering how long the trip was going to take.

As Maggie Grant drove she tried to find something on her radio to fill the stillness inside her car. She listened to one of the talk stations for a moment then changed to pop, tired rapidly of that and found classical. Finally, unable to settle on anything, she switched the radio off and drove in silence. For a moment she contemplated putting a CD on but decided against it. Her own muddled thoughts would have to suffice for company.

Behind her, careful always to remain inconspicuous, the black Audi kept within two car lengths.

32

Chapman felt hot and uncomfortable inside the van. He wasn't sure if it was because of the cramped conditions, the fact that the air conditioning inside the vehicle seemed to be malfunctioning or his fear of what might happen when he eventually reached his destination.

He hadn't checked his watch when they'd left the police station so he had no idea how long the journey had taken. He guessed at thirty minutes so far.

Sitting opposite him, the uniformed constable seemed similarly disenchanted. He moved about constantly, trying to get comfortable as the van fought its way through traffic, never, it seemed, able to increase its speed.

'You said you had a couple of kids,' Chapman offered, looking at the man.

'I've got a girl of ten and a boy of fourteen,' the constable said. 'What about you, sir?'

'Daughter. She's seventeen.'

'Growing up.' The constable smiled. 'They can be difficult when they're in their teens, can't they? My boy's an argumentative little sod at times but he's a good lad.

He's got trials with Spurs coming up soon. I told him that might be a bit of a problem with me being an Arsenal fan.'

Chapman forced a smile and nodded.

'Is your daughter still at school, sir?' the uniformed man asked.

No. She's run away from home because I told her she'd have to get an abortion.

'No,' Chapman confessed. 'She didn't want to stay on. Wanted to get out and earn herself some money. We tried to talk her out of it but . . .' The words faded away.

'What does she want to do?' the constable enquired.

'I don't know,' Chapman told him. 'I really don't know.'

The two men looked at each other in silence for a moment.

Then the van came to a halt again.

Maggie saw the large yellow DIVERSION sign up ahead and sighed wearily.

She brought the Ford to a stop behind the police van, lowered her window and peered out in the direction of the hold-up. There was water covering the street.

'Burst pipe,' she muttered to herself. She could only guess at how long the workmen she could see had been present. There were two of them hanging around one of the overflowing drains while another was standing beside a Thames Water van speaking animatedly into a mobile.

She wondered how much more time this was going to add to the journey. If the chosen route was now closed to the small convoy, then they'd have to find a more circuitous one. She cursed under her breath as she saw the police car ahead of the van attempting to reverse.

137

The DIVERSION arrow was pointing to a road to the right, but that too appeared to be blocked, judging from the ROAD CLOSED sign barring access.

Behind her, the driver of the black Audi lifted a two-way radio and spoke a few words into it.

'What's going on?' Chapman asked as the van showed no sign of moving.

The constable could only shake his head. He took a step towards the grille in the centre of the partition separating the cab of the van from the rear and pressed his face against it.

'What's the problem?' he asked the driver.

'Bloody road works or something,' the other man informed him, cursing as he crunched the gears of the van into reverse.

Maggie also jammed her car into reverse, inching back slowly, giving the vehicles behind her time to attempt the same manoeuvre.

She could see the black Audi in her rear-view mirror. It didn't budge.

Maggie hit the horn lightly to show that she needed to reverse but still the Andi remained immobile.

She stuck her head out of the window and waved back in the direction of the Audi.

'Move,' she shouted.

The large black car continued to block her path.

Muttering to herself, Maggie stuck her own car in neutral and hauled herself out from behind the wheel. She advanced towards the Audi.

'You're going to have to move back,' she said irritably, 'or no one in front of you can get out of this bloody street.'

For a split second neither the driver nor his passenger even seemed to acknowledge her presence.

'Move the car,' Maggie shouted again, standing in front of the black Audi.

At last, it reversed three or four feet.

'About time,' Maggie muttered under her breath. 'You're going to have to go further than that,' she added, raising her voice again. 'Go right back. As far as you can.' She gestured with both hands.

The Audi rolled back another foot or so then stopped again.

'Jesus,' Maggie said through clenched teeth.

The engine of the Audi suddenly roared. The back wheels spun madly for a second and then, as Maggie watched in horror, it accelerated straight at her.

33

Like a gleaming black bullet, the Audi shot forward.

Maggie had only a split second to react, but to her it seemed as if time had frozen. As if she was moving in slow motion.

She saw the black car coming at her and flung herself to one side to avoid it, but she was only partially successful. As she threw herself towards the pavement, the offside wing of the Audi caught her leg.

Maggie felt a tremendous impact that catapulted her into empty air. She hit the concrete with a sickening thud that knocked the breath from her.

The Audi ploughed on, slamming into the back of Maggie's Ford so hard that it propelled the vehicle into the police van.

Inside, Chapman and the constable were shunted from one end of the vehicle to the other by the impact.

'What the fuck's happening?' the detective snarled, pulling himself upright.

The constable didn't get the chance to tell him. A second thunderous impact sent the van lurching several feet across the blocked street, struck so hard that one of its rear doors swung open. The constable fell backwards, cracking his head hard against the floor of the van, the impact powerful enough to stun him. Chapman fell heavily on top of him.

Ahead of the van, the occupants of the police car saw what was happening in their rear-view mirror and the passenger began to clamber out.

'Call for assistance,' he shouted, as he pushed open his door.

The driver snatched up the radio and prepared to follow instructions.

From his right, from the other blocked road, a silver Land Rover roared into view.

It hit the flimsy ROAD CLOSED sign, sending it spiralling into the air, then slammed into the front of the police car, spinning it ninety degrees.

The passenger was sent sprawling across the tarmac by the impact, the driver thrown sideways. He dropped the two-way.

The Land Rover reversed a few yards then shot forward again, hitting the police car even more violently. The rear bumper disintegrated under the impact as the 4x4 slammed into it. The shattered lights and, indicator housings skittered across the street like plastic confetti.

Lying semi-conscious on the pavement, Maggie was aware of the impacts but with her head spinning and the agonising pain from her leg she couldn't immediately pinpoint where the sounds were coming from. At first she thought that the Audi, which had now manoeuvred past her car and was a few yards behind the police van, was responsible. She gritted her teeth and tried to rise, but it was useless. The smell of petrol and rubber was strong in her nostrils.

At the front of the convoy, a man had leapt from the

141

back of the Land Rover and was now dashing towards the police van.

Maggie saw him and wondered what it was he was holding in his right hand. She was sure it was a gun but it didn't look like any weapon she'd ever seen before.

She saw the driver of the van step out in an effort to block him.

The man raised the gun he held and fired.

There was no muzzle flash. No deafening report. Just a loud crackle and then a scream of agony from the police driver as he hit the ground clutching his chest.

The twin barbs from the taser had caught him squarely in the solar plexus, pumping fifty thousand volts into him.

He lay helpless, his body twitching uncontrollably, as the man from the Land Rover vaulted him and ran on towards the back of the van.

The constable, looking dazed, emerged. He stared round in bewilderment, shaking his head to clear his thoughts.

It was then that the Audi hit him.

The black car careered into the back of the van, carrying the uniformed man with it. It smashed him against the vehicle, pinning him, shattering both his legs just above the knee. He slumped forward onto the bonnet of the Audi, sliding off as it reversed again.

Chapman hauled himself towards the open door and found himself confronted by the man carrying the taser.

For interminable seconds they gazed at each other; then Chapman felt paralysing pain as the barbed projectiles hit him, penetrating his clothes and his flesh. The jolt of electricity that followed the twin punctures almost blew him off his feet.

He dropped to his knees then fell forward into the

142

street, cracking his head on the tarmac. Through his pain and the growing darkness of approaching unconsciousness, he saw his assailant reach inside his jacket and slide something free.

Chapman could see that it was a hypodermic needle and, seconds later, he felt a sharp pain in his arm as the steel cylinder was rammed into his flesh.

Blackness hurtled in from all sides. His head spun and he felt as if someone had filled his veins with iced water. He tried to speak but his mouth only flapped like a freshly caught fish.

He felt himself being lifted up by powerful arms, dragged from the van towards the waiting Land Rover by a man stronger than he could ever hope to be.

The tailgate of the Land Rover was open; he was being pushed across it. He heard the engine revving loudly, detected voices shouting excitedly, felt the vehicle turning in the road.

Then there was only darkness.

34

'You were lucky.'

DS Maggie Grant heard the words but, for a moment, she wasn't sure where they were coming from.

'You could have been killed,' the voice continued. 'The doctor said apart from some cuts and grazes and some bad bruising to your left leg you're OK.'

'Where am I?' she wanted to know.

'Portland Street hospital,' the voice told her and, at last, she recognised it.

Detective Sergeant Michael Bradley was standing at the end of her bed.

'I don't remember getting here,' Maggie said, pulling her flimsy gown more tightly around her.

'You cracked your head too, apparently,' Bradley informed her. 'You blacked out in the ambulance.'

Maggie touched her forehead tentatively with two fingers and winced.

'What do you remember?' Bradley asked, stepping closer to her.

'A car, an Audi,' she began, pulling the bedsheet up so that it covered her chest. 'It rammed my car into the van carrying Joe.' She sat up slightly, wincing in pain as she felt some discomfort from her left leg. 'What happened to him? To Chapman?'

'We don't know,' Bradley told her. 'He was taken from the van and put in a Land Rover, according to some workmen who saw what happened. After that . . .' Bradley could only shrug.

'Someone must have seen some number plates.'

'If they did they're not telling. We've got shit. Apart from the makes and colours of the two vehicles involved in the attack we've got nothing.'

'What about the other policemen? The ones in the leading car? The ones in the van?'

'Cuts and bruises apart from the ones in the van with Chapman. The uniform's in a bad way. Two broken legs and a shattered pelvis. Some kidney damage too, apparently.'

'I don't understand what happened.'

'It was a set-up,' Bradley said. 'It looks like someone wanted Chapman out of there.'

'Like who? I'm telling you, that looked like a professional job.'

'I agree.'

'Then someone had inside information, because whoever set it up knew we'd be going that way and they knew the best place to hit us.'

'The only people who knew the route were the guys in the police car and the van and they're all clean as far as we know. No axes to grind. It took them as much by surprise as it did you. Especially the poor bastard lying upstairs with both his legs in plaster.'

'Why the hell would they want to take Joe?'

'Until we know who they are, we're not going to know why.'

145

Silence descended for a moment, broken by Bradley.

'Perhaps Chapman set it up himself,' he offered.

'From inside his cell?' Maggie said incredulously. 'Get real, Bradley.'

'He was a murderer on his way to prison.'

'He was a suspect on his way into remand,' she snapped.

'Whatever he was he's disappeared now,' Bradley said. 'But he can't get far. He's a wanted man.' The DS turned towards the door of the room. 'I just nipped in to check you were all right. I'd better go now.'

'You could have brought some grapes,' Maggie told him, looking at the empty fruit bowl on the nightstand beside her.

Bradley laughed. 'You'll be out of here by tomorrow,' he said, and was gone.

He headed down the corridor towards the lifts and rode one to the ground floor. Once there he made his way out into the car park and climbed behind the wheel of his Astra. Before he started the engine he reached for his mobile phone and tapped in a number, glancing around as he waited for it to be answered.

An ambulance arrived and Bradley watched as a small child, its head wrapped in bandages, was lifted out by a paramedic. The man carried the child towards the main entrance of the hospital. He was followed by a young woman who, Bradley noticed, was carrying a white fluffy rabbit. The toy was splashed with blood.

The phone was answered and Bradley's attention shifted rapidly from the woman.

'It's me,' he told the voice at the other end of the line. 'I'm just leaving the hospital now.' He paused a moment. 'Have you taken delivery yet?'

The voice said that it had.

Bradley smiled. 'I hope that my help will be suitably

146

appreciated,' he said. 'Perhaps we should call it a hundred thousand this time. After all, the merchandise is worth more to you than usual, isn't it? And you wouldn't have got it without me. No one else would have told you the route that was going to be used.'

There was a pause at the other end of the line before the voice finally agreed.

Bradley slipped his phone back into his pocket and started the engine.

Fifty miles away, the receiver had just been replaced in its cradle. 'One hundred thousand. Who does he think he is? Doesn't he know who he's dealing with?'

Anthony Seymour shook his head in annoyance.

35

When he woke he was naked.

DI Joe Chapman tried to force his eyes open but, at first, it felt as if someone had glued the lids shut. He sat up, his head thumping.

He grunted, aware also of a pain in his right ear. He raised a hand and touched it, feeling wetness there. He parted his eyelids enough to see that there were two spots of blood on his fingertips.

He rubbed his eyes, his surroundings swimming slowly into view.

Why, he wondered, was he naked?

Wherever he was it was cold. Who the fuck had taken his clothes and why?

Chapman felt something rough beneath his bare buttocks and realised that he was sitting on a blanket. He ran his palms over it, the knowledge gradually dawning on him that he was sitting upright on a single bed. He felt the cold metal frame, then swung his legs over the side until his feet touched something else cold.

There was concrete beneath his toes.

He tried to rise but a wave of dizziness engulfed him and he fell backwards, muttering irritably to himself.

He lay on the bed until the feeling passed then he hauled himself upright once again, took a deep breath and held it. This time when he stood up, the dizziness subsided quickly. Chapman let the breath go and massaged the bridge of his nose between his thumb and forefinger. There was still that awful dull thumping inside his skull and the pain in his right ear. After-effects of the drug he'd been given, he wondered?

He shivered again, and pulled the thin grey blanket from the bed to wrap round himself. Then he sat down on the mattress and again looked round the room.

About twelve feet square. Low cciling. Bare walls. A single wooden door in the wall to his left. Inside the room itself there was the bed and a small, unvarnished wooden bedside cabinet. That was it. Nothing else.

No. There was something else.

In the corner of the room, close to the door.

Chapman blinked hard, his vision now clearing properly.

It was a camera.

The type they used for CCTV. And it was working. As he stood up and moved towards it, the lens rotated and the aperture narrowed like the pupil of an eye. Chapman looked directly into the camera and waved a hand in its direction.

The lens moved once more.

The detective took a couple of steps to his left and then to his right.

The camera followed his movements.

Chapman turned and took a firm grip on the wooden bedside cabinet. Then, with a grunt, he lifted it and hurled it at the camera.

His aim was good.

The camera fell to the ground amid a desultory spray of sparks.

He grunted triumphantly, looking down at the shattered surveillance device. But what really caught his eye was what had fallen from inside the bedside cabinet.

Lying before him was a pair of jeans, a white T-shirt, a pair of thick-soled work boots and a mask.

A clown mask.

Chapman picked up the jeans and held them before him. They looked like the right size so he dropped the blanket and pulled them on. They were a couple of inches too long but who cared? Then he pulled on the T-shirt and stepped into the boots. They were a size too big but what the hell? He kicked the blanket to one side and headed for the wooden door, twisting the handle.

It was locked.

He muttered something under his breath and dropped to his knees to peer through the keyhole.

On the other side of the door, through the small opening in the lock, he could see a light, illuminating what appeared to be a narrow corridor. If he could get through the door he could get into the corridor and from there, who knew?

But where, he wondered, was he? Who had brought him to this room? And why? Who'd pumped him full of drugs and sedated him? Taken him from the police van and . . .

He looked down at the camera he'd smashed.

Who'd been watching him?

Chapman sat down on the edge of the bed again, his headache seemingly intensifying. And as that particular pain grew so did the one in his right ear. He touched it again and saw only tiny spots of blood this time.

150

He must, he reasoned, have been injured somewhere between the police van and wherever he was now.

Wherever the fuck that was.

Get out of this room. You won't know anything until you get out of this fucking room.

The detective got to his feet, aware now of a familiar smell.

Fresh paint.

Was it coming from the other side of the door?

There was only one way to find out.

He kicked at the already broken bedside cabinet and smashed it easily. It broke up into several large pieces of wood, one of which was about two feet long and thicker at one end than at the other. It would make a suitable weapon should he need one.

Chapman hefted it before him, then turned his attention to the door.

He was about to kick it down when he heard the voice.

36

'Why did you destroy the camera?'

Chapman spun round. His eyes darted about within the gloomy confines of the room, trying to pinpoint where the voice had come from.

'Why?' the voice asked again. 'Don't you like being watched?'

Again he looked around. There was nowhere in the room to hide. There was quite obviously no one in here with him. It must be some kind of radio.

Was the speaker under the bed?

He overturned the metal frame, the mattress falling away.

Nothing there.

'You seem to enjoy wrecking things, detective,' the voice chided. 'And I suppose you're wondering how I can still see you after you smashed the first camera.'

Chapman turned slowly, gazing into all four corners of the room.

'It's above you, in the air vent,' the voice told him. 'If you look up you'll see it.'

Chapman followed instructions and immediately

spotted the gleaming lens behind the metal slats of the vent.

'You can't get to that one, detective,' the voice continued. 'Well, you probably could if you stood on the bed and hit it with that piece of wood you're holding but I can't really see the point. For the time being, I would think you'd be more interested in where you are. And why.'

'Who are you?' the DI said, still looking round.

'I'd been contemplating whether or not to reveal that now,' the voice informed him. 'Or whether I should perhaps leave that little surprise until later. But, as you've asked, I'll tell you. However, before I do, there are some things that you should know.'

Chapman, still gripping the piece of wood like a club, moved back towards the overturned bed, pulled it back to its normal position and sat down.

'Go on then,' he said challengingly. 'Tell me what's going on, but before you do I'll tell you something. When I get my hands on you I'm going to kill you, whoever you are.'

'Exactly the response I expected,' the voice replied with something close to contempt. 'Well, I can tell you now that whatever you do to me couldn't match the pain I've had to endure for the last eighteen months.'

'Just talk,' Chapman snarled.

'The reason you can hear my voice is because there's a very small radio transmitter surgically implanted inside your right ear,' the voice told him. 'It was put there shortly after your arrival here. It's no larger than a thumbnail and all you need to know is that you'll be able to hear me but I won't be able to hear you.'

'How can you hear me now then?' Chapman snapped.

'Because there are microphones in the room with you,'

153

the voice told him dismissively. 'Once you're released from there I'll be your guide. But I'll also be your only chance of getting out of this. If you've got any sense, you'll listen to me.'

'Fuck you. You think I'm going to trust you? Forget it.'

'If you want to survive you've got no choice.'

'You'd better hope I don't survive, because if I do, you're dead.'

'Empty threats, detective. They're about as useful as empty promises. And you made me plenty of those eighteen months ago.'

'Who the fuck are you?'

'You promised me that you'd find the men who attacked my son. You promised me they'd pay for what they did to him. You lied.'

Chapman frowned, pressing one finger to his right ear where the voice continued speaking.

'You promised me justice and I never got it,' the voice went on. 'My son never got it. The men who almost killed him were never caught. They never suffered. Instead it was my son and my wife who suffered. She tried to nurse him but finally it became too much for her. Seeing the son she'd given birth to shambling around like a zombie. Brain-damaged so badly that he could barely feed himself. My wife killed herself because of that. Because of what had happened to our son. Because of you, Detective Inspector Chapman. You may as well have put the bottle of sleeping tablets in her mouth yourself.'

'Seymour,' Chapman said under his breath. 'Anthony Seymour.'

'Am I supposed to be flattered you remember my name, detective?' the voice snapped. 'Is it meant to be some kind of comfort to me that you can recall who I am?'

154

'You were big in the media. Owned a couple of newspapers here and in the States. Ran film and TV companies and publishers. You were worth millions.'

'I still am.'

'When your wife killed herself you disappeared from public life. Became a recluse. You made Howard Hughes look like a fucking party animal.'

'I didn't want to be a part of that world any more.'

'What the hell are you doing, then?'

'I'm creating my own justice, detective. Thanks to me, not just you but other criminals have already suffered the way the law could never allow them to suffer. They received the kind of punishment they deserved.'

'You made those snuff movies,' Chapman breathed. 'The ones on the Internet.'

'Very astute, detective.'

'Why?'

'I just told you. So that criminals would receive the kind of treatment they really deserved. They're not fit to live. They don't deserve life and freedom, not when my son still suffers and the men who attacked him still walk free.'

'What's that got to do with me?'

'You're a criminal too.'

'So is that why I'm here? Is that why you organised the attack on the van taking me to Wandsworth?'

'You're no better than those you hunted. You're a murderer. You have to be punished. But not just for what you did to the man you killed: for what you did to me and my family.'

'The investigation into your son's attack was taken as far as possible,' Chapman said. 'We had no witnesses. Not enough physical evidence. Do you know how many motiveless assaults there are in London every single night?'

155

'I don't care. My son wasn't even robbed the night he was attacked,' Seymour went on. 'They didn't pick on him because he had money. Or because his father was a multi-millionaire. They attacked him because they felt like it. For fun. No other reason.'

'Then perhaps you should have spent your money trying to find the men who hurt your son.'

'You were supposed to find them,' Seymour shouted. Chapman winced as the sound exploded in his right ear. 'You were the detective in charge of the investigation. It was your job to find them. Not mine.'

'I tried my best.'

'Well it wasn't good enough,' Seymour snarled. 'You didn't make them pay.' His voice calmed a little. 'So now, I'm going to make you pay.'

37

'Put on the mask.'

Chapman heard the command loud in his right ear.

'Why?' he said defiantly. 'What does it matter who knows what I look like? Your website is untraceable, isn't it?'

Seymour didn't answer.

'Why did the others have to wear masks?' the detective continued. 'You were punishing them. Wouldn't it have been more fitting if everyone knew who they were?'

'Having them in masks appealed to me,' Seymour told him. 'Especially clown masks. They seemed particularly appropriate.'

'But the men you had killed were petty criminals. Car thieves. Burglars. Drug dealers. If you wanted to make a point why not take out rapists, child molesters or murderers? Why stick with the small fry when you could have done everyone a favour and wiped out some real fucking scumbags? Or were the small fry the extent of your ambition?'

'They were more readily available.' Seymour laughed.

The sound was like a droning bee inside Chapman's ear. 'Anyway, when you die I will have taken care of a murderer, won't I?'

'Not you personally, Seymour. Or is that how you get your rocks off? Do you put on one of the masks and join in when the bastard finally gets caught? Who are the people who actually do the killing?'

No answer.

'Come on,' Chapman rasped. 'Tell me. If I'm going to die out there,' he motioned to the wooden door, 'what the hell difference does it make what I know? Who are the killers? Who are the ones that do your dirty work?'

'Everyone has a price, detective,' Seymour told him. 'It's just that some come cheaper than others.'

'What the fuck's that supposed to mean?'

'You should be congratulating not vilifying me. I've been doing what you and your kind have been unable or unwilling to do. Not only have I rid the world of five criminals no one will miss, I've also cleaned up the streets of London.' Again he laughed.

Chapman sat motionless on the edge of the bed, his eyes flicking round the room.

'Not everyone's life revolves around money, detective,' Seymour continued. 'The first time I was in New York I saw a man in Times Square begging. He was holding a piece of cardboard and on it he'd written, *Will work for food.* There are plenty of people like him in every city in the world. London seems to attract more than its share.'

'Very philosophical,' Chapman said dismissively.

'That man was willing to do anything for some food. There are plenty who will perform any task demanded of them for alcohol, drugs or simply for shelter. The only reason an alcoholic values money is so he can buy drink with it. Similarly a drug addict has no interest in cash other than for how much heroin or crack it can get him. People like that will do anything to satisfy their addiction. Don't forget, detective, I made my millions by seeing opportunities and taking them. By exploiting needs. The people who kill for me in the films I've made do so because of their particular needs. If they do as they're told they get what they want. If a drug addict uses the knife he's given, then he gets his drugs. If an alcoholic uses the axe he's presented with, he gets his drink. All of them have a place to stay because I put them there. I took them from the streets and gave them what they had to fight and steal for. In return, they perform for me.'

'And what happens when that performance has finished?' Chapman wanted to know.

'They stay here. Provided with what they need. Their life here is preferable to the one they knew on the streets.'

'You kidnap people from the streets of London, dress them up in stupid fucking outfits and make them kill for your entertainment. You do that and you think you're helping them?'

'They're not people, detective. They're drunks, drug addicts, the homeless. The dregs of society,' snapped Seymour. 'As worthless as those I persuade them to pursue. And if they're killed there are hundreds more waiting to replace them.'

'You're insane.'

'There's a thin line between insanity and genius, detective. I know which side of that line I stand on.'

'None of this is helping your son, Seymour. You can wipe out every criminal in the world but it'll never

159

bring your wife back. Your son will always be the way he is.'

'That's something I'll have to live with. It isn't your concern. Now, put on the mask.'

'Fuck you.' Chapman stamped hard on the cardboard face.

'As you wish,' Seymour conceded. 'Soon it won't matter anyway.'

'You won't get away with this,' Chapman snarled. 'Even if you kill me, or a dozen more people, in the end you'll be caught.'

'We'll see. Now, you've wasted enough time and I'm tired of talking. It's time for you to perform, detective.'

'And what if I don't move out of this room?'

'Then you'll die in it. If you follow my instructions you've got a chance of surviving.'

'Bullshit. There's no way you're going to let me get out of this alive.'

'That choice may be down to you. If you follow instructions. If you trust me.' Seymour laughed.

Chapman heard a loud electronic buzz and looked in the direction of the noise.

'The door is open, detective,' Seymour told him. 'You can leave the room.'

Chapman got to his feet and walked across the small room, pushing the wooden door with one fingertip. It swung open and he peered out into the corridor beyond.

'Time to go,' Seymour told him. 'Perhaps I should wish you good luck.' Again that laugh, deep inside Chapman's ear.

'Did you say that you wouldn't be able to hear what I said once I left this room?' the detective enquired.

160

'That's right.'

'Right, then there's one last thing I'd like to say. Fuck you, Seymour.'

Chapman stepped out into the corridor.

38

Still gripping the piece of wood in his right hand, the DI surveyed his new surroundings.

The narrow corridor was lit by one unshaded bulb that hung from the ceiling by its cord about ten feet ahead of him. Due to the low wattage of the bulb, it was difficult to see to the end of the corridor and Chapman had no way of knowing how long it went on for.

What he could see was another door. About three feet ahead of him on his left. He moved towards it and turned the handle. As he did so, he became more aware of the smell he'd first detected while inside the first room. He sniffed hard and nodded to himself. It *was* fresh paint.

The detective rubbed his index finger against the wall nearest to him and noticed that some of the paint came off. He returned his attention to the door before him.

It swung open, revealing another room almost identical to the one he'd just left.

About twelve feet square. A single bed with just a mattress. Paint peeling from the walls and—

There was a dark stain on the mattress, and similar

marks on two of the walls. It didn't take more than a second for him to realise that it was dried blood.

Hidden by the gloom in the corner of the room, a camera turned silently and focused on him.

'You're wasting your time in here,' Seymour's voice rumbled in his ear.

'Maybe I am,' he murmured, forgetting that his tormentor couldn't hear him.

'If you're wondering who the blood belonged to it isn't really important,' Seymour told him. 'Let's just say it was one of my other guests.'

Chapman looked round once more then backed out into the corridor, moving on.

'You'll find a door at the end of this corridor,' Seymour told him. 'Go through it.'

Chapman ignored the words in his ear, more intent on trusting what he could see with his own eyes. In the dull light of that single bulb, it wasn't very much. The corridor continued for another five or six feet and then he saw the door that Seymour had referred to.

He was pretty sure that beyond the door lay the location of the snuff movies. The starting point. The first thing that the other five men who had perished here had seen.

But where was here?

London? Some other large city? Chapman had no idea how long he'd been unconscious prior to waking in the small room behind him.

Long enough for them to implant an electronic device inside your right ear.

He touched his ear gently.

Surgically implanted.

The detective shook his head. What kind of organisation and planning had gone into this exercise he

163

could only begin to imagine. The scale of it was bigger than anything he or any of his colleagues had ever dreamed of.

'And you're a part of it,' he murmured to himself. 'Starring role.'

'Talking to yourself?' Seymour's voice was there again. 'I saw your lips move on one of the camera feeds, and wondered if you might be saying your prayers,' the voice went on, a low chuckle accompanying the words. 'Or perhaps apologising.'

Chapman gritted his teeth, hefted the piece of wood before him and stepped closer to the door at the end of the corridor.

There was an electronic buzz and the door opened a fraction.

'The door's unlocked,' Seymour told him. 'Go through.'

Chapman reached out and pushed the door, which opened wide enough to reveal what lay beyond.

'Jesus Christ,' he murmured.

39

'Miss Grant, I really must protest.' The doctor stood by helplessly as Maggie buttoned her blouse. 'It was recommended you stay in the hospital under observation at least for the night.'

'I was told I only had cuts and bruises,' Maggie reminded him, smiling. 'What's the point in my using up a bed when it could be given to someone who needs it more than me?'

'I can't stress strongly enough that I don't agree with your discharging yourself,' the doctor continued. He glanced at the bruise on her left cheekbone. 'You could have a concussion.'

'I realise that and if I collapse when I get home you won't be held responsible,' she assured him.

He stood by the bed, watching as the detective sergeant tucked her blouse into her skirt. 'This really is irregular, Miss Grant,' he said wearily.

'All I need now are my shoes,' she told him, padding round the bed to pull open the door of the bedside cabinet and retrieve them.

The doctor shook his head. 'Is there someone with you tonight?' he asked. 'Just in case.'

Maggie stepped into her shoes. 'I'll be fine,' she said.

'I know your tests showed no damage,' the doctor sighed, 'but I cannot express strongly enough how deeply I am opposed to this . . .'

He allowed the sentence to tail off as Maggie stood before him, now fully dressed. She picked up her handbag and put it on her shoulder, looking past the doctor.

'At least let me walk with you as far as the hospital exit,' he said, realising that further protest was futile.

'Thank you.'

They rode the lift to the ground floor, the doctor occasionally glancing reproachfully at her. As the lift bumped to a halt he shook his head again, trying to disguise the thin smile on his face.

'I shouldn't be condoning this behaviour,' he told her.

'You're not.' She smiled. 'You're just escorting me off the premises and I appreciate it.'

'Any problems at all, you come straight back,' he told her.

Maggie nodded.

A nurse came hurrying towards them, her attention fixed on the doctor. Outside, the strident sound of a siren cut through the night. Maggie was sure that she could hear the sound of a child crying somewhere close by. She looked first at the doctor and then at the nurse.

'Dr Hamilton,' the woman said urgently. 'They need you in A&E immediately.'

'There are obviously people who need your help a lot more than I do, Doctor,' Maggie said.

Dr Hamilton hesitated a moment then nodded and hurried away with the nurse. Maggie continued towards the exit. As soon as she reached it, she dug in her handbag and switched on her mobile phone.

There were six messages on her voicemail. As she headed round to the front of the hospital she played them back.

It was the fifth one that interested her most.

40

Chapman recognised the street as soon as he saw it.

It was wide and empty, occupied only by abandoned motor vehicles and piles of rubbish. There was refuse everywhere. Lots of the bottles, cans, newspapers and other detritus was scattered across the tarmac but much had also been gathered together in tall heaps lining the thoroughfare.

On either side of the road were shops, most with their windows boarded up or blacked out.

The detective gazed around, aware that he'd seen this street in every one of the five snuff movies he'd viewed. Behind him, the door closed and he heard another electronic buzz as it was locked.

No going back that way.

He glanced up towards the sky.

It was pitch black. Not a cloud in sight and also, he noted with a slight frown, no sign of any other natural light. Nothing to guide him.

To his left when he stepped out of the doorway, there was a tall brick wall that seemed to stretch up to and actually become a part of the black sky. He couldn't even see the top of it.

The street itself was lit by sodium lamps placed about twenty yards away from each other. They gave off pools of sickly yellow light that barely cut through the tenebrous gloom. Chapman crossed the street swiftly and sheltered in the doorway of a shop for a moment.

'If you walk to the end of the street you'll find an alleyway,' Seymour's voice told him.

The detective hesitated a moment and then headed briskly towards the first lamp post.

'You're in no danger just yet, detective,' Seymour added. 'That will come later.'

'Piss off,' Chapman said to the empty air, not caring whether his tormentor heard him or not.

As he walked he was immediately aware of two things.

First, the overpowering silence.

If this was a deserted or abandoned part of a city, Chapman thought, then it was a huge area. There was no background noise at all. No distant car hooters to disturb the solitude. Not even the hint of an aeroplane far up in the black heavens. The only sound that Chapman could hear as he walked was the heavy fall of his own footsteps.

The other thing that struck him was that there was no wind at all.

Not even a breath. No threat of so much as a breeze. The newspaper that lay on the street remained where it had been dropped, undisturbed by even the gentlest of gusts. The same was true of the piles of rubbish on either side of the road. They stood there like sentinels, untroubled by the elements.

Chapman kicked one, watching the refuse spill across the street.

A tin can bounced noisily over the tarmac.

'Presumably you had some reason for doing that?' Seymour asked.

Chapman kept walking.

He passed two large skips. Both were empty. Neither had the name of either a firm or a council printed anywhere on them. Nothing to give him any clue as to where the hell he was.

Ahead of him were two abandoned cars. The body-work on both was holed and rusted. They'd obviously been there for some time. Both were up on blocks: suspended on piles of bricks where their wheels should have been. He passed them and moved towards a battered taxi a little further along. At least this vehicle had its tyres and, what was more, they were intact. Fully inflated.

Chapman pulled open the driver's door and almost smiled when he saw a set of keys dangling from the ignition.

'You want me to try them, don't you?' he whispered. 'Want me to find out there's no fucking engine.' He stepped back and walked on. 'Well, fuck you.'

'Not going to try to drive off, detective?' Seymour chuckled in his ear.

Chapman moved on.

'Just up ahead on your right, you'll find the alleyway I mentioned,' the older man added. 'Take it. There's no other way out of this street anyway, as I'm sure you're already aware.'

Chapman stopped walking and stood motionless in the middle of the thoroughfare.

For fleeting moments he wondered if it would be worth shouting for help. The thought passed and he shook his head. If he was unable to hear anyone, he reasoned, then it was fairly safe to assume that no one would hear him.

Save your breath.

Just up ahead, he saw the entrance to the alleyway.

It was narrow and the walkway beyond was lit only by a single light mounted high on the side of the building beside it.

Chapman could barely see the end of the alley, but as he stood squinting into the gloom he was certain that there were some vaguely discernible pinpricks of light in the distance.

Street lamps or lights inside buildings?

He stepped into the alley and the blackness folded around him like a shroud.

As he moved slowly along, he stretched out his arms, aware that he could touch both sides of the alley it was so narrow. He looked up, wondering if Seymour could still see him in such dense gloom.

The electronic whirring he heard seemed to answer his question.

Any camera mounted in this alleyway must be infra-red.

'Walk to the end of the alley,' Seymour breathed into his ear.

'I haven't really got a lot of choice, have I?' Chapman said to the empty air.

As he moved towards the end of the alley the blackness began to retreat and the detective was aware of lights ahead of him now. There were half a dozen stone steps leading down towards what looked like an abandoned tennis court. The entire thing was contained within a tall wire fence.

Chapman walked up to the fence and rattled it, the sound echoing in the night.

Like everything else he'd seen so far, it looked run down and neglected. There was no net between the poles on either side of the court, just the white-painted outlines

171

of the playing area to remind people what it was once used for.

The detective walked along, looking for a way in. On the far side he could see more stone steps leading up between two high buildings.

'No advice from you, shithead?' Chapman said aloud, looking around for the cameras he knew were still trained on him.

He dropped the piece of wood he'd been carrying and pulled at the rusty wire with both hands. It came free easily and the detective slipped under it and on to the concrete of the tennis court.

'On the morning of his execution, King Charles the First wore two shirts.' Seymour's voice. ' "If I tremble," he said, on his way to the scaffold, "my enemies will think it is with fear. I will not expose myself to such reproaches."'

Chapman frowned as he heard the words in his ear.

'The steps ahead of you are the steps to your own scaffold, detective,' the older man continued. 'Mount them now.'

'Fuck off,' the detective grunted.

Ahead of him, he heard voices.

41

'I got here as soon as I could,' Maggie said, seating herself on the edge of DS James Mackenzie's desk. 'I came straight from the hospital when I got your message.'

The other detective nodded and smiled back at his colleague.

'You don't look too bad, considering,' he told her. 'Even with the bruises.'

'Thanks. Now tell me about the Audi.'

'It was spotted this afternoon,' he said. 'About an hour after DI Chapman was taken.'

'Where?'

'At Scratchwood services on the M1. Some guy scraped it with his car.'

'How do we know it was the same one used in the kidnapping? The one that rammed my car?'

'When the geezer hit the black Audi at Scratchwood he got out to apologise to the two guys in it. He wanted to give them his details, you know, for insurance and all that, although he said their car looked pretty well bashed up at the front already. They weren't interested — almost ran him down as they drove off, he reckons — so he took their reg number and rang 999. Since it was a black Andi they notified us, and Forensics checked the tyre marks at Scratchwood against the ones where the attack on you and the police van took place. They matched.' Mackenzie grinned. 'Same as the paint samples taken from the Ford you were driving and the geezer's car. It's the same vehicle. I ran the number plate through the computer but it didn't show up as stolen. It was bought. From a dealership in Surrey two days ago.'

'Who the hell buys a car to use in a kidnapping? Why not just nick one?'

Mackenzie could only shrug. 'It was bought with cash. Twenty-three grand in used fifties and twenties.'

'Name of the buyer?'

'False, as you'd expect, but the guy who sold the car and the geezer at Scratchwood both gave good descriptions of the purchaser and the driver. The artist's impressions are being run through the computer to see if there's any match-up with known villains.'

'I wonder why they didn't just dump the car at Scratchwood?'

'Perhaps it wasn't convenient for them.'

'Then why pull in there in the first place?'

'Christ knows. Could have been any reason. Perhaps they needed fuel, maybe. Could have been that.' He shrugged. 'Even villains have to pee, don't they? Who cares? All we know is that they were there.'

Maggie nodded. 'Does Bradley know about this?' she enquired.

'He's been out of the office all afternoon. I left a couple of messages on his voicemail but he hasn't got back to me.'

Maggie stood up, wincing slightly in the process.

'You all right?' Mackenzie asked.

174

'OK. A bit stiff.'

'You should go home. There's nothing more we can do until we get some kind of feedback on those artist's impressions anyway. And there's no telling when that'll be. It could be an hour or it could be tomorrow.'

'I'll wait,' she said distractedly. 'I wonder where Chapman is? Where they took him?'

'I'd like to know *why* they took him,' Mackenzie added.

Maggie raised her eyebrows. 'Me too,' she murmured.

42

Chapman was surprised at how far the voices carried on the still air.

He was also grateful.

For brief seconds he froze as he heard the sounds coming from the top of the stone steps ahead of him. Then the moment passed and he dashed across the deserted tennis court, heading for the deep shadows behind a skip. As he ducked into the gloom he realised his fists were clenched tight.

You forgot the piece of wood. You left your only weapon on the other side of the fucking wire.

'Shit,' he muttered under his breath.

His mouth felt dry and he was having trouble controlling his breathing. In such a deathly silent arena, he was beginning to wonder if even his laboured exhalations might give him away.

He strained his ears once more, trying to catch more of the words he'd heard. Trying to pick out exactly how many voices there were.

The sound of speech had been replaced by another, more furtive sound: that of footsteps on the steps ahead of him.

Chapman felt suddenly exposed, unsure that the shadows cast by the skip were dense enough to hide him, but there was nowhere else to hide. Not now.

He pushed himself back against the rusty metal, trying to become a part of it. To melt into the blackness of the shadows there.

The footsteps came closer.

Chapman gritted his teeth.

A single figure padded into view.

Slightly built, wearing trainers and jeans under a dark sweatshirt.

And the mask.

It looked horribly familiar to the detective. He'd seen ones just like it in each of the five snuff movies created by Seymour.

This newcomer, Chapman guessed, was in his late teens or early twenties. The sleeves of his sweatshirt were rolled up as far as his meagre biceps. The track marks in the crooks of both elbows were clearly visible, even in the dull light bathing the deserted tennis court.

Something else clearly visible was the length of metal piping that he carried. He held it in his right hand, swinging it back and forth every now and then. It made a loud swishing sound in the air.

Just one of them, Chapman thought. He was sure he'd heard two voices. Perhaps the other one was waiting at the top of the steps. Any movement by the detective would bring the other running.

The masked figure walked slowly across the expanse of concrete, heading for the wire fence.

Chapman stood up, wondering whether it would be better to run for the steps or to take the figure out.

'Can you see anything?'

The voice lanced through the stillness and the detective ducked hurriedly down again into the welcoming embrace of the shadows behind the skip. The words had come from the top of the stone steps to his right. Called by the masked man's companion.

Chapman waited to see if the second pursuer would also descend. One of them he could handle. Two might be a little more difficult. And the noise might bring more of them.

'I said, can you see anything?' the voice shouted once more.

'I fucking heard you,' the first man replied without looking round. Chapman watched as he reached the fence and kicked at several panels. They rattled loudly.

'He must have got past us,' the first man called.

'He can't have,' the other shouted back.

'Well, he's not here, is he?' the first said derisively. 'Check back there. Tell the others.'

Others, Chapman thought. How many more of them were up there?

'Let's just find this cunt and put him to sleep, eh?' the first figure said. He scratched at the crook of one elbow with a bony finger.

Chapman heard the footsteps at the top of the stairs fading away. He let out a breath slowly. One on one now. That was more favourable odds.

The figure turned and headed straight towards the skip. He hawked loudly and spat on the concrete ahead of him. Chapman could hear him humming tunelessly as he approached. The detective sucked in a deep breath.

Now or never.

The figure was five feet from him, still swinging the piping.

Chapman heard him sniff loudly then spit again. A large globule of mucus landed on the concrete a couple of feet away.

The detective rose slightly and edged towards the end of the skip that hid him.

Now. Do it now.

The figure stepped into view.

Chapman launched himself at it, slamming into it with all his weight. The masked figure went down under the attack, surprised by its ferocity. The detective pinned the figure beneath him, gripped the front of his sweat-shirt with one hand and drove a fist three times, hard, into the masked face. The impacts drove his opponent's head back against the concrete beneath and a groan of pain escaped from the lips under the mask.

Chapman hauled him up, preparing to strike again if he had to, but the figure's head lolled to one side and the detective realised his oppenent was unconscious. He pulled at the mask, ripping it away to expose the face beneath.

The man was in his early twenties. His face was pock-marked, and there was blood running from his split lip and smashed nose.

A kid.

The detective hurriedly rifled through the youth's pockets. There was no ID. There weren't even labels in his clothes.

Chapman reached for the length of metal piping, closing his fist around it. It would be more effective than a lump of wood, he thought.

'Well done, detective.' Seymour's voice rumbled in his right ear. 'First blood to you. But bear in mind there is an awfully long way to go.'

179

Chapman got to his feet, gazing down at the motion-less youth.

'Just one more thing to do before you press on,' Seymour continued. 'Kill him.'

43

Chapman hesitated, still looking down at the prone youth.

'Kill him,' Seymour repeated. 'If you don't he'll come after you.'

The detective prodded the body with toe of his boot.

'Do you think he would have hesitated to kill you if he'd got the chance?' Seymour went on. 'Him or any of the others waiting up ahead.'

Chapman shook his head.

'I would have thought killing would have been easy for you, detective,' Seymour said. 'After all, you didn't have any problem killing that paedophile, did you?'

The detective took a couple of steps away from the youth, his eyes now fixed on the stone steps ahead of him.

'Don't expect to get through this if you're not prepared to kill,' Seymour continued. 'It's your only way out. Personally, I don't care where you choose to die but you will die if you don't fight back. If you don't kill.'

Chapman spun away from the body, ducking low as he ran towards the steps.

Seymour laughed. 'Do you think you're depriving me of entertainment by not fighting back?' he asked. 'Do you think that your refusal to kill suggests some kind of nobility on your part? Well, if you do, you're mistaken, detective. And as you know, the object of these films was never entertainment. It was justice.'

Chapman tapped his right ear, as if to silence the voice. He was halfway up the stairs now, still ducked low, the length of piping held in his hand. He slowed his pace, noticing that there was more light ahead. If anyone was waiting for him he would be visible as soon as he reached the top of the steps. However, also at the top of the stairs he could see a number of dustbins, piled up on top of each other like the discarded building bricks of some gigantic child.

Chapman reached the top step and crouched down once more, peering through the gaps in the barricade of dustbins.

Beyond, lit by half a dozen street lamps, was a large paved area. There were a number of wooden benches dotted about the square and, at its centre, Chapman could see what appeared to be a large ornamental fountain. The perimeter of the square was formed on all four sides by tall buildings, some of which had lights glowing in their windows.

The detective scanned them, wondering if they actually had people inside. There were still no land-marks to help him identify the location. Nothing familiar about the architecture that enabled him to pin down which part of which city he might be in. Not even the church that faced him across the large open area.

182

He remembered the church from one of the other snuff movies. It was next to several partially demolished houses and there were two large lorries and a crane parked outside. The crane thrust upwards towards the heavens like the skeletal remains of some previously undiscovered species of dinosaur.

'You can try to make it across the square if you like,' Seymour told him. 'But I wouldn't advise it.'

Chapman thought for a second about telling Seymour to fuck himself but remembered he couldn't hear him anyway. He contented himself with raising two fingers into the air, sure that one of the many CCTV cameras would capture the gesture.

'It's more than five hundred yards from one side of the square to the other,' Seymour's voice went on. 'You've got to reach the church. Get inside it. If I were you I'd make my way through the buildings on either side. But it's your choice. Perhaps I should say it's your funeral.' The older man laughed. 'Or it will be if they find you.'

Chapman glanced to one side then the other. There was no sign of movement ahead of him. Perhaps, he reasoned, those hunting him might be inside the buildings waiting. In any case, he couldn't take the chance of running across the square with so little cover there. If two or three of them caught him in the open, that would be the end. Seymour was right about that at least.

But which way to go? Left or right?

Chapman went left and darted for the doorway leading into what looked like a Victorian town house. He ran up the steps towards the heavy front door and pushed against the partition, looking over his shoulder to see if anyone had heard him. The door opened enough for him to slip inside. He stepped in, pulling it shut behind him.

The detective found himself in a narrow hallway lit by a single unshaded bulb. Ahead of him was a wooden staircase, to his right an open door.

He edged towards the door and popped his head round the jamb. The room beyond was empty. Uncarpeted and unfurnished. No paint on the walls. He ducked back into the hallway and began climbing the stairs.

They creaked protestingly under his weight and the detective cursed to himself as he climbed higher, pausing every now and then to listen for sounds of pursuit. He reached the landing and turned to his right.

Again, there was no carpet on the floor. No furniture in sight. No wallpaper or paint to hide the plaster walls. He moved towards another door and pushed it open.

There was a sleeping bag on the bare floor.

Chapman crossed to it, aware now of a pungent smell which he recognised as stale urine. He assumed it was coming from the sleeping bag, but as he straightened up after bending to check he realised that the source was beyond the room. There was a large hole in the wall closest to him, so large that he barely had to duck to get through it. He moved through, realising that the hole connected the house with the next building.

The smell of urine grew stronger and he followed it, through two rooms that were almost pitch black. He pressed himself close to the wall, stepping over bricks and pieces of timber that had fallen across the floor, presumably when the wall was breached.

There was much brighter light a few feet ahead.

Fluorescent light. And still that smell of urine, now cloying and almost overpowering.

The floor of the next room dropped away sharply and Chapman found himself looking down into what had once been a public toilet. There was dirty water all over the floor, glistening in the light of the fluorescents. The tiles inside were yellowed in places, stained dark brown in others. He didn't even want to think what had caused the discoloration but the stench rising from the lavatory would seem to supply the answer However, on the floor outside one of the cubicles there was another splash of colour. Blood. Chapman smiled grimly. He had watched it being spilt.

The wall ahead of him was solid and unbreached.

Nothing else to do but go down there, eh? No other way round.

He stuck the length of piping into the back of his jeans and lowered himself down from the first floor, dropping as silently as he could into the tiled expanse of the toilet.

The metal pipe fell from his jeans, dislodged by the impact of his landing, and hit the ground with a loud clang that seemed to reverberate around the entire square.

The detective heard footsteps above him. Running. He snatched up the piece of metal and ducked into the farthest of the six cubicles, the footfalls now hammering more urgently towards him. He heard them come down a flight of steps.

Heard them on the floor of the room next to him.

'In there,' he heard a voice say.

The detective pressed himself back against the rear wall of the cubicle.

The footsteps entered the toilet.

'Check the cubicles,' said a second voice.

Before the last word had even been spoken, Chapman heard the crash as the door of the first cubicle was kicked open.

Another five and they would be on him.

44

The detective stepped up on to the seatless bowl of the lavatory inside the cubicle and waited.

He heard the second door slam open.

Then the third.

He gripped the metal piping more tightly, readying himself.

He'd heard two sets of footsteps outside. Just two. How many more were waiting beyond he couldn't begin to imagine but, for now, his only concern was the two people searching for him in this reeking hole.

The fourth door was kicked open.

Chapman pressed back against the tiles as if to melt into them.

The fifth door slammed back against the wall.

The detective could see a pair of dirty trainers outside his cubicle.

The door was kicked. It flew open.

Chapman launched himself from his perch, swinging the metal pipe as best he could in the confined space He caught the leading figure across the forehead, bringing the metal down so hard it splintered bone. The figure dropped to his knees, clutching at his head.

The one behind ran at Chapman.

The detective saw something metallic flash beneath the fluorescents and realised it was a knife.

The second man caught him across the right shoulder with the flailing blade. It cut through the material of his T-shirt and scraped his collarbone. Blood blossomed from the wound but Chapman managed to grab the man's outstretched arm and swing him round.

He flung him into the wall with a sickening crash that stunned the man long enough to leave him defenceless. Chapman hit him hard across the face with the metal piping and he went down in an untidy heap, blood spilling out from beneath his mask to puddle on the grimy tiles beneath.

The first man by this time was on his feet again. He shot out an arm in Chapman's direction and the detective hissed in pain as he felt something slice open the back of his left hand.

As his assailant swung the open razor again, Chapman ducked beneath the lunge and drove his shoulder into the man's solar plexus, knocking him backwards. The figure landed in a pool of urine and skidded two or three feet.

Chapman advanced on him, bringing the metal pipe down with thunderous force on the man's outstretched leg.

It splintered the shin bone easily and the man shrieked in agony, now more concerned with escaping from Chapman than killing him. As he tried to scramble to his feet, the detective caught him powerfully across the base of the skull. The man crashed forward on his face, gasping for breath, still trying to crawl.

Chapman hit him again.

This time he didn't move.

Chapman staggered back, gulping air, blood dripping from the cut on his left hand. He stepped aside to pull the mask off the man behind him, revealing another youth in his early twenties. Again, he went through the lad's pockets but found nothing. It was the same with his other assailant. However, he noticed that the second unconscious youngster was wearing a belt. Chapman undid it and pulled it free, threading it through the belt loops of his own jeans. That done, he took the fallen knife and jammed it into the belt. It was a big, broad-bladed weapon, very similar to a Bowie knife and lethally sharp. The open razor he left.

He knelt by each of the figures in turn and pressed his fingers to their throats, feeling for a pulse.

Both were still alive.

'Fuck you, Seymour,' Chapman rasped. 'I'm not killing anyone for you.'

He moved slowly out of the toilet.

45

Maggie Grant nudged the office door with her shoulder. She muttered to herself when some of the coffee slopped over the side of the plastic cups she was carrying.

DS Mackenzie didn't afford her so much as a glance. He was gazing raptly at his computer screen.

'Maggie, come and have a look at this,' he said, beckoning her forward. 'It just came through.'

She put the coffees down and moved over to Mackenzie's desk. 'What's so interesting?'

'The black Audi,' he told her. 'We've got positive ID on one of the occupants.' He gestured towards the screen. 'David Phelan. Ex-army. He did eight years in the paras. Got out ten months ago and went to work for a private security firm in London.'

'Has he got form?'

'He was court-martialled while he was in the army for supposedly torturing prisoners of war in Iraq. Apparently one of them died.'

'And he was convicted?'

'No. The case fell apart when two witnesses refused

to give evidence against him. He left the army two months later. Bought himself out.'

'How old is he?'

'Thirty-six.'

'How come the computer came back with his name if he's got no convictions since he came out of the forces?'

'He had them before he went in.' Mackenzie smiled. 'He did a two stretch for aggravated assault when he was twenty.'

'Who's this security firm he worked for?' Maggie asked. 'They must have details about him.'

'Gauntlet Security. They're based in London but they do work all over the country. All I could get out of them on the phone is that he's not employed there now.'

'You'd better circulate Phelan's description, Mack. Put out a directive to pick him up wherever he's spotted. The quicker we can interview him the better.'

'I've done that, but nothing so far. There's no trace of him from the time he left Gauntlet. No home address, nothing. It's like he took off his uniform and disappeared into thin air.'

46

Chapman clenched his left fist tightly. The cut on the back of his hand wasn't as deep as he first feared. The bleeding had stopped and, apart from a little stiffness around the wound itself, the hand was undamaged.

The skin on the knuckles of his right hand was bruised from punching his attackers but the discomfort was negligible. He pressed himself tight against the wall of the room where he now sheltered and waited.

There was a window just ahead of him and, from his position on the first floor of the building, he could see out over the square. He leaned forward slightly and gazed out into the open expanse of concrete.

There were four men moving about slowly around the fountain. They didn't go far from the central marker, not venturing into the dull, shadowed areas on the perimeter of the square. Perhaps, he reasoned, they were content to wait there for him, convinced that he would have to cross the open space at some point. Whether they'd heard the commotion earlier that had resulted in the disabling of two of their companions he could only guess.

The detective ducked as he passed the window. There was always the chance that the light from the sodium lamps outside might illuminate him.

He dropped to all fours and crawled the last few yards towards the hole in the wall before him. He grunted painfully under his breath as the shattered plaster and broken pieces of brick dug into his kneecaps but he continued doggedly, anxious to reach the next building.

There was light ahead. It was welling up from below, coming from a hallway. A set of wide stairs descended into the light. Chapman hesitated, one hand on the balustrade, wondering if it was safe to go down.

He hefted the piece of metal piping before him and tapped the knife wedged in his belt for reassurance.

Carefully he began to descend.

The stairs creaked loudly and the detective paused for a moment, listening for any sounds of movement either below him or from anywhere else on the first floor.

Satisfied that he hadn't been heard, he continued down, wincing at the brightness of the light in the hallway. A bank of fluorescents was shining in the ceiling, reflecting off the grubby tiled floor. The staircase turned at a right angle and Chapman paused at the halfway mark, trying to slow his breathing, ears alert for the slightest noise.

He moved down several more steps, still gripping the stair-rail to steady himself. There were doors leading out of the hallway to his left and his right. He reached the bottom and turned to his left.

The door he was facing burst open, slamming back on its hinges so hard it looked as if the whole frame was coming away from the wall.

The figure that hurtled through the door was big.

At least six feet tall. Dressed in jeans and a battered

leather jacket, it was holding a claw hammer in one fist.

Over the face, a thick black balaclava obscured the features. As the figure ran at him, Chapman could see only the eyes, glaring wide.

Such was the suddeness and ferocity of the attack, the detective barely avoided the first savage hammer blow aimed at his head. He heard the weapon part the air close to his right ear, then felt a numbing blow as it slammed into his shoulder. He went down.

White-hot pain shot down his arm and he hissed as he rolled to one side, desperate to avoid the next strike. The second blow missed him completely, smashing one of the tiles beside him instead. Chapman rolled again, trying to find some way of getting to his feet. He struck out blindly with the metal piping and caught his assailant across the shin.

The attacker yelped in pain and backed off. Chapman managed to get to his feet. He lifted the piping again, prepared to face the next onslaught. His assailant said something unintelligible and launched himself at the detective again. Chapman swung the pipe up to meet the downward swing of the hammer and the two im-plements crashed together with a loud clang.

Chapman kicked out, catching the other man on the ankle hard enough to unbalance him. Taking advantage of his temporary superiority, the detective struck again, catching the man across the left shoulder with a blow powerful enough to shatter the collarbone.

The man staggered backwards, his breath coming in gasps. Chapman pressed his advantage. He ducked under another swipe of the hammer and drove his shoulder into the man's stomach, knocking him over. Both of them slammed into the wall, landing with the policeman on top. He drove two powerful punches into the face of his opponent then brought the metal pipe down hard on his forehead.

The man groaned loudly, the hammer slipping from his grasp. As he reached out to try to retrieve it, Chapman smashed two of his fingers with the piping. Again the man shrieked with pain.

'Who are you?' Chapman demanded, tugging at the balaclava. 'Tell me or I'll kill you.'

The figure beneath him whimpered in pain and shock.

The detective pulled the woollen mask free and tossed it to one side. He found himself looking into the face of a man in his late twenties. His face was splashed with blood, his eyes wide with fear.

'Who are you?' Chapman snarled, grabbing the man by the throat. He raised the pipe above his head as if to strike.

'You'd better run.'

The voice was inside the detective's right ear.

He ignored it for a moment, more interested in the man he had pinned beneath him.

'Get out of there now,' Seymour's voice insisted.

Chapman hesitated then slowly got to his feet. 'You follow me and you're dead,' he snarled, pointing the metal pipe at the prone figure. 'Understand?'

The man raised both hands in a supplicatory gesture.

'Can I get out of here that way?' the detective demanded, indicating the door through which the other man had entered the hallway.

The younger man nodded.

'You haven't got time to stand around,' Seymour's voice said. Outside, Chapman could hear the sound of pounding feet coming closer. 'If you want to live, get out now,' the voice continued. 'They heard you. They're coming for you.'

195

47

Anthony Seymour allowed his eyes to flick from one of the four screens before him to another. Each monitor showed a different image. A different angle on what was happening. He moved forward in his chair a little and zoomed one of the cameras in for a closer look at the four masked men outside the building Detective Inspector Joe Chapman now occupied.

Seymour smiled to himself, noting the assortment of weapons the men carried.

Knives. Small hatchets. Chains and machetes. Each carried at least one of the weapons. In two cases, a combination of them.

They were at the front door now, slipping easily through the unlocked partition and spilling into the building itself.

Seymour checked to see where Chapman was and saw that the detective was already making his way through a hole in the wall into the next building. A camera inside the room he emerged into swung towards him. Like many of the others, it was motion-activated and the approach of the detective had triggered it.

The room Chapman was now in was filled with piles

of wooden planks, some stacked bags of plaster and other workmen's paraphernalia. In the centre of the room was a mound of broken bricks, looking like some kind of bizarre funeral mound. Seymour watched as the policeman considered the best place to hide.

There was a doorless gap in the wall to the far side of the room but Chapman seemed more intent on secreting himself somewhere.

'If I were you, I'd keep running,' Seymour said into the microphone on the desk he sat at. On one of the cameras he saw Chapman mouth something that he guessed was an expletive.

The next moment, the policeman ducked down behind a stack of plaster sacks, pushing himself against the wall behind them. Hidden by the shadows and the sacks, he waited.

'You can't hide for ever, detective,' Seymour told him. 'They'll find you. Better to run or fight.'

Two of the masked men were entering the room. Seymour sat forward excitedly, watching them as they blundered past the skulking detective.

'Bloody fools,' Seymour murmured, shaking his head. He watched them run out of the room through the doorless gap. Another angle showed him their ascent of the staircase beyond. He reached for the brandy glass on his desk and warmed the balloon in his hand, enjoying the aroma that rose from within. Then, smiling, he sipped the spirit slowly, his eyes still flicking from one screen to the next.

Chapman was now peering over the stack of plaster sacks, gazing in both directions, wondering whether or not to come out.

'You've got to reach the church, detective,' Seymour told him, leaning close to the microphone. 'If I were you, I'd press on. You haven't far to go.'

He saw Chapman duck back behind the sacks once more.

'I don't think this one likes our game,' Seymour sighed, looking to a chair on his right, where his son, eyes wide with wonder, pointed at the screens with a thick index finger. Thomas laughed raucously, a sound from deep inside his throat.

'Just keep watching, Tom,' Seymour said quietly. 'You watch what happens next.'

Thomas Seymour laughed again.

48

Chapman peered tentatively over the sacks of plaster, ears alert for any further sounds of movement. When he heard nothing he swung himself out from behind the makeshift rampart.

Gripping the metal piping, he moved cautiously towards the doorway through which his two pursuers had disappeared. The detective saw the steps leading upwards and put his foot on the first wooden stair, hesitating a moment before he began to climb. The stairwell itself was dark but there was a light burning on the landing above. It acted like a beacon for the detective and he moved slowly towards it.

He was halfway up the staircase when the two figures appeared on the landing above him.

They both hurtled down towards him, the leading one swinging the chain he carried like some kind of metallic bolas.

Chapman ducked beneath the swing, hearing the heavy links crash into the wall behind him. At the same time he swung a powerful arm and caught the attacker in the face with the metal piping, pulverising his nose and knocking him off his feet. The man pitched forward with a loud shriek and tumbled down the remainder of the stairs, landing with a thud at the bottom where he lay still.

The second man hacked frenziedly at Chapman with the machete he was carrying. The first wild swing caught the detective across his left side, tearing through the material of his T-shirt and opening a gash in the flesh below. Blood burst from the cut and Chapman hissed in pain, even as he ducked beneath another blow designed to split his skull.

He struck out with the metal piping and hit his assailant across the shoulder with it, deflecting the next blow of the machete. Frustrated, the masked attacker lunged again, shouting madly as he did so. The long blade sliced through the air. Chapman managed to parry the strike with the metal piping, deflecting it and causing his assailant to overbalance.

The masked man clutched at Chapman, trying to pull him down too, and the policeman brought a knee up into the man's groin. It connected so hard he felt it slam into the pelvic bone. His opponent groaned in agony and Chapman struck him again with the piping, catching him across the left temple. The figure grasped at empty air for a second then toppled backwards down the stairs.

The detective followed him, hitting him again as he sprawled at the foot of the stairway. The man flopped backwards, the machete slipping from his hand.

Chapman took the machete and slid it into his belt along with the broad-bladed knife. The man, he noticed, was still groaning quietly, raising his head from the floor a couple of inches. Chapman put one hand to his gashed side and saw the blood on his palm when he pulled it away. He glared at the figure lying before him, trying to rise, then stamped hard on the back of his skull.

The savage impact drove the man's face downwards. Chapman repeated his action, his breath now coming in gasps, the sweat running down his face.

'Why not finish him off?' Seymour said into the detective's ear. 'He's helpless now. They both are. They would have killed you. What have you got to lose?'

Chapman looked down again at the wound in his left side. It wasn't as deep as he'd first thought. The blade had missed his pelvis and, despite the fact that it hurt badly, the bleeding wasn't too severe.

Lucky it caught one of your love handles, eh? No muscle damage. It just cut into fat.

He wiped his bloodied palm on his jeans and made his way back up the stairs, knowing that there were at least two other men close by. He would have to either fight them or outrun them. How soon that decision would arise, he had no idea.

He moved on.

49

Detective Sergeant James Mackenzie spotted a parking space and hurriedly swung the Mazda into it.

'Tell me again why this can't wait until the morning?' he said, looking across at his passenger. 'There's been no trace of David Phelan for months. Turning up at the place he used to be employed isn't going to make him suddenly appear, is it? You'd have been better off going home and resting. We could have checked this out tomorrow.'

'I appreciate your concern, Mack,' Maggie Grant said. 'But I can rest when this is over.' She turned from her inspection of the buildings in Brook Street to meet his enquiring gaze. 'If Phelan was an employee of Gauntlet Security until a few months ago then they might know where he is. Or at least the place where he was employed after he left them.'

Mackenzie shrugged, swung himself out of the car and hurried round to help Maggie out of the vehicle. She smiled at her colleague, a look of amusement on her face.

'I can manage, Mack.'

'You've spent most of today in hospital,' he said. 'I was just trying to help.'

'Thanks,' she said. 'Your thoughtfulness is touching.'

He smiled and raised two fingers in her direction.

Maggie chuckled.

Mackenzie locked the car and the two detectives set off along the street looking for the address they sought.

'This one,' Maggie said, nodding in the direction of a black-painted front door.

There was a panel beside the door bearing the names of the occupants. Maggie pressed one index finger to the list and drew it slowly down.

'Got it,' she exclaimed.

She rang the appropriate bell and leaned closer to the panel. As she did so, a CCTV camera turned to track her movement.

'Gauntlet Security,' said a metallic voice.

'Police,' she announced. 'We'd like to speak to whoever's in charge.'

'Can you hold your ID up to the camera, please?' the metallic voice requested.

Both detectives produced their identification and did as instructed. There was a loud droning sound and the door opened. Maggie walked into the hallway, heading for the lift directly ahead. Mackenzie followed her and the two of them rode the lift to the third floor. It bumped to a halt and the two detectives stepped out into a cream-coloured hallway. Ahead of them was a white painted door with a gold nameplate on it. GAUNTLET SECURITY.

'Business must be good,' Mackenzie said, glancing around.

Maggie knocked on the door and it was opened immediately by a tall, dark-haired man in a charcoal-grey suit who ushered them inside. They followed him through to a large office where he pointed in the direction of a calfskin sofa before seating himself behind the desk.

'What can I do for you?' he said.

'Are you in charge?' Maggie asked.

'At the moment. Mr Wells doesn't come in until the morning. He owns the business.'

'And who are you?' Mackenzie asked.

'My name's Lane. Andrew Lane.'

'We're looking for a former employee of this firm, Mr Lane,' Maggie told him.

'I can't give you information like that,' Lane said flatly. 'Mr Wells wouldn't like it.'

'He doesn't even have to know,' Mackenzie assured him.

'Run a computer check now,' Maggie added, 'and we won't have to come back in the morning with a warrant.'

'I can't,' Lane repeated.

'If you make us come back with a warrant, it'll be in a patrol car,' she said. 'Probably with the lights flashing. That wouldn't look so good for business, would it? Especially not around here and certainly not if your boss had clients in. You give us what we need now and we won't have to do that.'

Lane looked at the two detectives for a moment longer, then nodded.

'Who are you looking for?' he enquired.

'A man called David Phelan,' Maggie said. 'Our records show that he started work here ten months ago.'

Lane gazed at his computer screen for a moment, tapping various keys in the process.

'He did work here,' he said finally. 'But only for two months.'

'Where did he go?' Maggie asked. 'Is there anything

on your files about the job he went to after he left here? Have you got a home address for him?'

Lane frowned as he tapped more keys.

'And what if I don't tell you?' he grunted. 'Will you still be back in the morning with a patrol car?'

Maggie smiled. 'And the lights flashing.'

Lane eyed her warily. 'He went to work for a previous client,' he said. 'That happens in this business. Someone gets on with an operative, likes their attitude and the way they work, and employs them full time.'

'Who was the client?' Mackenzie enquired.

'Anthony Seymour.'

'The multi-millionaire?' Mackenzie exclaimed. He turned to look at Maggie. 'Wasn't his son attacked a while ago? Almost killed?'

Maggie nodded. 'And his wife killed herself,' she said quietly. 'He's been a recluse ever since.'

'And Phelan's working for him?'

'He lives on Mr Seymour's estate,' Lane told them. 'The man employs about seventy bodyguards. Three other guys who worked here are on his payroll too. Do you want their names as well?'

Maggie shook her head. 'Thank you for your co-operation, Mr Lane,' she said. 'We'll leave you in peace now.'

She got to her feet and headed for the door, followed by Mackenzie. Lane watched as they headed for the lift that would take them back to the ground floor.

'In the morning we drive out to Seymour's estate,' Maggie said as they waited for the lift to arrive. 'Talk to David Phelan.'

The lift doors slid open and the two police officers stepped in.

'Seymour owns half of Buckinghamshire, doesn't he?'

205

Mackenzie said. 'Perhaps that's why he needs so many security men.'

'Seventy of them,' Maggie noted. 'That's not security, that's more like a private army. Makes you wonder what he's got to hide, doesn't it?'

'Didn't someone say that behind every fortune there's a crime?'

'Maybe we should find out if they're right.'

'Tonight?'

'It shouldn't take us more than a couple of hours to reach Seymour's place,' Maggie said. 'If we leave now.'

Mackenzie nodded.

They hurried back to their waiting car.

50

Chapman thought his lungs were going to burst.

As he ran he could feel his heart hammering against his ribs so hard he feared it might explode from inside.

It wasn't going to be the masked man chasing him that ended his life, it was going to be a heart attack.

Sweat was pouring down his face, mingling with the blood from the cut on his left cheek. It was a deep one. The knife that had been drawn down his face had carved a path from his hairline all the way to his top lip. He'd been fortunate it had missed his eye.

He hadn't seen the attack coming. He'd been too busy fighting off the other assailant. The one who was now chasing him. The one who had cut into his right thigh with a kitchen knife.

Chapman could feel the pain from his wounds as he ran but it seemed to spur him on. Even without turning he knew the attacker was gaining on him. He had to be. He was younger, stronger.

Bastard.

The detective could see the church ahead of him.

Less than a hundred yards away, but could he make that last stretch?

Would he be better off turning and fighting? He had the machete in his right hand. The metal piping had fallen from his grasp as he'd smashed it across the neck of the man who had cut his face. The blow had laid the masked man out, but even before he'd had time to enjoy his victory this other maniac had gouged open his thigh.

Cunt.

Chapman chanced a look over his shoulder. He could see that his pursuer was gaining.

Turn and fight him.

In the gloom, the church door seemed to shine like a beacon to the DI. If he could only get inside. Hide. Ambush this fucker so intent on killing him.

'Run faster, detective,' Seymour said in his ear. Chapman heard the words as he run. 'Or is it all going to end here?'

The policeman was close to the steps leading to the door of the church now. Again he looked behind him. The masked man was still pursuing him but it didn't look as if he'd got any nearer. Perhaps he was running out of breath too. Maybe he was losing the stomach for a fight.

Chapman tripped on the steps and went sprawling.

The machete fell from his grasp and skittered across the pavement.

Chapman rolled over on to his back, dragging the knife from his belt, seeing that his pursuer was now within feet of him.

The man skidded to a halt and looked at the detective, who got to his feet as quickly as he could, the knife now lowered in the direction of his attacker.

They faced each other across a few feet of concrete.

'You don't have to do this,' Chapman gasped, wiping sweat and blood from his eyes.

The masked man glared at him and shifted the Stanley knife he held from one hand to the other.

'Turn and walk away,' Chapman said.

'I can't,' the man told him. 'He'll know. He's watching.'

Chapman took a couple of steps backwards, moving slowly up the steps leading to the church. The masked man followed, still keeping his distance.

'Did you help kill the others?' the detective asked, still backing away.

The figure nodded.

'Because he was watching?'

'Because I wanted to.'

Chapman frowned.

'They were valuable,' the masked man grunted. 'Just like you.'

'In what way?'

The man ran at him.

Chapman tried to avoid the lunge but his right leg buckled beneath him and his assailant crashed into him hard. They both went down, the masked man trying to pin the detective beneath him. Chapman struck out with his right hand, using the hilt of the knife as a bludgeon. He slammed the metal into the side of his attacker's head twice, powerful blows delivered with a strength born of desperation. The first splintered the man's jaw, the second smashed through the mask and knocked out two of his teeth. Chapman pushed him off, scrambled to his feet and kicked him hard in the face.

'Cunt,' he snarled as the man's head snapped violently backwards. Pieces of the mask spun into the air, shattered by the impact.

'Good,' Seymour purred in his ear. 'Now kill him.'

209

'Fuck off,' roared Chapman, his voice echoing across the square.

He didn't know how many of the men hunting him were left. He didn't care if it brought them running.

'Do it,' Seymour insisted. 'He's helpless. Use the knife on him.'

Chapman looked down at the prone figure of his assailant, then jabbed it with the toe of his boot.

The masked man didn't move.

Gasping for breath, the detective hurried to the bottom of the steps and retrieved the machete. Then he made his way back towards the church entrance.

He pushed against the heavy door, almost surprised when it opened. He stepped inside, his footsteps echoing within the cavernous building.

'What the fuck is this?' he murmured to himself.

The church was empty. No pews. No pulpit. No lectern. No font. Even the spaces in the walls where the stained glass windows should have been were bricked up. The detective walked slowly through the building. Down what should have been the central aisle towards the nave, then on to the chancel and the altar.

Set into the back wall was a small, unpainted wooden door.

'Go through the door, detective,' Seymour told him.

Chapman hesitated.

'You'd better hurry,' Seymour insisted. 'Before anyone else comes.'

The detective pushed open the door and stepped through.

'You should have let him die.'

Anthony Seymour shook his head. 'He was always to be afforded the same chance as the others had,' he said

210

quietly, watching the bank of monitors before him. 'He's already got further than any of the others.'

'I still say you should have let him die,' the other voice insisted.

'There's plenty of time for that,' Seymour said quietly. 'Relax.'

'And what if he makes it? What if he gets out?'

'You know that's impossible. He's already injured. They've slowed him down. He won't escape. Just sit back and watch.'

'You'd better be right.'

Seymour turned to face the owner of the voice. 'He won't get out alive,' he said flatly.

Detective Sergeant Michael Bradley chewed one bitten-off fingernail and gazed nervously at the screens.

51

Chapman couldn't see a thing in front of him.

The darkness beyond the door at the rear of the church was so total he feared, for a few seconds, that he'd gone blind.

He put out a hand. It connected with something solid, and he paused a moment, his breathing ragged, squinting into the impenetrable gloom. He rubbed his eyes with one hand but saw only white stars behind his own eyelids. Keeping his hand against the wall on his left, he edged slowly through the cloying blackness.

If one of those fuckers is waiting in here, you haven't got a chance.

The thought struck him like a thunderbolt.

He could cut your throat before you even knew he was there.

The detective stopped dead, trying to control his breathing, attempting to slow the savage beating of his heart.

Think. Be logical. If you can't see, neither can they.

He took another step forward.

Or can they?

Chapman edged forward again, left palm still pressed

to the wall. What if they were equipped with infra-red goggles or something? Some of the cameras had to be built for infra-red. Why wouldn't Seymour have equipped his maniacs with the same device?

The detective swung the machete in the darkness, hearing it swish through empty air.

It didn't strike anyone.

Well, it wouldn't, would it? If there's someone in here with you, using infra-red to watch you, they would have seen what you were doing and got out of the way, wouldn't they?

He swung it again, spinning round to aim it behind him this time. The blade cut through the air and clanged noisily against the wall beside him. Several bright sparks leapt from the impact point: minute sparks of brilliant light in the all-enveloping gloom.

Chapman moved on, the machete now held before him at arm's length.

He had no way of knowing how long this walkway was, although the fact that the machete had connected with stonework when he'd swung it led him to believe that it was less than ten feet wide.

What if there's some kind of trapdoor in the floor?

He shook his head. That was too simple. Seymour was watching his predicament for entertainment. The bastard wouldn't want him to die in the dark just by falling down a fucking hole. No. He wanted to see him die. Out in the open in full, glorious technicolour.

Shithouse.

Chapman gripped the handle of the machete more tightly and moved on, jabbing the weapon ahead of him.

The wall he was pressing against felt dry, not the damp wetness he expected. He wondered if he was under-ground, but he doubted it. He hadn't descended any steps to reach this impenetrable gloom. He looked up but

213

could see nothing. No night sky. No stars. It had been the same when he'd been out in the square in front of the church or walking the street when he'd first been released from inside the holding cell. And, as in the street and the square, there was no sound either. No distant traffic. Not even a hint of a breeze. He stopped walking and dropped to his haunches, wiping one hand across the ground beneath his feet. It was smooth. Not stone but something man-made. Linoleum, possibly?

He got up once more, wincing at the growing pain from his slashed right thigh.

The sudden noise just ahead of him was deafening inside the black and silent corridor. A strident shriek of metal on metal.

Chapman gripped the machete more tightly and prepared himself to reach for the knife with his left hand. If they were going to rush him from the front he wouldn't go down without a fight. If—

'Jesus,' he hissed, shielding his eyes.

Bright light filled the corridor, spilling from behind the sliding metal door that had just opened. It rolled aside on hydraulic runners, finally slamming into a wide crevice on the right-hand side of the corridor. The darkness retreated before this invasion of radiance and Chapman glanced behind him to see that he had barely advanced fifteen feet. He could see the door by which he'd left the church behind him.

He was, he noted with relief, alone in the corridor.

As his eyes became accustomed to the brightness, he walked on, pausing at the threshold of the electronic metal door, peering ahead to what awaited him.

There was grime all over the floor in every direction. Chapman could see what looked like excrement. Even blood. There was graffiti sprayed on some of the

214

shop fronts that were visible from where he stood. Many were boarded up or had their windows painted black but the detective could see that some had their doors open. Some were lit inside; others looked as dark and gloomy as the corridor he had just left. High above him, banks of fluorescents cast a blinding white glow over everything. About fifty yards ahead of him was an abandoned escalator leading up to another level of shops.

He realised he was gazing at a shopping mall.

Who had shopped here and when, he wondered? Would he find some clue within as to where he was?

He was still wondering when he heard the screams.

52

As he dashed from the cover of the corridor into the glaring brightness of the mall, Chapman had one thought.

Was this all part of the game? Were the screams meant to bring him running?

He wondered if Seymour was sitting watching him at this very second, smiling. Congratulating himself on the whole set-up. Thinking how fucking clever he'd been. Chapman glanced up at the shop fronts as he ran, wondering if there were cameras mounted there that were now picking up his image. He knew they'd be somewhere. Watching.

The screams had come from his right and he'd followed them without hesitation. Only now, as he slowed his pace, did he hear another.

It seemed to rise on the air then die quickly. As if something had stifled it.

The sounds were unmistakably female; that much he was sure of.

Who's to say Seymour hasn't got girl killers patrolling this fucking place as well?

Then there was a deeper, guttural sound he recognised as male laughter.

The detective skidded to a halt and ducked into a shop doorway, his breath rasping in his throat. He tried to pinpoint exactly where the sounds were coming from. There was a deserted clothes shop opposite him, its windows boarded up. To his right was a sports shop, to his left an empty building. The doorway he now sheltered in was boarded up too.

The detective heard groaning, then some more laughter. Then what sounded like a cheer. It was followed by some sporadic clapping.

What the fuck was happening?

He gripped the machete tighter and inched his way out of the doorway towards the sports shop, certain by now that that was where the sounds were coming from. Keeping low to the ground, he ran towards the entrance of the shop, drawn by the noises coming from within.

The door was open and Chapman slipped inside, using some display units as cover. There were more of them further down the shop, leading to where the tills had once been. The detective moved to the next unit, straightening slightly to peer between the shelves. From this vantage point he could see the back of the shop.

There were three men there. Two were standing up, leaning on the counter, smoking. The third, his jeans and pants round his knees, was crouched behind a fourth figure.

She was in her teens, naked from the waist down, her blonde hair obscuring her face as she shuddered on all fours. Her head was bowed, and she had stopped screaming now. The man behind her continued to drive his penis into her, each thrust accompanied by

217

a grunt of delight from him and a moan of despair from her.

'Give it to her up the arse,' said one of the figures at the counter. His companion laughed.

'*You* give it to her up the arse,' said the third man, gripping the girl's hips more tightly. 'I'm staying where I am. This cunt feels like liquid velvet.' He chuckled throatily, then groaned approvingly.

Chapman gripped the machete more tightly, the knot of muscles at the side of his jaw pulsing angrily.

Is it a trick? Are they waiting for you? Do they know now that you're watching them?

'I want to come on her face,' said the second man, excitedly unzipping his jeans.

The girl groaned unintelligibly.

'No,' the first one protested. 'Come in her mouth. Make her suck your cock.'

The second figure pulled his erection free of the confines of his jeans and knelt in front of the girl, masturbating slowly.

'You wait until I'm finished,' the third figure grunted. 'I don't want her getting distracted.'

All three men laughed.

Chapman clenched his teeth, desperately trying to think what to do next. He was about twenty feet from the little group. If he rushed them he'd take them by surprise. The two with the girl didn't appear to be armed; or, if they were, their weapons didn't seem to be within easy reach. That just left the third guy. Chapman could see that he had a knife stuck in his waistband and there was a baseball bat lying on the counter next to him. Apart from that, he had nothing.

How can you be sure it isn't just a fucking set-up?

He sucked in a deep breath. He couldn't take that

218

chance. And, even if it was and the girl was part of it, then he'd just have to deck her too.

The third man was speeding up his thrusts now, his fingers digging more tightly into the girl's slender hips, his jagged nails scraping her skin so hard that he left angry red weals on the flesh.

The second figure pushed his engorged penis towards her face, his own hand still moving quickly up and down the shaft. 'Get her head up,' he grunted. 'I'm going to come in her fucking mouth.' He edged closer to the girl. 'Get your fucking head up, bitch.'

'Go on,' rasped the first figure. 'Let her have it. Both ends at once.' He moved closer to the little tableau, chuckling loudly.

Chapman got up on to his haunches then eased into a crouching position, steadying himself. He'd be upon them in two or three strides. He raised the machete a little higher.

'Ready, bitch?' the third man rasped, driving into her faster and harder. 'I'm going to fill you up.'

'Get your fucking head up,' the second snapped again, grabbing a handful of her blonde hair. 'Suck this.' He pushed his penis towards her.

Chapman was on his feet now, ready to strike.

'Do it, do it,' urged the first figure, now only a foot or so from the other three bodies. He was rubbing the front of his jeans, massaging his own erection. Waiting his turn.

'Get your fucking head up, cunt, or I'll cut you,' the second man hissed. Again he tugged at her hair, this time wrenching her head up so that her face was level with his penis.

Chapman could see her clearly now. The scratched and bruised face, the smeared make-up and the grubby, tear-stained cheeks. The detective felt as if someone had suddenly wrapped him in a freezing blanket, shrouded him in material that sucked every ounce of warmth from his body.

He was looking at his daughter.

53

As he jumped to his feet, Chapman could see nothing except the three men before him.

The men raping his daughter.

My daughter.

Anger filled his veins like liquid fire, coursing through every inch of his body. Driving him on. He opened his mouth in a silent scream of rage, his face contorted.

Even if the three men had been ready for his attack it was highly unlikely they would have been able to prevent it, such was its ferocity.

Chapman swung the machete with a savagery born of incandescent fury. The initial blow caught the watching man across the chest, laying it open to the bone and shattering part of the sternum in the process. Blood burst from the wound and the man fell backwards, away from Carla, sprawling on his back. Chapman kicked him hard between the legs, stamping so hard that he split the man's scrotum. Simply burst the soft skin.

The man screamed in agony, clutching at his groin, blood gushing through his fingers.

Chapman caught the first rapist across the face with

a powerful backhand stroke that splintered three of his front teeth and sliced off part of his lower lip. As he reeled from the wound, the detective caught him again, this time with a downward cut that severed the man's left ear and drove two inches into his shoulder. Blood ejaculated from the wound and the man dropped to his knees, one hand raised as if in surrender. Chapman cut at the hand, hacking off two fingers and splitting the palm from knuckle to wrist.

Carla, still on all fours, lunged forward, her lips closing around the penis of her other tormentor. She brought her teeth down hard on the stiff shaft, the strength of her bite shearing through muscle and veins with ease.

The man shrieked in agony as she tore off the top of his penis, spitting it out contemptuously as his blood showered her face.

He rolled on to his back, clutching what was left of his manhood.

Carla was on her feet instantly, reaching for the baseball bat on the counter. She grabbed it and stepped back until she was standing over the fallen figure beneath her. He was still screaming, writhing like a fish on a hot skillet as he held his torn penis.

'Bastard,' she roared and brought the bat down on his head.

The first blow split his forehead just below the hairline. The second shattered his skull. The third split it. She kept hitting him, her aim unerring and her strength ferocious.

Chapman drove a foot into the face of the first fallen man, splintering his jaw and knocking him out. He used the flat of the machete to strike at the other rapist, slamming the bloodied metal hard against the man's temple.

The blow knocked him sideways, unconscious before he hit the ground.

His own quarry immobilised, the detective jammed the machete into his belt and put out a hand, trying to grab the blood-spattered baseball bat from his daughter's hold.

'Carla,' he snapped. 'Stop.'

She shook loose and hit the fallen man again, unconcerned by the fact that there was now little more than a puddle of blood, pulped brain matter and pulverised bone where his head used to be.

'Carla,' Chapman snarled. 'He's dead.'

She spun round to look at him, eyes wide.

The detective stepped back as she swung wildly at him. He felt warm blood spray from the baseball bat as it arced through the air, droplets of it spattering his face.

'Get away from me,' she shrieked frantically.

'Carla, stop,' he urged, backing off. 'Put the bat down.'

She swung again, tears now pouring down her face. 'I'll kill you,' she whimpered.

'Carla,' he said quietly. 'It's me, sweetheart. It's Dad.' He lifted his hands towards her, palms up. 'Look.'

She raised the bat again but at last he saw something approaching recognition in her eyes.

He stood with his arms outstretched.

'It's Dad,' he said again.

She dropped the bat and ran into his arms.

He felt her body shaking uncontrollably, her sobs torn from the depths of her soul. Chapman held her to him, enveloping her in his arms, tears now rolling down his cheeks too. For what seemed like an eternity, they cried together. A shared suffering.

'It's all right,' he whispered. 'It's all right.'

Still she cried.

'No one's going to hurt you now,' Chapman assured her. 'I won't let them.'

'How touching.' The voice was inside Chapman's right ear. Seymour's voice. 'How very gallant of you to save the girl, detective,' it went on.

Chapman looked round, trying to spot one of the cameras he knew were trained on him.

'Unfortunately, deciding to help her may well have doomed you both,' Seymour continued. 'Others are coming.'

The detective kissed the top of his daughter's head and hugged her as he felt her still quivering against him.

'We've got to get out of here, babe,' he said softly.

She clung to him.

Chapman stroked her hair with one bloodied hand, oblivious of the fact that the crimson gore was matting the fine strands.

'Everything's going to be fine,' he assured her. 'But we've got to get out of here now.' He stroked her hair again. 'You just do as I tell you and we'll be all right.'

'Time's running out, detective,' Seymour said.

'Carla,' Chapman said more forcefully. 'Sweetheart, come on. Let's go. We've got to move.'

She pulled away from him slightly and he looked down at her face.

There was a rack of tracksuit bottoms behind him. He felt round and pushed a pair towards her, not wanting to look at her scratched and bloodied lower body.

'Put them on,' he told her.

She nodded and did as he instructed.

'Come on,' he urged, picking up the baseball bat and heading towards the door.

'No, Dad,' she said, shaking her head. 'This way.'

She pointed to a door off to the left.

'It leads to the stairs,' she told him.

Outside he heard the sound of pounding feet.

Carla was already heading towards the door. Chapman followed her.

54

Chapman hurried up the narrow staircase behind his daughter, glancing over his shoulder, waiting for the first of their pursuers to crash through the door below.

'Where are we going?' he gasped as they continued to climb.

'We can hide up here,' she told him.

Carla pushed open the door at the top of the steps and dashed through it. Chapman followed a second later, ducking low among the clothing rails.

Through one of the large picture windows at the front of the shop he could see the first floor of the mall. Carla was already heading towards the door.

'There's a toyshop over there,' she said, pointing ahead of her. 'We can hide in there until they've gone.'

Chapman was about to tell her that they wouldn't go. That they'd hunt them down no matter how long it took. Instead, he merely followed her as she hurried towards the exit. She paused and glanced to her left and right, ensuring there was no one around, then darted out of the shop, across the tiled floor towards the line of shops opposite.

Chapman waited a moment then sprinted after her, moving as quickly as he could on his injured leg. Below him he could hear raised voices and shouts. He had no idea how many of the bastards were down there or if they'd found the three men inside the sports shop yet. All that mattered to him at present was reaching the toyshop that Carla was hurtling towards.

He saw her push open the glass double doors and press on into the welcoming gloom within. She waved at him to join her and he ran across, ducking low.

Carla padded towards the back of the shop, weaving amongst large stuffed bears and other cuddly animals. Chapman thought that it was reassuringly claustrophobic inside the shop: lots of shelves and toys to hide behind if the need should arise. The closer to the back of the building they got, the darker it got too – something else that the detective was grateful for. He glanced to his right and left and found hundreds of eyes trained on him. The sightless glass eyes of dolls fixed him with unblinking stares as he passed in front of them. They watched his progress silently and impassively.

'Just up here,' Carla said quietly, motioning him to join her.

They turned a corner, passing two full-size cuddly reindeer. Chapman ran his hand over the soft fur of the closest as he passed.

The figure loomed out of the gloom in front of them.

Instinctively, the detective stepped in front of Carla to shield her, raising the baseball bat, preparing to strike.

'Dad,' Carla said. 'It's OK.'

Santa Claus looked back at him.

'Ho fucking ho,' Chapman muttered, lowering the bat.

Carla touched his arm and stepped inside the grotto that the red-clad mannequin was guarding.

The room was ten feet square, the floor dusted with about an inch of polystyrene fragments to simulate snow. On the mock timber walls hung a collection of masks. Mickey Mouse. Donald Duck. Goofy. Bugs Bunny. Sylvester. Every imaginable comic character, all with smiling faces. Chapman didn't feel like smiling and he certainly didn't want to see any more fucking masks for a long time. But at least the grotto offered temporary respite from the savagery outside. He slumped against one wall and slid down in a corner, removing the machete from his belt and putting it and the baseball bat on the floor next to him. Carla sat down beside him.

'How do you know about this place?' he asked her quietly.

'I know lots of places to hide in here.'

They sat in silence for a moment, Chapman gazing at his daughter.

'How long have you been here?' he asked finally.

'Five days,' she told him. 'Maybe longer. It's hard to keep track of time.'

'Do you know where we are?'

She shook her head.

'How did you get here?' he asked.

'Two guys, I don't know who they were, put me in a van. Me and five others.'

'Where did they take you from?'

'Oxford Street. It was late one night. I was going back to the squat where I was living. Me and another girl. These two guys pulled up beside us, started talking. Next thing, they were pushing us into the back of their van. When I woke up I was in this place.'

'They drugged you?'

'They must have.'

228

'What happened to the girl you were with? The others in the van with you?'

'I don't know. The same thing that happened to me, I suppose.' She sniffed and wiped one eye with a bloodied finger. 'At the beginning, they told us that we could live here. We'd be given food and whatever we needed.'

'Who told you?'

'Just some guys. I don't know who they were. They said that if we did as we were told we'd get what we wanted. They supplied drugs to the junkies, booze to the alkies. They handed it out every morning and every night along with the food.' She crossed one slender leg over the other and rubbed some dirt and blood from her bare foot. Chapman saw that she was shivering.

'Those bastards that attacked you,' he began softly. 'The ones . . .'

'Raping me?' she murmured. 'You can say it, Dad.' She wiped a tear from one cheek. 'They said I'd stolen food from them. They said that was my punishment.'

Chapman reached out to touch her hand.

She looked at him, her face impassive. 'You're being hunted, aren't you?' she said flatly. 'Like the others.'

'What do you know about that?' he asked, his hand resting lightly on hers.

'We were told that if we managed to kill the men we found we'd be given whatever we wanted. Money. Drugs. Anything.'

'Did you see anyone killed?'

'No. I got told about it, though. They said they cut his head off.'

'What happened to the body? How did they dispose of it?'

'I don't know. I didn't ask.'

She continued rubbing dirt from her feet for a moment

229

then looked at him. 'Did you come looking for me?' she said.

'I've been looking for you ever since you left home,' he told her.

She moved closer to him and Chapman snaked an arm round her shoulder, pulling her nearer.

'We're going to get out of here,' he whispered. 'I promise you.'

'You used to say that when I was a little girl,' she reminded him. 'You said you'd never break a promise you made to me.' She sniffed back tears.

'I tried not to,' he told her.

'I want to go home, Dad,' she said, tears rolling down her cheeks.

Chapman enveloped her in both arms, holding her as tightly as he could.

55

'She's a pretty girl isn't she?'

The detective heard Seymour's voice in his right ear and jerked his head round as if expecting to see the older man standing there.

'Quite a catch,' Seymour went on. 'Is that why you saved her? Would you have saved her if she'd been fat and ugly?' He laughed. 'Are you planning to do to her what the others were doing? Perhaps if you had more time.'

'You sick fuck,' he hissed.

'You've already put on quite a show, detective,' Seymour continued. 'I suppose anything else would be too much to ask.'

Chapman held Carla more tightly to him, his initial anger gradually subsiding as the realisation hit him.

'He doesn't know you're my daughter,' he said softly, his lips barely moving.

Carla didn't answer. She was still clinging to her father, her tears soaking into his already stained T-shirt.

'I'm afraid it's time to end this touching little scene,' Seymour said. 'It's becoming boring. You might want to prepare yourself, detective. You've got visitors.'

Chapman scrambled to his feet, snatching up the machete and the baseball bat.

'Dad,' Carla gasped in surprise, looking up at him.

'Come on,' he said quietly. 'We've got to go.'

'But they won't find us in here,' Carla protested.

Chapman could hear voices but he wasn't sure how many or how far away they were. Inside the shop or outside? He couldn't be sure. Couldn't take the chance to wait and find out.

'They already have,' he said flatly.

'But how could they?' Carla protested, clambering to her feet.

Chapman didn't answer her. He was already moving towards the door of the grotto, disturbing the fake snow once again.

'We've got to get up on to the roof,' he said. 'If we can do that we might be able to see where we are and we'll be able to move from building to building without them seeing us.'

'There're air vents up there,' she said, pointing to several metal grilles in the ceiling. 'Perhaps we can get up through those.'

'We've got to try.'

He stepped out of the grotto, pausing close to the figure of Santa Claus. Carla followed.

'How do we get up into those vents?' he mused, looking into the darkened shop, trying to pick out any signs of movement.

'There's a door at the back of the shop,' she told him. 'It leads to some kind of stockroom.'

'Show me,' he whispered, allowing her to step past him.

Carla ran across the shop, dodging a display of doll's prams. She found the door she sought and turned the handle, relieved to find it wasn't locked. She turned and beckoned Chapman. He nodded then moved as swiftly as he could towards her.

The bang was made all the more thunderous by the solitude inside the shop. The head of the doll closest to him exploded as the bullet hit it.

'Jesus, they've got guns,' he snarled, diving to the floor as he reached the door.

There was another deafening blast and a portion of the door was punched in as if by an invisible fist. Pieces of wood spun into the air, one landing at Chapman's feet. He propelled himself into the storeroom and slammed the door behind him. His daughter was already halfway up the ladder on the far wall.

Chapman began pulling boxes across the door in a desperate effort to block it.

'Come on,' Carla called as she reached the top.

'You go on,' he told her. 'I'll catch you up.'

She hesitated, one hand on the grille above her head.

'Go,' he snarled, piling more boxes and crates against the door.

Carla pushed the grille and found that it opened with very little resistance. She scrambled up, pulling herself into the compartment above. It was pitch black and the metal on all four sides felt freezing cold against her skin. It was barely wide enough for her to squeeze her slender body into. She started crawling, unable to see a hand in front of her, not knowing where she was going or what lay further along the vent. All she wanted was to be away from those who pursued her and her father.

Chapman looked in the direction of the grille and nodded to himself. Then he felt the first impact against the stockroom door. There was shouting from the other side and then another blow.

233

The detective spun round and dashed towards the ladder on the wall, hauling himself up as quickly as he could. He glanced back and saw the door shudder again as it was struck.

He shoved the machete and the baseball bat through the hole where the grille had been then pulled himself up after them, cracking his head on the ceiling of the air vent. He cursed under his breath, hearing another hard collision against the door. Another minute or so and they would break it down.

He dragged himself up, kicking at the ladder, knocking it away from the wall. Even if it only gained them a few seconds it might be crucial. Then he began crawling along the metal culvert, his breath coming in gasps.

Below, three more tremendous blows finally splintered the door and it crashed inwards. His pursuers dashed into the stockroom and Chapman heard their angry shouts as he continued to crawl along the air vent. In his mind's eye he could picture them clambering up the ladder, following him into the tunnel. What if the one with the gun merely climbed to the top and began firing?

The detective tried to push the thought from his mind as he crawled on, barely able to drag himself along in such a restricted space. The sweat was already pouring off his face, soaking his T-shirt. He was having trouble breathing. It felt as if the four metal walls were closing steadily around him.

Up ahead, Carla crawled as fast as she could, knowing her father was only feet behind her. She pulled herself along in the impenetrable gloom, praying for some chink of light or some opening somewhere close through which they could both escape this metal coffin.

Two feet ahead there was light spilling upwards into the dark vent.

234

Spurred on by this welcome sight, she dragged herself more quickly, and finally came to a grille. It was another air vent and, peering through the metal slats, she could see down into another shop.

The grille was large enough for both of them to slip through.

She pulled at it.

It didn't move.

She was about to shake it loose when she realised that any such noise would bring their pursuers below running. Perhaps, she thought, her father might be able to pull it open.

She crawled on, her hands out in front of her. Pushing with her feet, she managed to propel herself forward, blind in the unforgiving darkness.

Pushing against the metal with her feet, she, slid further forward.

Then her hands connected with something solid. Something metal.

She realised with horror that she'd reached a dead end.

56

Behind her, Chapman heard her groan softly. He scrambled forward a few more feet, seeing the light from the grille in the metal floor ahead.

Like Carla, he pulled at it, but was unable to shift it. He shuffled on. Ahead of him, his daughter wasn't moving. Now he could hear her harsh breathing.

'It's a dead end,' she panted. 'We can't go any further.'

The detective swallowed hard, the hopelessness of their situation closing around him as surely as the metal confines of the vent. He tried to control his own breathing, his heart hammering against his ribs. He felt as if an invisible hand was slowly squeezing more and more tightly around his upper body, forcing the breath from him. The crawlspace was too narrow for him to turn round in. It had him pinned like a rat in a trap.

The air was stale, thick with the smell of sweat, tinged with the odour of cold metal from the vent walls.

'We'll have to go back,' Carla called.

'We can't,' he told her.

His boots scraped against the floor of the vent and he tried to push himself back but it was difficult to obtain sufficient leverage in the cramped space. And, he reasoned, even if they managed to backtrack, God alone knew how many masked maniacs would be waiting for them by now.

'We'll suffocate in here,' Carla called, the first hint of panic tinging her words.

'No, we won't,' he told her, wondering if he was trying to reassure himself as much as his daughter.

Who says you're not going to suffocate?

He pushed himself back another couple of inches, trying to get above the grille he'd seen moments before. There was air coming through that, he thought. Surely there was enough circulating inside the vent to prevent them both from dying through lack of air.

Ahead of him, Carla groaned loudly and spoke some unintelligible words.

'We're going to get out of here,' he called to her. 'Just take it easy.'

He pulled again at the grille, using as much strength as he could muster in his restricted position. Beneath him he could see the shop they were suspended over. It looked like a bookshop. He could see the shelves and their literary cargo. Perhaps if he could prise the grille free he could lower himself down.

If there was anyone waiting down there he'd deal with that when he had to. For now, Chapman's main concern was getting them both out of the vent.

He grabbed for the machete, dragging it back towards him. He closed one hand round the hilt, trying to work the blade into the grille, trying to work it loose.

More sweat ran down his face from the effort. Every

237

movement, cramped and constricted as it was, seemed like a monumental effort. He jammed the blade between two of the slats and pulled it back and forth, trying to loosen the screws that held the grille in place.

'Come on,' he murmured to himself, willing the metal to give.

'Dad.' Carla's plaintive cry echoed inside the shaft.

'It's all right,' he called back, still rocking the machete as best he could. He pushed himself back another couple of inches and paused for a moment, the effort sapping his rapidly failing strength.

It was like being buried alive. Encased in such a small space, desperately attempting to get out. Nothing but their own sour air to breathe. He closed his eyes for a second, wanting badly to just lie down and rest.

'Dad,' Carla called again.

He nodded to himself.

'I've got to get out,' she said, more urgently. 'I'm coming back that way.'

'You can't,' he told her. 'It'll take us twice as long to go back and fuck knows what's waiting for us.'

'I can't stay in here,' she wailed tearfully. 'I'm going to turn round.'

'I'll get this grille off,' he told her. 'We can get through it. Just hold on.'

She banged despairingly on the floor of the vent. The sound reverberated along its length.

'Carla, stop,' he snapped. 'They'll hear us.'

'They'll hear us anyway,' she groaned.

Chapman tried to swallow but his throat was parched.

Come on, think, he told himself, blinking hard as a droplet of salty sweat rolled into his eye. 'What's above you?' he called. 'Can you reach the top of the shaft?'

238

There was a moment's silence.

'Carla,' Chapman called again.

'There's nothing there,' she called back. 'There's no top. I can stand up.'

Another long silence.

'I can feel something against the wall,' she called back excitedly. 'A ladder or something.'

'Can you climb up?'

There was another silence, then he heard several impacts against the metal. The sounds echoed loudly in his ears and the whole shaft seemed to shake.

'Dad, crawl through to where I was,' Carla shouted. 'There's a way out. The vent turns upwards. It's like an L shape. It must lead to the roof.'

Chapman gritted his teeth and began hauling himself along the vent, pushing the baseball bat and the machete in front of him. Inch by inch he moved, like some huge human slug, wriggling on his belly to slide along the pipe. Pushing himself with his feet to negotiate the dark, metal crawlspace.

'Up here,' Carla called and he glanced up in the direction of her voice, up into the blackness. 'The shaft's only as wide as the vent but we can get up it.'

'What's at the top?' he asked. 'Is there anything blocking it?'

There was a moment of silence; then he heard Carla grunting as she pushed against an object he couldn't see.

'There's like a trapdoor,' she said. 'But I can move it.'

'Get through,' he instructed her. 'I'll follow you.'

He reached the dead end and waited, sucking in huge lungfuls of stale air. His head was spinning with the heat and the effort of dragging himself on. He felt a tightness across his chest.

Not a fucking heart attack. Not now. Not here.

The detective lay still, trying to control his breathing. Somehow, he had to turn his body enough to work himself upright in a space no wider than the tunnel in which he lay. Both his arms were trapped beneath him, confined by the small space inside the vent. For a second, he wondered if he'd be able to slide his left arm out from under him. He gasped and cursed under his breath.

Even if you manage to get both arms out, how the hell are you going to turn over in such a narrow passage?

The detective thrust out his left arm and it smacked against the side of the shaft. He repeated the movement with the right arm. If only he could reach the bottom of the ladder, perhaps, he reasoned, he could pull himself up. But how to reach that elusive bottom rung? He could see nothing in the pitch darkness. He had no clue how far above him the ladder was.

'Come on, Dad,' Carla called from the top of the shaft.

Again he felt the tightness across his chest and he closed his eyes, waiting for the sensation to subside. Hoping that it would.

He slipped his right arm beneath him again and managed to move on to his left side. If he could now just turn on to his back he could reach up and grab the first rung of the ladder and pull himself up. He sucked in a deep breath and raised himself just enough to slip his left arm under too. The movement caused him to slide on to his back. He reached up with both hands and grabbed the bottom rung, gripping as hard as he could, using all his strength to pull himself up. Muscles already starved of oxygen seemed to burn painfully as he pulled.

240

He dropped back, bumping his head on the bottom of the vent.

'Carla,' he called. 'I can't move. I'm stuck.'

'I'll help you,' she called down the shaft.

'No, you go on. Get out of here,' he urged, but even as he spoke he heard movement in the darkness and her footfalls on the ladder above him.

'I'm not going without you.' Her voice was close now. Two or three feet above him.

Chapman clenched his teeth, readying himself for another effort. He knew he had to get out of this vent if he was to survive and he also realised that he wasn't going to do it without his daughter's help.

He felt something brush against his chest and realised that it was her hand, groping blindly in the pitch blackness. He shot up his own right hand and it touched Carla's.

'Let me pull you,' she told him. 'If you can get your back against the side of the shaft you'll be able to stand up.'

He dug his heels hard against the metal base of the vent and pushed as Carla pulled on his hand. Chapman felt himself beginning to rise a few inches. Carla clung to the ladder, using all her strength as she tugged on her father's outstretched hand.

Chapman grabbed for the ladder again and this time he hung on to the bottom rung. He pushed with his heels again, propelling himself further up the shaft. Above him in the the darkness, Carla climbed higher, allowing her father to rise. He drove upwards with his legs until he was able to turn and grip another rung of the ladder.

He began to climb.

Carla clambered out on to the roof of the building,

241

followed moments later by Chapman. He dropped to his knees, gulping in air, relieved to be free of the claustophobic grip of the vent.

'Shit,' he gasped, looking around.

Carla was close to the edge of the roof, peering down at the shopping mall below. Light from the complex offered only a dull illumination but anything was welcome to the detective after the pitch blackness of the vent. He walked across to join her, also looking down briefly before inspecting the sky.

'Where are the stars?' he murmured.

Carla looked at him in bewilderment for a second, then turned her attention to the cloudless sky.

'There aren't any clouds,' Chapman went on. 'Why can't we see the stars?'

'Does it matter?' she grunted. 'I thought we'd got more important things to worry about.'

Chapman didn't answer her. Instead, he reached for the baseball bat, lifting it skyward, his brow furrowing.

'What are you doing?' Carla wanted to know.

There was a dull thud as the bat connected with something solid.

'Jesus,' Chapman exclaimed. 'That's why there're no stars.' He gestured above them. 'It isn't the sky above us. This whole place has got a ceiling.'

'Of course it's got a ceiling,' Carla said. 'We're in a shopping mall. They've all got ceilings.'

'No, you don't get it. The tops of the buildings inside the mall should be joined to the canopy that covers the place, right? We're standing on the roof of this building. We're above the canopy. All that should be above us is the sky.' Again he reached up with the baseball bat and again Carla heard the dull thud as the wood struck something overhead. 'This shopping mall. The streets, the

242

buildings and everything else we've encountered is inside. That's why there could be wet streets and dry streets a hundred yards apart in the films. That's why there's no breeze. That's why we can't see lights from any other part of the city. We're not in a city. We're on one huge enclosed film set.'

57

Carla looked at her father incredulously then peered skyward once again.

'That's impossible,' she said.

Chapman merely shook his head. 'It must have cost millions,' he mused. 'But where the fuck did he put it?'

'Who? I haven't got a clue what you're talking about.'

'Anthony Seymour. The man who built this fucking place. The man who brought us both here. Us and the bastards hunting us.'

'I don't care where we are or who built it. I just want to get out.'

Chapman nodded. 'We're going to,' he assured her, looking round. He glanced over the edge of the parapet then walked to his left. 'If we use the roof, they can't get at us so easily.'

'They'll know we're up here. They saw us go into that storeroom, and they'll find the open vent,' Carla reminded him.

'But they don't know if we slipped out of the tunnel into another shop. We can go another hundred yards just by staying up here on the roof.'

'We'll have to go down again eventually, won't we?'

'Maybe, but at least they won't know whereabouts we are. We can get ahead of them. Hide.'

'What if there's no other shaft leading back down into the shops? We'll have to come all the way back here. Go back through that vent.'

'There must be one somewhere,' the detective decided, hefting the baseball bat before him. He stuffed the machete into his belt, with the knife. 'Come on.'

They began walking.

'Don't I get a weapon?' Carla asked.

He glanced at her, then continued across the flat roof. 'Would you know how to use one?'

'I can look after myself, if I have to.'

'He sighed. I noticed.'

'Give me the knife, Dad.'

He hesitated a moment, then slid the sharpened blade from his belt and passed it to her. Carla gripped it in one fist, reassured by its weight.

'How many of them have you killed?' she asked.

'None, so far. I'm not going to give Seymour that satisfaction if I can help it.'

'Who is this Seymour guy anyway? How can he control something like this?'

'Because he's got money and power. There's nothing that his sort of money can't buy.'

'But why's he killing people?'

'Because he can. This is all a fucking game to him. He's watching us. Everything we do. He's got cameras set up all over the place. He's filming. Creating snuff movies.'

'Why couldn't you stop him? You're a policeman.'

Chapman grunted. 'Thanks for reminding me.'

'Very clever.' The words were in Chapman's right ear.

245

A dull drone, like a trapped bluebottle. 'Climbing on to the roof was an inspired idea, detective. And taking the girl with you too. Very cunning. You should leave her behind now, though. She'll slow you down.'

Chapman continued walking.

'You're doing well,' Seymour went on. 'No one's ever got this far before. I'm impressed. But your triumph will be fleeting, I'm afraid. Eventually you'll have to come down.' There was a note of irritation in Seymour's voice that the detective wasn't slow to pick up. 'You can't hide up there in the dark for ever. When you come back down they'll be waiting for you. If not here, then further on.'

The detective wandered close to the edge of the roof and glanced down. He could see several dark shapes moving about in the aisles and walkways of the mall.

'Just because I can't see you now doesn't mean I don't know where you are,' Seymour snapped.

Chapman glanced round rapidly.

He can't see us.

'First they'll kill the girl while you watch,' Seymour rasped. 'I might get them to rape her first. Give them a little extra for that.' He chuckled. 'Then, when she's dead, they'll kill you and it'll be over.'

'There aren't any cameras up here,' Chapman exclaimed.

Carla looked round at him. 'Who are you talking to?'

'Just because I can't see you now doesn't mean I don't know where you are.'

Chapman touched his right ear, digging his index finger as deep as he could as if he was trying to reach the receiver implanted there.

'The last thing you see will be the girl's death,' Seymour told him. 'The last voice you hear will be mine.'

'Give me the knife, Carla,' Chapman said, stopping in his tracks.

246

'Why?'

'Just give it to me.'

Carla handed over the blade.

'He can't see us up here because there are no cameras,' the detective explained. 'But he says he still knows where we are.'

'I don't understand what you're going on about.'

'Perhaps this fucking receiver in my ear doesn't just receive. Maybe it's a transmitter too. That's how he's tracking us when he can't see us.'

Carla shook her head.

Chapman sat down on the roof then raised the point of the knife until it was level with his right ear.

'Dad, what are you doing?' Carla gasped, taking a step towards him.

As she watched, the detective pushed the point into the cartilage at the centre of his ear, turning it as he probed. The razor-sharp blade sheared off the central section of his outer ear and it dropped to the ground close by. Blood spurted from the cut as Chapman dug deeper with the metal, his face screwed up in pain. Blood was pouring down his face and neck, staining his already grimy T-shirt. He pushed harder, the pain keeping him conscious. He felt something touch the needle-sharp point as he pushed the blade into his auditory canal.

Chapman tilted the blade slightly, gouging more deeply into flesh and cartilage, prising the obstruction from inside his ear. Fresh blood spattered the blade and dripped on to his leg as his head lolled forward slightly but he continued with his movements.

'Stop,' Carla gasped, her stomach contracting as she watched, unable to tear her gaze away from the bloody spectacle before her.

Chapman groaned and pulled the knife free, dropping it. He inserted his thumb and forefinger into the blood-choked hole he had cut into his own ear. He felt the searching digits close over something cold and metallic and he pulled it free like a splinter leaving soft flesh.

Gripping it triumphantly before him, he sucked in several deep breaths. Carla peered more closely and saw the small object he held.

'Seymour put it there,' the detective gasped. 'I could hear his voice through it.' He swayed uncertainly and shot down a hand to support himself, feeling the knife under his palm. Carla knelt beside him, putting an arm round his shoulder. 'Not any more.' He grinned crookedly and dropped the receiver on the roof. As Carla watched he brought the handle of the knife down on it, shattering it.

'Fuck you, Seymour,' he gasped, pulling off his T-shirt.

He cut it in two with the knife then balled up one of the strips and pressed it against the bleeding hole where what remained of his right ear was. Then he wrapped the other piece of material round his head to hold the blood-soaked wad in position. Carla fastened it at the back of his head then helped him to his feet.

Chapman handed her the knife. She wiped the blade on her joggers and gripped the hilt more tightly.

'There must be a chemist's shop down there somewhere,' he said. 'Somewhere with bandages.'

'If you're right and this is only a film set, then how can you be sure?' Carla asked, holding his arm to support him. 'I told you not all of the shops have stuff in them.'

'I'm not sure about anything any more,' he told her, putting a hand to his stomach as a wave of nausea swept through him. 'Sorry.'

Carla looked down at the crushed remains of the transmitter he'd cut from his ear.

'Come on, Dad,' she urged.

Chapman nodded.

They moved on.

58

'Still no answer.' Detective Sergeant Maggie Grant sat back in the passenger seat of the car and looked accusingly at her mobile phone. 'Where the hell is he?'

DS James Mackenzie swung the car round the round-about, towards the exit he needed. 'Have you tried his home number?' he asked.

'Twice,' Maggie told him. 'When did you say he left the office?'

'He was out all afternoon,' Mackenzie reminded her. 'I told you I'd left a couple of messages on his voicemail and he hadn't got back to me either.'

'And he didn't say where he was going?'

Mackenzie shook his head.

Maggie glanced out of the side window at the countryside speeding past in the darkness. They'd left the outskirts of London behind about ten minutes ago, she reasoned. Another hour or less and they'd be at the home of Anthony Seymour.

The car sped on.

★   ★   ★

'Now what are you going to do?' Bradley got to his feet and glared angrily at Seymour.

'Sit down, Bradley.'

Bradley hesitated a moment then slumped back in his seat.

'He's removed the transmitter, that's all,' Seymour said. 'He's still trapped inside. He can't get out and there's no way he's going to escape. Now, if you're finding this all too stressful, I suggest you leave.'

Bradley stroked his chin thoughtfully and looked around the screens in the control room. 'Where the hell is he?' he demanded. 'He's not on any of these fucking monitors.'

'He's on the roof of the shopping mall. Either that or he and the girl have made their way back down into the shops. Wherever he is he won't get much further.'

'I wish I was as sure as you are.'

'Do you want to go in and kill him yourself?'

'Why not send some of your men in? Make sure it gets done.'

'My men have got better things to do, Bradley. I'm getting sick of telling you, he hasn't got a chance. There are more than thirty hunters left before he reaches the end. Even if he makes it out of the mall alive, there's no way in the world he'll get past the next area.'

'How many men have you got in there?'

'It isn't the men in there he's got to worry about,' Seymour said flatly. 'It's what they've got with them.'

Chapman leaned back against the counter of the pharmacy department as Carla bandaged his head.

There were a couple of strip lights on inside the store but at the rear, in the area where he and his daughter sheltered, it was reassuringly gloomy.

'Have you got any idea how much further we've got to go before we reach the end of the mall?' the detective asked quietly.

Carla shook her head and fastened the bandage with some double-sided tape.

As he sat there, Chapman pulled the top from the painkillers he'd taken from the pharmacy shelf. He swallowed two, feeling the bitterness as they rolled over the back of his tongue. He crunched one, wincing.

'Get yourself some trainers,' he suggested, glancing down at Carla's scratched and filthy bare feet.

'When I've got you patched up.'

'And see if you can find me a bottle of whisky too.' He grinned. 'Purely medicinal.'

Carla smiled and inspected her handiwork. There was blood already seeping through the gauze pad she'd placed over her father's ravaged right ear but, other than that, the dressing was relatively neat.

'That's good,' he said, touching it with his left hand. 'You should have been a nurse.'

'Can you hear anything in that ear?' she asked, pointing at the damaged appendage.

'Enough.'

She got to her feet, the knife gripped in her fist. 'I'll be back in ten minutes,' she told him, ducking low as she edged out from behind the counter.

'You watch yourself,' he told her. 'If you see anyone moving about down there, get back here as quick as you can.'

Carla nodded then moved off, melting into the shadows.

Chapman watched her as she ducked in and out of the shelving units and the clothes rails. He glanced around him, wondering where the cameras were situated. When he looked in Carla's direction again, she was heading for the escalators that would take her down to the ground floor.

'Be careful,' he whispered.

59

As Carla descended the immobile escalators, the metal steps felt cold beneath her bare feet. She moved slowly, one step at a time, peering down towards the ground floor of the store.

It was lit by several fluorescent lights set into the ceiling, two of which were flickering. However, as she reached the halfway point of the frozen staircase, she saw that it was only the central aisles of the shop that were brightly lit. The outer areas closer to the walls were in reasonably deep shadow. Large windows made up the broad frontage of the store and she noted that they would make her easy to spot for anyone passing. As she reached the bottom of the escalator, she crouched as low as she could, listening for any telltale sounds of movement.

Satisfied that she was alone on the ground floor, she sprinted to her right, towards a sign that proclaimed *Menswear*.

There were several shelf units, most of them empty but some containing cheap cellophane-wrapped shirts and T-shirts. She glanced at the garments then snatched two T-shirts from the nearest shelf and tucked them under her arm.

She saw the figure as she turned.

Tall. White-faced, dressed in jeans and a leather jacket.

Carla swung the knife up, ready to strike, her heart thundering against her ribs. It took her a second or two to realise that the figure was a mannequin. She sucked in a grateful breath, looked irritably at the dummy and walked on.

Ahead of her were more shelves and a sign above them saying *Electrical Goods*.

Apart from an antiquated-looking cassette player, the shelves were empty. There were a few CDs in racks close by to add to the illusion that the store was frequented by shoppers. Carla moved on towards the footwear section, pausing to check that no one had entered the building while she'd been preoccupied with her shopping spree. Satisfied that she was still relatively safe inside the store, she jammed the knife into her belt and began taking trainers from the display shelves, pressing each one against her foot for size. Those that looked too big or small she tossed away. Finally she found one that seemed as if it might fit.

Carla pushed her left foot into it, relieved to have something to protect the battered appendage. Now all she had to do was find another for her right foot. Muttering to herself, she went through the other trainers, discarding them all because they were either too big or also for the left foot. Finally, she looked across to a cardboard bin full to the brim with cheap trainers held together by their laces. The smell of their rubber soles was overpowering. She found a pair that fitted, removed the other from her left foot and slipped them on, tucking the laces inside.

Whatever else they needed she could find on the first floor, so she turned and headed back towards the escalators.

She almost tripped over the sleeping bags.

They lay side by side next to a high shelf stacked with notebooks and pencils. Carla looked down at the grubby bags, noticing that there were cigarette burns in one of them.

An empty beer bottle lay on the other. They both smelled strongly of sweat and unwashed bodies.

She was still contemplating where the owners might be when she heard movement outside the shop.

Carla spun round and saw four men through the wide picture windows.

All were masked, all carrying weapons. The leading man was wearing a faded denim jacket. He was holding a knife in his right hand. The second of the newcomers, a baseball cap pulled down tightly over his head, gripped a crowbar. The third, a stocking pulled taut over his head, was holding a pistol. The fourth, a short, stocky youth dressed in a hooded fleece, was brandishing a shotgun.

Carla ducked down behind a clothes rail, listening to the sound of their footsteps as they entered.

'Why can't I have a gun?' one voice asked.

'Because you'd fuck things up and shoot us by mistake,' another answered.

Carla heard their raucous laughter, feeling her own breath coming in gasps. She tried to control it, fearful that they would hear her.

'I need some gear,' the third voice announced. 'I'm fucking strung out.'

'If we get this bastard you'll be sorted,' the first voice said.

Carla heard their footsteps coming closer and pushed herself further beneath the rail.

'Wait,' one of the men grunted. 'I've got to have a piss.'

'Fuck that,' one of his companions called. 'We'll check upstairs. You and Tylan check down here then catch us up.'

Carla's heart jumped.

Two of them were heading for the escalators. She had to warn her father somehow. She swallowed hard. How the hell was she going to make it up to the first floor without being seen? She knew she could run. She knew she could probably beat them up there. But what if the two with the guns were going up? Carla knew she couldn't outrun a bullet.

She rose slightly, trying to see where the men were positioned.

The one in the stocking mask was near the back of the store. Baseball cap had his back to her about ten yards away. Denim jacket was heading towards the escalators. The one with the shotgun was nowhere to be seen.

Carla gripped the knife more tightly, wondering what to do.

Run for it and risk getting shot?

Stay put and chance being found?

Either way, her father was upstairs alone.

She made her choice.

60

Chapman heard the shotgun blast and the furious shouts from below him.

'Carla,' he murmured.

He jumped to his feet, grabbing the machete and the baseball bat, and hurried in the direction of the escalators. A second later he saw his daughter reach the top of the metal stairs. She stumbled and fell, sprawling on the floor, but she rolled over and scrambled to her feet, anxious to be away from her pursuers.

'Over here,' Chapman hissed, beckoning her towards him 'How many?' he wanted to know.

'Four,' she panted. 'Two with guns.'

The detective heard footsteps pounding up the escalators and he looked round desperately for somewhere to hide.

'There,' he snapped, pulling her along with him as he ran towards an area marked *Garden Supplies* at the back of the first floor. He glanced over his shoulder to see that two figures had already reached the top of the escalators. The first of them, squinting through his stocking mask, held his pistol in front of him, ready to fire.

Chapman and Carla dived among the high shelves of the garden supplies area, seeking refuge behind piled-up bags of fertiliser. The detective watched as the first two men separated, one of them heading towards where he and Carla sheltered, the other seeking them at the front of the shop.

'You can't hide for ever,' stocking mask shouted, waving the gun around. 'The only way out is through us.'

Chapman peered at it in the gloom, trying to make out the manufacturer. As far as he could tell it was no bigger than a .22. However, he reasoned, at such close range, even a weapon with a calibre so small could kill. Stocking mask walked closer and Chapman gripped the baseball bat more tightly, waiting for the moment to strike. Carla, too, held her weapon before her, ready to use the blade if she had to.

Stocking mask stopped walking and glanced around, seeking any telltale signs of his quarry. There was a low platform for the display of lawnmowers about ten yards further on. He took a couple of steps towards it.

Chapman leapt up from behind the bags of fertiliser like some malevolent jack-in-the-box. He swung the baseball bat with furious power, the thick wood connecting with stocking mask's head. The impact was so powerful, it sent the masked man sprawling.

It also broke the bat.

Chapman tossed the lump he still held to one side and advanced on the fallen figure, driving a foot into the man's temple. Bone crumbled under the thunderous assault, blood bursting from the wound that opened there.

Chapman snatched up the .22, inspecting the pistol. It was a Smith and Wesson model 617 with a six-inch barrel. He flipped open the cylinder.

'Shit,' he hissed.

'What's wrong?' Carla asked.

'It's supposed to hold six shots,' the detective told her. 'There're only two in here.' He glanced at the prostrate body of stocking mask. 'Check his pockets for ammo.'

Carla did as she was instructed, rolling the body over and digging in the man's jeans for hidden bullets.

'Nothing,' she gasped.

There was a thunderous explosion and the bird table close to Chapman disintegrated.

As he dived for cover, he saw two more men at the top of the escalators. The one in the hoodie had fired at him and was even now working the slide of the shotgun to chamber another round.

Chapman swung the .22 up and sighted quickly, squeezing off a shot.

It missed, drilling into the wall behind the man.

The detective fired again and, this time, his aim was better. The bullet caught hoodie in the right knee. It shattered the patella and erupted from the back of the leg carrying fragments of flesh and cracked bone with it. Hoodie went down screaming and clutching the damaged knee, the shotgun skidding from his grasp.

Baseball cap grabbed for it, dropping his crowbar in the process. He raised the shotgun to his shoulder and fired off two rounds in quick succession. The first blasted a hole in the floor a foot to Chapman's right. The second shredded the air just above his head. Again, baseball cap worked the slide, his finger tightening on the trigger.

There was nothing but a loud click.

Chapman realised that the man was out of shells and sprinted towards him, the machete now clutched in his right hand.

Baseball cap swung the shotgun like a club but Chapman ducked beneath the swing, striking out with the machete in the process. The thick blade hit baseball cap across the right forearm.

He shrieked and dropped his weapon but now Chapman was aware of another figure hurtling towards them. Denim jacket was running from the front of the shop, his knife brandished before him.

Carla snatched a shovel from the shelf next to her and ran to meet the onrushing attacker. Using all her strength, she swung the implement, slamming the metal into the face of denim jacket. He dropped like a stone and she hit him again across the base of the skull.

Chapman drove one fist into the face of baseball cap, knocking him backwards towards the escalators. He over-balanced, clutched at empty air for a second and then, with a despairing wail, he fell. The detective watched as the man tumbled down the metal steps, his head cracking on three of them before he slumped motionless at the bottom.

The detective grabbed the crowbar and advanced on hoodie, who was more concerned with his shattered knee than with the fate of his companions.

'Give me the other shells for the shotgun,' Chapman snapped.

'I need a doctor,' hoodie whimpered.

'You'll need a fucking undertaker if you don't give me those shells,' Chapman rasped, pressing the crowbar beneath the man's chin.

Hoodie looked up at the detective for a moment longer then dug in his trouser pocket and pulled out four cartridges.

'Is that it?' Chapman grunted.

Hoodie nodded, returning his attention to his pulverised knee, while the detective thumbed the four cartridges into the magazine then worked the slide, chambering a round.

'Help me,' Hoodie gasped. 'You can't leave me here like this.'

Chapman held his gaze for a moment.

'I had to try to kill you,' the younger man blurted. 'We all did. We didn't have a choice.' There were tears running down his face, dripping from beneath the mask. 'I'm sorry.'

'He'll tell the others where we are,' Carla said, still clutching the spade.

'No, I won't, I swear,' hoodie wailed.

Carla hit him once with the edge of the spade. The blow split his skull from forehead to crown. He sagged forward, blood pumping from the savage wound.

Chapman looked emotionlessly at her.

'Now he won't tell anyone,' she said through gritted teeth. She dropped the spade and put out her hand for the crowbar. 'You've got to carry the shotgun,' she reminded him. 'Give that to me.'

Chapman jammed the machete back into his belt and handed the length of iron to her.

'We'd better go before the others come.' She was already heading for the escalators.

Chapman glanced round at the fallen attackers, all unconscious, two of them in spreading pools of blood. At the bottom of the escalators, baseball cap lay still, his head twisted at an impossible angle. Chapman could tell by the dark stain spreading across the front of the fallen man's jeans that he was dead.

'Dad,' Carla said, pausing on the first metal step.

He nodded and followed her.

61

'Where did you find those?'

Chapman watched as Carla pulled a packet of cigarettes and a disposable lighter from the pocket of her joggers.

'They were in that guy's jeans,' she told him. 'The one with the gun.'

The detective nodded. 'I didn't see you take them,' he admitted.

'You had other things on your mind.'

She lit one for herself then offered him the packet. Chapman took one gratefully, lit it and sucked hard on it.

'Christ, I needed that,' he murmured, allowing himself to slump back a little further against the counter of the hardware store where they now sheltered.

Even in the poorly lit interior of the shop he could see hammers, chisels, saws and all manner of electrical tools hanging up. Any of them could be used as weapons. His eyes strayed to a chainsaw for a moment, then he returned his attention to Carla, who was gazing blankly into space.

'Are you all right?' he asked.

She nodded distractedly. 'I thought you were going to tell me off for smoking,' she said, managing a thin smile.

'Under the circumstances, you smoking seems pretty fair,' he answered. He took another drag on his cigarette, blowing out a long stream of blue smoke. 'Listen, Carla, this isn't the right place or time, I know, but what happened between us . . . I mean, the reason you left home. You've got to understand that I was only doing what I thought was best for you.'

'You mean, throwing me out? Thanks.'

'I didn't throw you out, you left.'

'Because you said I had to have an abortion.'

'I didn't want you ruining your life. Having a kid at seventeen, it's no way to start. I wanted more for you than that.'

'Like the life you've had?'

'Christ, no. My life's been a fucking waste. I've been a shit husband, a useless father and not much of a son either for that matter.'

'You're good at your job.'

Chapman smiled humourlessly. 'But that's all I had. Or thought I had. If I hadn't been so wrapped up in my work perhaps I'd have realised how important you and Mum were to me. I'd give anything to change what happened, Carla. I'd give anything for one more chance, but I know I won't get it.'

'Why?'

'Because what's done is done and I can't change that. I can't put right the mistakes I've made. I can't help the people I've hurt. Not now.'

He took another drag on the cigarette.

'What happened with the baby?' he said finally, his voice low, the words faltering.

'I lost it,' Carla told him. 'Miscarriage. About two days after I left home.'

'I'm sorry,' he breathed. 'I wouldn't have wanted that.'

She nodded, a single tear running down her cheek. She brushed it away almost angrily. 'Like you said, what's done is done.' Her voice cracked.

Chapman moved closer to her and snaked out an arm, pulling her to him. She allowed her head to rest against his chest, ignoring the splatters of blood and the sweat.

She looked down at his torso. It was decorated by dozens of cuts, bruises and abrasions.

'You're getting fat, Dad,' she told him, trying to smile.

'I don't think this is the time and place to be discussing my middle-age spread, do you?' he said, tapping her gently on the back of the head.

'You're not middle-aged. You're old.'

'Cheeky sod.'

They smiled at each other and got to their feet, retrieving the weapons they so badly needed.

'Can he see us now?' Carla asked, looking round. 'That Seymour guy? The one who put you here?'

'There'll be cameras watching us wherever we are but it looks as if I was right about that transmitter he put in my ear. The others haven't been able to find us as easily since I took it out.' He touched the blood-soaked gauze over his right ear. 'The only way Seymour can direct them is by trying to figure out where we are and telling them.'

Chapman looked again at the walls hung with so many lethal devices. There was a pile of rucksacks behind the counter and he reached for one, strapping it on.

'What are you doing?' Carla wanted to know.

'We need all the help we can get to make our way out of this fucking place. I know there're more of those bastards out there waiting for us but at least we can even things up a bit.'

He reached for a hedge-cutter and inspected it, touching the oiled and savagely serrated blades with a satisfied look on his face.

'It's electric, cordless,' he remarked. 'It'll work if we need it.'

Carla took it from him and put it in the rucksack, the blade protruding. She watched as he pulled down a nail gun. He opened it and saw that there were dozens of steel spikes inside the tool.

'We'll take this too,' he said, passing it to her.

Carla hefted it before her, keeping her finger off the trigger.

Finally, the detective reached for a small chainsaw. He could smell the oil on the fifteen-inch blade and the chain of the machine. He shook it and heard some petrol slopping around inside.

'See if you can find some more petrol,' he told Carla. 'Just in case.'

She hurried off towards the back of the hardware store, returning a moment later with a small, green plastic container. Chapman took it from her and emptied it into the tank of the savage-looking implement. He ran his thumb over the starter switch, careful not to trip it for fear of bringing their opponents running.

'Put that in too,' he told Carla, allowing her to slip the 40cc Husqvarna into the rucksack.

He picked up the shotgun and looked around once again. 'If Seymour insists on leaving these things lying around, it seems a shame not to use them,' he grunted. He put his arm round Carla's shoulder and the two of them walked slowly towards the double doors that led from the store.

'How much further do you think we've got to go?' she enquired, ducking low as they both gazed out of the window towards the open spaces of the mall.

'I wish I knew,' Chapman murmured.

'Just along this road,' DS Maggie Grant said, squinting through the gloom towards the high stone wall that formed the perimeter of Anthony Seymour's estate.

'Not too keen on visitors, is he?' Mackenzie remarked, spotting the razor wire and broken glass that topped the formidable barrier.

He swung the car off the narrow road towards the two ornate metal gates that barred the way to the estate.

Maggie pulled herself out of the car and walked over to the intercom set in one of the stone pillars supporting the gates. She pressed the visitors' button and waited.

Above her, a CCTV camera turned towards her, fixing her in its cyclopean glass stare.

Maggie pressed the button again.

62

Detective Inspector Joe Chapman held up a hand as he edged out of the shop doorway. He stepped a few paces into the aisle of the mall, looking to his right and left. Satisfied it was clear, he beckoned with his hand.

Carla dashed from the cover of the shop and hunkered down beside a wooden bench and an overflowing dustbin.

Twenty yards ahead of them were the glass doors of a cinema.

The area in front of the latest obstacle was worryingly open, especially, Chapman reasoned, if the doors were all locked. He looked up at the front of the building, noting that there were a couple of posters in the frames outside. One of them caught the detective's eye and he stood gazing at it, his brow furrowing.

'What is it?' Carla said, noticing his apparent interest but not realising what it was directed towards.

'*The Hounds of Zaroff*,' Chapman murmured. 'There's a poster for it in that frame there.' He nodded in the direction of the cinema.

Carla looked but only shook her head. 'Haven't seen it.'

'It's an old film about this bloke who lives on an island,'

Chapman told her. 'He captures the people who are ship-wrecked there and hunts them for sport. Looks like Seymour's a fan. Perhaps that's where he got the idea for this shit.'

'What are we going to do?' Carla asked, looking nervously around her.

'Let's see if we can get inside there. We might be able to find our way out. This looks like the end of the shopping mall.' He glanced around, noticing one camera high up on the front of the cinema. It turned slightly as the detective moved.

'He's seen us,' he said quietly. 'He knows we're here.' He took a few steps towards the front of the building. 'Come on.'

They both hurried towards the first of the four sets of double doors.

Chapman tugged at the handles.

Locked.

He tried the next set.

Also locked.

Carla turned and looked behind her, back into the mall. She could hear voices and they were getting closer.

'They're coming,' she breathed.

Chapman pulled on the next set of doors.

They opened and he held them apart for Carla, who slipped past him into the foyer.

The detective followed her, cursing under his breath as he struggled to get the rucksack through. He finally managed it, the dust inside the large open area beyond clogging his nostrils.

The floor of the foyer was carpeted, and the two of them walked with an eerie lack of sound.

'Which way?' Carla said.

To their left and right there were steps leading up to

269

the first floor of the building. Straight ahead were more stairs, this time leading downwards. *Screens 1–4* boasted the sign above them. Screens 5–8 and screens 9–12 were indicated by wall-mounted signs beside the stairs to the left and right.

Chapman hesitated a moment, aware now of the sound of voices outside the building. Still a hundred yards or more away but closing too rapidly for comfort.

'Did they see us come in here?' he whispered.

Carla could only shrug. 'Where do we go, Dad?'

'Up,' he suggested, jabbing a finger at the left-hand set of steps.

The two of them hurried up the carpeted stairs, Chapman grunting with the effort of lugging the rucksack on his back. The wound in his right thigh was giving him a lot of pain, too, but he struggled on, anxious to find somewhere to hide. They reached the first floor and saw four sets of double doors to their right, each one with a number above it.

There were more film posters on the walls too. Chapman saw one for *Mission Impossible.*

'Very funny, Seymour,' he muttered as he passed it.

He ducked into the first of the screens, holding one of the doors open for Carla to join him.

'Shit,' he grunted, barely able to see a hand in front of him in the gloom within. He blinked hard, his eyes gradually adjusting to the almost palpable blackness within the room. At the bottom of the single aisle leading towards the screen there was a door marked EMERGENCY EXIT.

'Check that,' he told Carla. 'See if we can get through it.'

She hurried off, the knife in one hand and the crowbar in the other.

As he waited for her to return he pressed his ear to

the double doors they'd just passed through. The sound of footsteps inside the cinema would be muffled by the thickness of the carpet, he assumed. Was that all part of the game? So they couldn't hear their pursuers drawing closer? Were they, even now, standing in the wide corridor outside, ready to strike?

Chapman gripped the shotgun more tightly and pushed gently against one of the doors.

Be careful. You've only got four rounds. There could be half a dozen of the bastards out there.

He swallowed hard and nudged the door open a little more.

The hand touched his shoulder.

Chapman spun round, swinging the shotgun wildly, trying to level it at his assailant. His finger touched the trigger.

Carla stepped back as she saw the barrel yawning at her.

'Shit,' hissed Chapman, lowering the weapon. 'Don't do that.'

'There's no way out through that exit,' she told him.

He nodded, his heart slowing its frantic pounding a little.

'Are they inside yet?' Carla whispered.

'I don't know. We'd better check the other screens. There must be a way out somewhere.'

'What if it's through one of the screens in the basement?'

Chapman didn't answer. He merely licked his lips.

He pushed open the door again and peered out into the corridor beyond.

'It's clear,' he said. 'You check the other screens. I'll watch the stairs.'

Carla nodded and sprinted off towards the doors leading into screen six.

271

Chapman walked slowly towards the top of the stairs and ducked down behind the low guard-rail there. From his position he could see the staircase and part of the foyer. He raised the shotgun to his shoulder and squinted down the sight.

If they came for him now, he was ready.

63

'How many million is this guy worth?'

DS James Mackenzie gazed raptly at the impressive façade of Anthony Seymour's house as he guided the car along the last few hundred yards of driveway.

'No one's sure,' Maggie told him, herself staring with awe at the huge structure looming before them.

The building was lit from the outside by a series of spotlights mounted in the bushes close to the walls. There were other spotlights on the house itself aimed at the drive and the surrounding grounds. Batteries of CCTV cameras covered every visible yard of garden and the vast expanse of gravel before the ornate front door.

As Mackenzie slowed down, two figures in dark suits directed him to where he should park.

'I wonder where the runway is,' he muttered.

Maggie looked at him and smiled.

'Geezers this rich always have private planes,' Mackenzie added.

'These two must be bodyguards,' Maggie offered, watching the besuited individuals who were shepherding Mackenzie to a suitable parking spot.

'And them,' Mackenzie added, nodding at two more of the men who were standing on the roof of the house itself. Illuminated by the spotlight close to them, they were peering over the parapet at the top of the building, one of them speaking into a two-way radio.

'Perhaps they're letting Seymour know we're here,' Maggie said.

'I bet he knew before we turned into the driveway,' Mackenzie muttered.

He turned off the engine and swung himself out of the car, his feet crunching on the gravel beneath.

Maggie followed his example, nodding amiably at the security man who approached her.

'Can you follow me, please,' he said curtly.

He turned away and headed for the main door of the house. The two detectives followed.

'Do you know them?'

Anthony Seymour pressed the lever that allowed the camera to zoom in and looked at the monitor.

He and Detective Sergeant Bradley both surveyed the black and white image of Maggie and Mackenzie as they approached the front of the house.

'Of course I know them,' Bradley said agitatedly. 'I work with them.'

'Are they here looking for you?'

'Why should they be?'

'Could they be looking for Chapman?'

'It's possible, but why would they come here? There's nothing to link him to you, is there?'

'You mean apart from the fact that he was the investigating officer when my son was nearly killed.' Seymour looked fixedly at the policeman for a moment, but Bradley's gaze was still on Maggie and Mackenzie.

274

'Are you going to speak to them?' he enquired.

'It'll look a little suspicious if I don't,' Seymour said coldly.

'What about Chapman?' Bradley asked, shifting his gaze to the other bank of monitors.

'He's almost reached the end of this section,' Seymour told him, examining the image of Chapman on the screens before him. 'He won't get much further.'

'You sound very sure of that.'

'I am.'

'I wish I was as confident.'

'Shall I show you where he's going, Bradley? Perhaps it might help to calm your nerves a little.'

Seymour reached over the control panel before him and pressed two red switches. The images of Chapman immediately disappeared from the screens, to be replaced by what looked like a scrap metal yard. Piles of cars and the rusted hulks of other vehicles were stacked as high as small buildings. They looked like the unwanted toys of some huge child, left to rot in an area fenced off by barbed and razor wire. There were also several figures moving around, all carrying guns.

'What makes you think they'll stop him?' Bradley asked. 'None of the others could.'

Seymour pointed to the monitor closest to him.

Bradley glanced at the enlarged image of what else waited inside the scrap yard, and swallowed hard.

'Satisfied?' Seymour challenged him, a slight smile on his lips.

'Oh my God,' Bradley murmured softly.

He felt the hairs on the back of his neck rise.

275

64

'This way.' Carla's voice echoed along the wide corridor and Chapman snapped his head round to look at her. 'There's a way out.'

'You go,' he told her, the shotgun still pressed against his shoulder. 'I'll follow you.'

She ignored his instruction, instead hurrying across to join him.

'I told you to go,' he snapped.

Standing beside him, Carla could hear movement below them in the foyer of the abandoned cinema.

'How many?' she asked, a look of fear on her face.

'At least four, as far as I can tell,' Chapman told her.

Even as he spoke, he saw a figure at the bottom of the steps: a tall, thin man dressed in black jeans and a navy sweatshirt. He glanced up in their direction and they saw that he was wearing a skull mask.

'Up there,' the man shouted. He was immediately joined by two other figures.

Chapman didn't hesitate. He pulled the shotgun in tight to his shoulder to absorb the recoil and fired once.

The blast blew a hole in the floor close to the leading figure's feet. All three jumped back out of sight.

'Go,' Chapman said, waving Carla away.

She hesitated as the detective fired another blast, the thunderous discharge momentarily deafening both of them. The shots seemed to have acted as a suitable deterrent to their pursuers. There was no sign of them on the stairs. A thin veil of bluish-grey smoke hung in the air and both Chapmans could smell the stink of gunpowder in their nostrils.

They ran towards the doors leading into screen eight.

'Down here,' Carla told him, leading the way through the darkened cinema towards the door to the right of the screen.

She pushed up the bar of the emergency exit and Chapman was delighted to see that there was a narrow but brightly lit corridor beyond it. He slammed the door shut behind them and they both ran on, until the detective slowed his pace slightly and turned to check that there was no one following them. After a moment he stopped completely and stood watching the emergency door.

'They're not going to follow us in here,' he said finally.

'How can you be so sure?' Carla snapped.

'If they haven't come by now it means Seymour won't let them. It's obviously not part of the game.'

He lowered the shotgun and sucked in a deep breath, slumping against the concrete wall beside him.

'So what do we do?' Carla demanded.

'We carry on until we find another door,' Chapman told her, noting that the corridor turned in an L shape just ahead of them.

'And what if there isn't one?'

'There will be.'

277

He wiped sweat from his face and walked on. Carla trudged along beside him.

'He's not going to let us out of here alive, you said that,' she persisted. 'They'll kill us somewhere.'

'They'll try.'

He turned the corner and saw that the corridor stretched away another twenty or thirty yards. At the end of it there was a metal door, above which a red light blinked atop a small camera.

'Told you there'd be a door,' Chapman said, smiling at his daughter. He put a hand on her shoulder.

'I don't want to die, Dad,' she said quietly, a tear cutting through the grime on her cheek.

'You're not going to. We're going to get through this. Both of us.'

Two feet from the metal door they heard a loud electronic buzz. The door opened a foot or so.

Chapman held up a hand and signalled Carla to wait. Then he used the barrel of the shotgun to gently push the door back on its hinges.

The smell of damp earth filled his nostrils.

'We must be outside,' he murmured, stepping through the door. He looked up but there were still no stars or clouds. Only the unending and unbroken darkness that he'd seen everywhere else on his journey.

Beneath his feet, the ground was soft. The detective knelt and scooped up some of the earth, digging deeper until his fingers connected with something more solid.

'Concrete,' he said, looking down at the little hole he'd excavated. 'It's just another set.'

Carla tapped his shoulder and pointed to something about twenty yards away. It looked like a metal Nissen hut. On either side of it there were battered wrecks of cars and piles of tyres.

'A scrap yard,' Chapman murmured.

They walked on, glancing around them in the darkness, watchful for any signs of movement, ears alert for the slightest sound.

They reached the Nissen hut and Chapman peered round the frame of the open door. It was clear inside, empty except for a battered portable television with its screen smashed.

'We can rest here for a while,' he said, unhooking the rucksack from his back. He sank down on to the dirty floor, laying the shotgun down beside him.

'Perhaps we should just keep walking,' Carla suggested.

'Just give me a few minutes,' he said, sucking in deep lungfuls of air. 'And one of those cigarettes would be nice.' He smiled. Carla fished in the pocket of her joggers for them.

She sat down beside her father and handed him a cigarette, screwing one between her own lips too.

Chapman was about to light up when he heard the sound.

Distant but still loud.

Getting closer.

Carla heard it too and she looked at her father with an expression of fear on her face.

The sound was drawing nearer by the second.

'Dogs,' Chapman breathed.

279

65

The sitting room wasn't as vast as Mackenzie had expected it to be.

It was, however, as opulent and as indicative of wealth as any room he'd ever set foot in. The walls were decorated with various paintings, most of which he fancied were originals costing hundreds of thousands each. Antique tables supported objets d'art of similar value. The detective sergeant negotiated a path round the vases and crystal, careful not to knock any with his arm. He had a feeling his yearly salary wouldn't even come close to replacing one should he be unfortunate enough to break it.

The floor was polished wood covered by large hand-woven rugs that were so thick his feet sank into them as he walked. Beside him, Maggie's heels clicked ominously on the gleaming surface and she herself glanced down on more than one occasion to ensure that the tips weren't scatching the flooring. She had the unshakeable feeling that one of Seymour's body-guards was about to ask her to remove the offending footwear.

Both police officers sat when offered a seat by the man who had led them into the room.

'Would you like a drink?' he asked. 'Mr Seymour will be with you soon.'

Maggie shook her head.

'I'll have a glass of water, please,' Mackenzie said, watching as the man crossed to a drinks cabinet on the far side of the room, poured a glass of mineral water and brought it back to him.

Mackenzie took a sip then put the glass down, afraid he might drop it. The absence of a coaster on the dark wood table beside him was also a concern to him and he glanced anxiously towards the glass, hoping he hadn't left a ring on the table beneath.

'Where is Mr Seymour?' Maggie asked.

'He's got some business to see to,' the suited man replied.

'I thought he'd retired,' Maggie said. 'Sold all his business interests.'

'He has,' the man told her, standing in front of the open fireplace with his hands behind his back.

'How long have you worked for him?'

'Three years.'

'Do you live on the premises?' Mackenzie interjected.

'All his security personnel do.'

'It must get a bit boring,' Maggie said. 'I mean, he doesn't go out much, does he? There can't be that much for seventy of you to do every day.'

'It's a big estate,' the man told her. 'We've all got individual duties to perform.'

'And I suppose the wages make up for the boredom.' Mackenzie grinned, reaching for his glass and taking a sip. He was relieved to see there was no mark on the surface of the wood.

The suited man merely glanced indifferently at him.

'How many other staff are employed here, besides the seurity people?' Maggie continued.

'I'm not sure of the numbers,' the man answered. 'Mr Seymour will be able to tell you.'

'You must have a rough idea,' Maggie persisted. 'Ten? Twenty?'

'I honestly don't know,' the man said curtly. 'That's not my concern.'

'You must act as security for the other staff while they're here, though. Do they all live on the premises too?'

'Most of them.'

'How many medical staff does it take to look after Seymour's son? It can't be easy. He's brain-damaged, isn't he?'

'I told you, I don't know figures,' the man snapped.

'You can leave now.'

All three occupants of the room turned their heads in the direction of the newest voice. The suited man nodded and headed for the door out of the sitting room. Mackenzie got to his feet to welcome the newcomer. Maggie also rose, her eyes appraising the figure standing in the doorway.

'We were expecting Mr Seymour,' she said.

'He'll be here shortly,' the latest arrival announced. 'In the meantime, I'm sure I'll be able to help you.'

66

From the low, echoing pitch of the barks and growls, Chapman guessed that the dogs were large.

Probably Alsatians or Rottweilers, he thought with a shudder. How many of them he couldn't begin to imagine.

'What are we going to do?' Carla said frantically. 'They'll know where we are. They'll sniff us out, won't they?'

Chapman didn't answer, but gripped the shotgun more tightly, wishing to God that he had more than two rounds inside it.

Outside in the gloom, the barking of the dogs grew louder.

The detective poked his head a few inches outside the Nissen hut, squinting in the gloom, trying to catch sight of anyone or anything moving in the cloying blackness. He looked in the direction of some wrecked car chassis piled on top of each other about twenty feet away.

'We can climb up there,' he said, jabbing a finger towards the battered vehicles. 'If we stay above them we've got a chance.'

'What chance? 'We don't know how to get out of here. We can't avoid them for ever.'

'It's better than nothing,' he told her, stepping out of the door. 'You go first.'

Carla hesitated for a moment, but the frantic barking of the dogs spurred her into action. She ran swiftly towards the stacked cars, looking back at Chapman as he followed her across the open area.

'Go,' he told her, nodding towards the topmost vehicle.

Carla began to climb, using the doorless frames like the rungs of a bizarre ladder. Satisfied that she was safely beyond the second vehicle, Chapman pushed the shotgun up on to the back seat of the wreck and began to clamber up behind her. The piles of vehicles were at least thirty feet tall, the hulks pushed bumper to bumper for the full length of the scrapyard. Getting to the top of them wasn't going to be a problem. How stable the stacked-up vehicles were when they started to move along the elevated platform, he thought with a shudder, might be.

Carla reached the bonnet of the highest car and sat on it, watching as her father hauled himself up to join her. They waited there, catching their breath and looking down at the scrapyard.

The first of the dogs rounded a corner to their right. It was huge.

Fully three feet high at the shoulder, a squat and incredibly powerful-looking animal with a large, heavy head, it was smooth-haired and, to Chapman, looked like a cross-breed. Some unholy union of Rottweiler and wolfhound. Bred for just this purpose by Seymour, he guessed. It was joined seconds later by another.

Both were on chain-like leads held not by masked figures but by men in dark overalls and heavy boots. Men carrying two-way radios and guns. The detective immediately recognised the Spas automatic shotguns they held.

'Who are they?' Carla asked quietly, watching as the men dashed off in the direction of the Nissen hut, almost dragged by the huge dogs.

Chapman could only shake his head. 'They must work for Seymour,' he said. He turned his attention from the men in overalls and their dogs and jabbed a finger in the direction of the next set of shattered cars. 'Come on. We've got to keep moving.'

He led the way across the small gap between the two stacks of vehicles, stepping tentatively on to the twisted bonnet of the next car. It took his weight and he held out a hand to help Carla across.

Chapman moved up over the roof of the car and on to the next pile, cursing under his breath when he heard the buckled metal groan beneath his feet.

He stood still for a moment, looking back in the direction of the Nissen hut. The dogs were both inside, barking frenziedly, and Chapman guessed that they'd picked up his and Carla's scent.

He moved on more quickly, Carla hurrying along behind him, also peering back worriedly towards the Nissen hut.

Below them, in one of the walkways between the rows of disused cars, something moved.

Chapman held up his hand to stop Carla, his gaze fixed on the figure below.

It was dressed in T-shirt, trainers and jeans and, for a fleeting second, the detective thought that he recognised the face. He narrowed his eyes, certain that he knew the contours of that visage. Then he shook his head slightly as he realised the features were indeed recognisable. The figure was wearing a Michael Jackson mask.

285

As Chapman watched, the figure walked slowly along the aisle between the piles of derelict cars, a Smith and Wesson automatic jammed into his waistband. In his hand he carried a hatchet. He stopped and took a step back when he heard the dogs approaching.

'Hey.'

The voice caused Michael Jackson to look up. The two dog handlers were walking towards him, dragging hard on the leashes of their animals to hold them back.

'Have you seen anything?' the first handler asked him.

Michael Jackson shook his head. 'Shouldn't you have found him by now?' he said. 'You're the fucking experts, aren't you? You and those dogs.'

The dogs barked madly at him, straining at their leashes.

'Can't you keep those fucking things under control?' the masked figure asked, gazing at the furious animals. He raised the hatchet and imitated the dogs' loud barks.

'I wouldn't do that,' the second handler said reproachfully. 'The dogs don't like it.'

'Tough.'

'You'd better watch your mouth,' the first handler reminded him. 'You're as expendable as the guy we're hunting.'

'Fuck you,' Michael Jackson sneered.

The first handler simply released his grip on the leash.

The dog leapt forward with a speed that belied its size and bulk. It was upon the masked figure in two huge bounds.

He shrieked in fear as the dog slammed into him, its huge jaws closing over his right forearm like a spittle-coated vice. It snapped its head from side to side, forcing him to drop the hatchet. The weapon flew from his hand and he went down under the weight of the dog. It released his forearm and went for his face, tearing at the mask, ripping portions away and biting into the flesh of his left cheek. Skin and muscle were torn free with ease, great bloodied slivers of them flying into the air. Blood spurted from the wounds and the figure screamed in pain and fear as the huge dog savaged his chest and neck.

He managed to get a hand up to block its lunge at his neck but the dog merely clamped its jaws shut over two of his fingers, severing them easily just below the first knuckle. It swallowed them without chewing. The taste of blood served to excite it further and it bit frenziedly into anything within range.

Beneath it, the figure struck back weakly, his legs kicking feebly as he tried to dislodge the monstrous animal.

The other handler smiled and dropped his own leash.

The second dog hurtled straight for the fallen man's legs and clamped its jaws round one thigh. Long canine teeth punctured the leg and gouts of blood erupted from the savage wounds. The dog struck again, biting hard into the victim's groin, its teeth closing over his genitals. It twisted its head violently to one side and the scream that exploded from the doomed man's throat was one of pure agony.

The dog tore off both his testicles and most of his penis. It swallowed both of the bulging orbs, tendrils of flesh and portions of vein sticking between its already stained teeth. The muzzles of both animals were awash with spittle and blood, the gory mixture spraying in all directions as the dogs continued with their attack.

Transfixed by the spectacle, Carla felt her stomach contract and her head began to spin. She wanted to vomit, to scream, to faint, all of those things.

Chapman grabbed her and held her close to him, forcing her head into his shoulder so she could see no more of the slaughter below.

The dogs were pulling agitatedly at the motionless figure now, angered by its lack of movement but still excited by the massive quantities of blood soaking into the ground around them, most of it spurting from the gaping gash in the dying man's groin.

The first handler stepped forward, snapped a command and retrieved the leash, dragging his dog away from the mutilated corpse. His companion did the same, the dog growling at him as he did so.

Chapman watched as the men moved off, the dogs now walking along quietly, sniffing the air. Only when they'd disappeared into the gloom did he relax his hold on his daughter.

He wiped some tears from her face then kissed her on the forehead.

'I've got to get that gun,' he whispered, nodding down at the bloodied remains below.

'You can't go down there,' she said breathlessly. 'You'll end up like him.'

Chapman put a finger to her lips to silence her.

'We need that gun,' he said softly.

'Dad, please don't.'

'We need it.' Chapman stroked her hair. 'They've moved on. They don't know where we are.'

Carla swallowed hard, watching as her father laid the shotgun on the roof of the battered car.

'Please be careful,' she breathed.

Chapman nodded.

He began to climb down.

67

Stella Crane smiled at the two detectives as she entered the room. Walking effortlessly on four-inch heels, she headed straight for the drinks cabinet, aware of the appraising eyes that followed her. She ignored the ID presented to her.

Detective Sergeant Maggie Grant was struck by the woman's stunning figure, accentuated as it was by the black dress clinging to her curves. Similarly captivated, Mackenzie took a sip of his water, the scent of Stella's perfume almost intoxicating as she walked past him.

'Can I get you a drink?' she asked, helping herself to a Jack Daniel's.

'We're fine,' Maggie said, glancing at Stella's face and, more particularly, the small white grains around her left nostril.

Stella smiled, showing off about ten thousand pounds' worth of immaculate dental work.

'You missed some,' Maggie said quietly, touching her own nostril with one index finger.

Stella's smile slipped and she brushed anxiously at her perfectly shaped nose.

'We're waiting for Mr Seymour,' Maggie explained again.

'He's busy,' Stella told her, sitting down on the sofa close to Mackenzie. 'Surely I can be of assistance?'

'Well, it is him we need to speak to,' Maggie persisted.

'I'm his partner. I'm sure I can help,' Stella assured her.

'How long have you and Mr Seymour been together?' Mackenzie asked. He glanced at her unadorned ring finger. 'Miss . . . ?'

'Crane. Stella Crane.' She recovered her smile. 'I've been with Anthony for nearly a year now.'

'Did you know his wife?' Maggie asked.

Stella shook her head. 'I know I can never take her place,' she said. 'But I don't think anyone should be alone, do you? If I can bring some joy into Anthony's life after what happened then I'm happy.'

'Are you involved in any way with the staff in the house, Miss Crane?' Maggie enquired. 'Their management and organisation?'

'Anthony asks for my opinion of their suitability, if that's what you mean,' Stella answered.

'How many staff are there?' asked Maggie.

'Other than the bodyguards,' Mackenzie added.

'Fifteen. That's not including the gardeners or Anthony's helicopter pilot. They don't live here. All the other staff do, of course.'

'Of course.' Mackenzie smiled, hoping that Stella hadn't noticed him running an approving gaze over her shapely legs.

'What about the medical staff?' Maggie interjected. 'How many of those are there?'

'Four nurses and a doctor,' Stella told her. 'They live in the same wing of the house as Anthony's son.'

'Do you have much contact with them?'

'There isn't much I can do, really. I wish there was more. It's so sad what happened to Thomas.' She sipped her drink, her smile fading. 'I do what I can, but . . .' She allowed the sentence to trail off.

'Do you know a man called David Phelan? He's one of Mr Seymour's bodyguards.'

'I'm not familiar with the name.'

'Then I'm afraid you can't help us, Miss Crane,' Maggie snapped. 'We really need to speak to Mr Seymour.'

'I told you, he's busy.'

'It's very important,' Maggie insisted, her patience finally at an end. 'Could you please get him?'

Stella regarded her evenly over the rim of her glass. 'He'll be here as soon as he can,' she said.

Maggie glanced at her watch. 'Ten minutes,' she said flatly. 'We've wasted enough time already.'

'Miss Crane's with them now.'

The security man stood close to Seymour's chair in the control room, his eyes occasionally flicking towards the banks of monitors on the wall ahead.

'Go and speak to them, for Christ's sake,' DS Bradley urged. 'Before they get suspicious.'

'Of what?' Seymour snapped.

'Of you,' Bradley insisted. 'Talk to them. Get rid of them.'

'Don't tell me how to handle this, Bradley,' Seymour hissed, turning to face the policeman.

'Shall I say you're on the way, sir?' the security guard enquired.

Seymour nodded, his gaze drawn back to the monitors once more.

On one of them, he could see that Chapman had reached the base of the pile of cars he'd climbed down. He was kneeling over the torn body of Michael Jackson.

'This will be over in a few moments,' Seymour said. He zoomed the camera in and looked closely at the bloodied face of the detective. 'By the time those dogs have finished, there won't be enough left of Chapman or the girl to put in a matchbox.'

He leaned closer to the microphone nearby and flicked another switch.

'Let the dogs go,' he said evenly. 'Let them off the leads.'

68

Chapman hung from the chassis of the car like an over-developed ape, looking around him in the darkness for a moment longer. Then he dropped the last three feet to the ground. He almost slipped in the puddle of blood that had spread out around the corpse.

Above him, Carla peered down anxiously from the rampart of cars.

He remained in a crouching position for a second, checking that no one had heard him, then he held his thumb up, signalling to her.

'Hurry,' she whispered.

Chapman looked at the body before him, aware of the stench of excrement and blood clogging his nostrils. He lifted the Michael Jackson mask and inspected what was left of the face beneath. Most of the flesh and muscle of the left cheek had been torn off to expose the shining white of bone. The left eye had been partially pulled from its socket by the ferocity of the attack. The detective could see it dangling by the deep red tendril of the optic nerve.

Forcing his gaze from the remains of the face he quickly

pulled the automatic from the waistband of the dead man's jeans. He hefted it before him. It was a Smith and Wesson .459 automatic. Nine-millimetre. The grips felt reassuringly bulky in his fist and he nodded approvingly. He pressed the magazine release button and the slim metal clip slid from the butt. He counted twelve bullets in there then slammed it back into place, working the slide to chamber a round.

The metallic sound echoed round the silent scrap yard and Chapman glanced about again to ensure he hadn't been heard.

'Come on,' Carla said quietly from above him.

The detective nodded and stuffed the .459 into his belt, freeing both hands for the climb back up.

He never even heard the dog.

It rounded a pile of cars about twenty feet away, paused for a second then hurtled at him.

Even as it ran, it made no sound except a low, guttural growl deep inside its throat.

Carla saw it before her father knew it was there.

'Dad,' she shrieked, her voice echoing ominously in the stillness.

The dog launched itself at him.

Chapman felt searing pain in his left ankle as the dog clamped its jaws round the top of his boot and his trailing leg. He shook the limb madly, trying to dislodge the animal that was now growling ferociously as it clung to him, its teeth slicing easily through the denim of his jeans and then the flesh of his leg. He felt one of its canines grate against his ankle bone and blood burst from the wound.

The weight of the dog was too much to resist and Chapman fell, slamming hard against the ground. He rolled as best he could with the rucksack still on his back. The dog dived at him once more, snapping at his face and neck.

Chapman drove his right foot into its chest and managed to push it backwards. The dog's feet scrabbled wildly on the ground as it tried to launch itself at him again. The detective dragged the automatic from his belt and squeezed the trigger just as the dog came hurtling through the air, its huge bulk threatening to crush him.

He fired twice and, from point-blank range, couldn't miss.

The first bullet caught the dog in the flank, the second hit it just below the left eye. The projectile, travelling at a speed in excess of thirteen hundred feet a second, blew away most of the left side of the animal's skull. Bone fragments, blood and brain sprayed into the air as the bullet exited. The dog hit the ground next to Chapman with a loud thud and didn't move.

The detective struggled to his feet, wincing as he put weight on his left ankle. Blood was pooling in his boot and the wound felt as if it was on fire. He stuffed the .459 back into his belt, feeling how hot the barrel was against his flesh. Then, trying to ignore the pain, he climbed towards Carla.

'Drop the rucksack,' she called.

Chapman ignored her and continued climbing.

Somewhere in the distance he could hear more dogs barking, the sound mingled with shouts as the pursuers raced towards the source of the gunshots he'd just fired.

He gritted his teeth and clambered up on to the bonnet of the car at the top of the pile. Carla looked down at the wound on his ankle, her eyes wide with shock.

'We've got to move,' Chapman said, almost pushing her towards the next stack of ruined vehicles.

'The shotgun,' she protested, seeing the weapon lying on the roof of the car.

'Leave it,' he told her. 'We've only got two shells anyway.'

Carla nodded and moved quickly but cautiously across the small gap to the next car. Chapman followed. On to the bonnet, up over the battered roof and down on to the boot. Then across again to the adjacent stack of cars. On again. They moved with a swiftness born of desperation, anxious to put as much distance between themselves and their pursuers as possible.

In the walkways below, Chapman could see several dark shapes moving about. Dogs and men, some of the men masked, others wearing the dark overalls he'd seen earlier.

Up ahead there was another pile of cars but it was taller than the rest, fully forty-five feet. Cars, vans and even the battered cab of a lorry had been crushed together to form this latest tower of twisted metal. The crane that had lifted the abandoned vehicles into place stood to its right, the jib dangling uselessly, unstirred by recent use or any semblance of breeze.

'Can you reach it?' Chapman asked, noting that there was about four feet between the rear of the car they were balanced on and the bonnet of the vehicle they had to climb on to. Below there was a thirty-foot drop to the dark aisle of earth that squirmed through the scrapyard.

Carla nodded, stretching out one leg to step on to the bonnet ahead of her. She teetered precariously for a second then swung herself over, clutching at the rusted metal to prevent herself from falling.

There was a loud metallic clang as she shifted the rest of her weight on to the vehicle.

'Oh, Christ,' Chapman breathed, his eyes widening in horror.

The tower of battered vehicles had swayed visibly.

296

Carla looked round anxiously at her father, before ducking through the shattered windscreen into the driver's seat of the car she had climbed on to. She too had felt the movement.

'Keep moving,' he urged her as another loud clang echoed through the stillness.

Perched on the top of the stack of vehicles, a battered black Audi began to slip forward.

Carla felt the entire structure begin to shake. The car she was in lurched to the left and it was all she could do not to scream. The black Audi slid another couple of inches.

'Get out!' Chapman shouted, seeing the movement of the tower. 'The whole lot's going to fall.'

69

As the teetering pile of scrap metal continued to sway, Carla hauled herself out of the driving seat and back on to the bonnet.

'Jump,' Chapman urged, holding out his hands to her, wincing when he put a little too much weight on his savaged left ankle.

At the top of the adjacent pile, the black Audi slid a little further, the harsh screech of metal on metal cutting through the stillness.

Carla steadied herself on the quivering bonnet of her vehicle, preparing to launch herself the few short feet to safety.

'Come on,' Chapman said, his voice cracking.

The pile of vehicles swayed more violently.

The Audi slipped off the top and plummeted to earth.

It struck the ground with a thunderous crash, its head-lights splintering and its radiator splitting open.

It fell backwards, banging the already unsteady stack of vehicles and completing the work of demolition. Slowly, as if pushed by a giant, invisible finger, the pile began to fall sideways.

Carla jumped.

She hung in mid-air for breathless seconds, then landed heavily on the car where Chapman was standing.

He grabbed at her, trying to prevent her from sliding off the metal and falling to the ground below. With a grunt, he gripped her arm, stopping her momentum.

Both of them ducked as the tumbling pile of cars hit the ground. Lumps of twisted metal met earth. Some tyres still attached to one or two of the vehicles were forced loose by the impact. The rubber circlets spun into the air or rolled forlornly away.

The thunderous impact caused several of the other piles of cars to wobble and Chapman wondered, for a second, if the whole lot would fall like oversized dominoes.

He was still considering that possibility when he heard voices and loud barking below them. Four men and three dogs had gathered around the fallen vehicles, some of the men checking inside the battered hulks for any sign of life.

Chapman pulled the .459 from his belt and aimed it at the rear of the black Audi, drawing a bead on the petrol tank.

Carla looked at him uncomprehendingly as he squeezed the trigger twice.

Both shots slammed into the car, the first punching through the chassis and drilling into the tank, the heat of the second igniting the petrol inside.

There was a huge explosion and the Audi disappeared beneath a searing ball of yellow and red flame.

Even thirty feet up, Chapman felt the concussion blast and he shielded his face from the fire and the mushroom cloud of choking black smoke that rose into the air. Men and dogs were lifted bodily from the ground by the blast, tossed in all directions like leaves in a gale.

Chapman grabbed Carla by the wrist and pulled her along with him as they both made their way back along the piles of vehicles, using the confusion to mask their escape.

'It'll keep them occupied long enough for us to find another way through,' the detective breathed, wincing again as he felt the pain from his left ankle.

Carla looked back over her shoulder at the rising pall of black smoke.

Detective Inspector Michael Bradley watched in shock as the explosion filled the screens, until the monitors went suddenly black.

'The explosion must have affected the cameras,' Seymour said irritably. He flicked several switches but the screens remained blank.

Bradley got to his feet and began pacing back and forth anxiously.

'Sit down, Bradley,' Seymour snapped. 'Everything will be working again in a minute.'

'We don't know what they're doing, Chapman and the girl,' the policeman muttered. 'How do we know what they're doing if we can't see them?'

'Well, we know they're not going anywhere.'

'Mr Seymour, the police are still waiting downstairs,' the security man reminded his employer.

Seymour nodded. 'Get that fixed,' he ordered, jabbing an impatient finger in the direction of the monitors. He brushed a speck of fluff from his sleeve and made his way towards the door of the control room.

'I'd better speak to your colleagues, Bradley,' he said. 'See what they want. Would you like to come with me?'

He shot the detective a contemptuous look, then paused to look back again at the monitors.

They were still blank.

70

'Take that,' Chapman said, pushing the nail gun towards Carla.

She hesitated, then accepted the tool her father had taken from the rucksack, surprised at how light it was. She ran her index finger over the Tacwise 50mm coil nailer, touching the trigger gently.

'Careful,' Chapman said. 'Touch that too hard and you'll pin me to the floor.' He managed a slight smile. 'Anyone comes near you, just squeeze the trigger and keep squeezing until they run or drop, got it?'

Carla nodded. 'Will it stop a man?' she asked.

'It fires thirty-millimetre nails at two hundred feet a second. You put enough into him he'll stop. Aim for the face if you can.'

They were seated in the front of a discarded jeep. All four wheels had been removed and the bonnet was up to reveal an empty cavity where the engine had once been. From where they sat, they could see a tall wire mesh fence topped with razor wire. Beyond it there was an open area leading to a large grey building that resembled a warehouse.

'What about you?' she asked.

'I'll stick with these,' he told her, holding up the .459 in one hand and the chainsaw in the other. 'We'll leave the rest of the stuff.'

'Tell me again why you think we have to get to that warehouse,' Carla said. She reached for the cigarette packet in her joggers and flipped it open. There was one left. She lit it and took a couple of drags.

'Because that's part of Seymour's game,' Chapman told her. 'The doors leading into and out of every portion of the set have been inside buildings. That warehouse is the only building I can see round here.'

'What if you're wrong?'

'Then I'm sure you'll keep on reminding me.'

Carla managed a smile.

'How's your leg?' she asked, looking down at her father's badly gashed ankle.

'It hurts like hell,' he confessed. 'But I can walk on it, that's all that matters.'

Carla slumped back against the seat and closed her eyes for a second. She allowed her head to rest on Chapman's shoulder. He gently touched her cheek with one blood-spattered hand. When he withdrew his fingers, he left two red smudges on her skin.

She sat up and took another drag on the cigarette.

'Are you going to smoke all of that?'

She handed him the cigarette and watched as he took a drag before handing it back to her.

'It's the last one,' she told him.

'Good,' he said, hauling himself out of the jeep. 'Those things will kill you.'

He glanced around, then began moving carefully towards the fence, the automatic gripped in one fist, the chainsaw in the other. Carla kept pace with him, her eyes darting to left and right in search of anything that might be moving in the darkness.

They were a hundred yards away from the fence when they heard the dogs.

Chapman's injured ankle gave out. He slipped and fell, the chainsaw falling from his grasp.

'You go on,' he told her quickly. 'Get through the fence. Get to that warehouse.'

'I'm not leaving you here,' she said, trying to help him up. He managed to haul himself upright, taking most of his weight on his uninjured ankle.

'Go,' he snapped. 'I'll keep them back. Give you time to get through.'

Again she hesitated.

'I can't keep up with you, Carla, not with this fucking leg,' he insisted, holding the Husqvarna close to him.

The barking was louder now.

'I'll catch up with you,' he said, through gritted teeth. 'Now go.'

She ran.

Chapman placed his finger on the starter button of the chainsaw and waited.

71

As the noise of barking dogs grew louder, Chapman retreated across the dirt towards a rampart of piled-up tyres. He chanced a look behind him and saw that Carla had already reached the wire fence. She was pulling at the bottom of the barrier, trying to find a way through.

The detective ducked down lower as he saw two of the large dogs bound into view from behind the wreck of an overturned bus.

One of them made straight for Carla, while the other growled viciously and ran towards where Chapman sheltered.

He raised the .459 and aimed it at the former.

His first shot missed, sending up a geyser of dirt when it struck just behind the animal. The second caught the beast in the side, punched in two ribs and bowled it over, but he barely had time to enjoy his triumph before the second dog launched itself at him.

It cleared the rampart of tyres with ease and slammed into him, knocking him over. The automatic spun from his grasp, landing two or three feet behind him.

The dog skidded on the soft earth, battling to keep

its feet. As it turned to face him, Chapman flicked the starter switch on the chainsaw.

The machine roared into life, petrol fumes spewing from the engine as it vibrated madly in his grip. The jagged chain spun at over seven hundred and fifty revolutions a minute and a film of oil rose into the air around the blade.

Startled by the sound, the dog hesitated a moment, then jumped at Chapman once more.

He thrust the chainsaw forward to meet it.

The churning blade tore through the dog's body, hacking through bone and rending muscle and internal organs. A vast spray of blood splattered Chapman as he lifted the thrashing dog higher, impaled on the blade and torn by the spinning chain. Its head flopped forward limply as he tore the blade upwards, practically splitting the animal in half from the belly to the neck. A sticky mass of intestines fell from the riven cavity, landing with a splat on the ground. Chapman shook the animal loose of the blade and stepped back, wiping blood from his face with the back of one hand. He slumped back against the piled-up tyres and flicked the chainsaw off. The sound died slowly in the stillness.

A thunderous blast filled the void and Chapman ducked down again as part of one of the tyres near him was blown away. A lump of rubber spiralled into the air as another shot struck the ground to his right.

He peered in the direction of the shots and saw one of Seymour's men preparing to fire again.

He looked round frantically for the dropped .459 and dived to reach it, pulling himself back behind the rampart of tyres.

The third blast from the Spas shredded one of the car tyres to his left and, instinctively, he ducked again, thrusting the pistol through a gap in the rubber circles. He fired twice, the empty shell cases spinning into the air.

Both shots missed but they were enough to send the overall-clad man scampering for cover.

Chapman pressed the magazine release button and the hot metal clip slid from the butt of the gun.

Just four rounds left.

The detective was breathing heavily, blood and sweat stinging his eyes. His heart was hammering against his ribs and he was having difficulty swallowing. He muttered something under his breath and glanced in Carla's direction.

He saw her slipping beneath the wire fence.

'Good girl,' he murmured to himself, aiming the automatic through the tyres to fire one more shot.

He could see his daughter running frantically towards the warehouse now.

At least she would escape.

He heard other voices in the distance. He knew more of Seymour's men would be arriving any time.

Three bullets.

You haven't got a fucking chance.

From where he crouched, Chapman could see the man with the Spas hunkered behind a battered car chassis. The man's body was protected by the wrecked vehicle but his feet and ankles were visible.

It was a slim chance but it was better than nothing and time was running out.

Chapman swung the .459 up before him and squinted down the sight. He swallowed hard, steadying his breathing and his aim. Then he squeezed off one round.

The bullet hit the man in the ankle, shattered the bone and exploded from his leg. He shouted in agony and fell backwards.

Chapman didn't wait to savour his victory. He turned and ran as fast as he could towards the wire fence, gritting his teeth against the pain from his gnawed ankle. He ran on, not daring to look back.

When he reached the fence he threw himself down and dragged his body under the mesh, ignoring the metal prongs that dug into the flesh of his calves as he pulled himself through.

He was on his feet immediately, hurrying along as best he could, seeing the warehouse ahead, knowing that Carla was already inside.

There were two loud blasts and the discharges tore through the air close to his head.

Chapman kept running.

Another shot. He felt the pellets pepper his left forearm and shoulder. Like a dozen red hot needles jammed into his flesh.

Someone shouted something but he didn't hear the words. He was only yards from the main doors of the warehouse now. At least there'd be cover inside, somewhere to hide. A place to mount an ambush if necessary.

He crashed against the door just as another shotgun discharge tore into the metal close to his face. It shredded the steel of the door and Chapman ducked instinctively, sliding into the welcoming stillness of the building itself.

'Carla,' he called breathlessly.

There were crates all around him. All shapes and sizes, but most made of wood and as tall as a man. Some were piled up like building blocks, others lay where they'd been dumped. What they'd held he couldn't imagine. That they'd never contained anything he thought more than likely.

Just part of the game.

The ceiling was high and Chapman could see two cameras up there, both trained on him.

'Carla,' he said again, slumping against the nearest crate.

She emerged from behind some boxes to his left.

He smiled and lowered the pistol.

'There's a room through there,' she told him, gesturing towards a wooden door set in the wall behind her. 'And a cellar.'

'That should be the way out,' Chapman said, licking his lips.

'There're more men down there,' she said quietly. 'I've seen them.'

'I apologise for having kept you waiting.'

Anthony Seymour swept into the sitting room, nodding respectfully in the direction of Maggie and Mackenzie as they showed their IDS. Stella smiled at him but he didn't smile back.

'How can I be of service?' he enquired, seating himself in one of the huge armchairs close to the open marble fireplace.

'We're looking for one of your employees, Mr Seymour,' Maggie began. 'A man named David Phelan. We'd like to speak to him.'

'I have a lot of staff, Miss Grant,' Seymour told her. 'I'm afraid I don't remember all their names. It's rather remiss of me, I know, but my memory isn't what it was. Age, no doubt.'

'He's one of your security men,' Mackenzie interjected.

'And why do you want to speak to him?'

'We have reason to believe he was involved in a kidnapping earlier today,' Maggie said.

'My word,' Seymour murmured. 'And you think he works for me?'

309

'We checked with his previous employers. As far as they're concerned he does.'

'I'm sure I'd know if I had a criminal on my payroll.' Seymour smiled. 'But if you want to speak to Mr Phelan, I'm sure that can be arranged. If indeed he does actually work for me.' Again the older man smiled. 'May I ask when this kidnapping took place?'

'This morning,' Maggie said.

'And who was the victim, or is that top secret?'

'The victim was a policeman,' Maggie told him. 'Someone you know. Detective Inspector Joe Chapman.' She watched for any flicker of emotion on the millionaire's face. 'He was the detective in charge of the case involving your son.'

'I know,' Seymour said briskly, his thin smile fading rapidly.

'How is your son?' Mackenzie asked.

'You didn't come here to discuss my son's well-being, did you? You came here to find out if one of my employees is a criminal. I suggest we set about dispelling or confirming that notion.' Seymour got to his feet. 'If you'd like to follow me,' he said.

Maggie and Mackenzie also rose.

Led by Seymour, the little procession moved out of the room.

72

'Which men?' Chapman looked almost despairingly into Carla's eyes. 'Seymour's?'

'They all work for this Seymour guy, don't they?' she said wearily. 'What difference does it make?'

'Are they armed?'

Carla looked blankly at him.

'Carla, have they got guns?' the detective persisted, resisting the urge to shake her.

There seemed to be nothing behind her eyes. He could see himself reflected in the grey-blue orbs and it was as if he was looking into glass. As if all the life had drained from her. And he couldn't help but sympathise with her. If she'd given up hope then he understood. He could appreciate that she had accepted her fate. It was hard to find hope when none seemed forthcoming any more. For them to have come so far and yet to be confronted yet again by men intent on killing them seemed almost too much to him as well.

'How many are there?' he continued, still gripping her by the shoulders.

'Five or six,' she snapped, pulling angrily away from

him. 'What fucking difference does it make? If we get past them there'll be more.' She stepped back. 'This won't end until they kill us.' Her voice cracked a little.

Chapman took a painful step towards her, his arms outstretched. 'Listen,' he urged. 'There are men chasing us too. You know that. If we don't get out of here we'll be caught in the middle. Then we're finished.'

'We're finished anyway,' she yelled at him, tears pouring down her face. 'We never had a chance of getting out of here. You lied to me when you said we did.'

'No, I didn't. We've come this far and we've done it by sticking together. By helping each other.'

'So it's taken us both nearly being killed to bring us together,' she blurted. 'Is that what this has been for you? A fucking bonding exercise? Trying to get close to me like you could never do on the outside?' She moved further away from him.

'This isn't the time, Carla,' he said, his voice low.

She looked at him angrily.

Chapman was about to say something else when he heard movement to his left. He waved a hand in Carla's direction, urging her to back off, and she sought refuge behind some crates.

Chapman himself ducked back into the shadows cast by a pile of crates behind the door, aware that the wooden partition was opening.

The figure that stepped through seconds later was dressed in the same dark overalls that the dog handlers behind them had worn. The man moved unhurriedly into the warehouse, the heavy boots he wore echoing on the concrete floor as he walked. Chapman could see the MP5K sub-machine gun that he carried in one gloved fist.

He was heading in Carla's direction.

312

The detective tried to control his breathing, wondering what his own next move should be. If he ran at the man then there was a chance that the others in the next room would hear. An even stronger possibility that his target would spin round and open fire. If he did that would be it. End of story. Even if he managed to start the chain-saw there would be no chance of using it before the man saw him.

The dark-overalled man was now only feet from the crate where Carla was hiding.

Chapman felt his heart beating madly.

Think. Come on. Do something.

The armed man stopped and peered round the inside of the warehouse. Chapman dropped lower behind his own rampart of crates, peering at his enemy through a gap in the wood. The man was standing two or three feet from where Carla was hiding, his back to her.

She popped up from between two crates. Chapman saw the nail gun gripped in her hand.

She squeezed the trigger three times in quick succession.

All three nails thudded into the skull of the dark-clad man, tearing through his cranium and penetrating his brain. He turned slowly, almost drunkenly, to face his attacker, his mouth open silently.

Carla fired two more nails at him. The first punctured his left eye. The second drilled into his skull squarely in the middle of his forehead, snapping his head back.

For interminable seconds he swayed uncertainly, then dropped like a stone to the concrete floor.

Chapman hurried from his hiding place and pressed two fingers to the man's throat, searching for a pulse he was already sure wasn't there.

Carla stepped out from behind the crates, looking

313

down indifferently at the prone man, her eyes flickering over the 30mm nails embedded in his skull. There were thin trails of blood running from the base of each one, forming a small puddle around his head.

Chapman pulled the sub-machine gun from the man's grip and checked the magazine. It was full. There were two more of the thirty-round clips in a holder on the dead man's belt. The detective took those too and jammed them into his pocket. Then he looked at Carla, who was still staring down at the body.

'Come on,' he whispered, closing his fingers round her forearm.

She hesitated for a moment then nodded and followed him towards the door that led through into the next room.

High above them, a camera turned to follow their movement.

73

Chapman pushed the door with one hand and stuck his head round the jamb.

No sign of movement in the room beyond.

He stepped through and beckoned Carla after him.

The room they were in now was slightly smaller than the one they'd just left but it was more brightly lit. Powerful wall lights bathed the entire place in a cold white glow. Chapman glanced swiftly round and saw a flight of stone steps leading down to a subterranean level.

'Are they down there?' he whispered. 'The other men?'

Carla nodded and stepped away from him, heading towards the centre of the room, beckoning him to follow.

There was a rectangular hole in the floor before them, covered by thick wire mesh. There was another to the right of where they stood and one more behind, Chapman noticed. Through the closest he could see metal walkways beneath them. Narrow corridor-like passageways with handrails on either side. He nodded and moved silently across to the hole on the right.

This one had much thinner mesh over it and there was a metal ladder attached to the edge. As Chapman knelt there he could hear a slow but rhythmic pumping sound. Like a giant mechanical pulse below him.

He stepped back rapidly as he heard footsteps echoing on the metal walkway beneath.

Another armed guard dressed in the now familiar dark overalls went by, whistling tunelessly to himself.

Chapman waited until the man had passed then ducked down again, peering into the subterranean depths once more. The pumping sound was more insistent now and he moved towards the rear wall and the last of the gaps in the floor in an effort to locate the source of the sound.

Carla stood motionless, watching him, the nail gun still gripped in her fist.

He signalled for her to remain where she was and then looked down through the hole in the floor at the back of the room.

'Jesus,' he murmured to himself.

The smell of hot oil and petrol rose from beneath him and Chapman finally realised what he was looking at.

'A generator,' he breathed, gazing at the panel of small flickering lights on the machine below him.

Carla walked over to join him and he pointed it out.

'That's where the power must come from for the whole set,' he told her softly.

They ducked back as they heard footsteps below them, both Chapmans involuntarily holding their breath as another man passed beneath them.

The detective took a couple of steps back, looking anxiously around him.

'What are we going to do?' Carla asked, her voice low. 'They're going to come looking for that guy I shot eventually.' She hooked a thumb in the direction of the door.

Chapman nodded but his attention was riveted on several dozen metal cans in the far corner of the room.

He crossed to them and lifted the nearest, the smell of petrol already strong in his nostrils. He unscrewed the cap of the container and sniffed.

'Fuel for the generator,' he told her.

More footsteps below.

Carla gazed at him with a look of incomprehension on her face as he tipped up the first of the petrol cans, the reeking fluid spilling across the concrete floor.

'What are you doing?' she gasped.

'Help me,' he said. 'If Seymour wants a show, we'll give him one. We're going to put this whole fucking place into orbit.'

The room was to the rear of the main house.

About fifteen feet square, the only item of furniture it contained was a dark wood desk with a laptop perched on it. Every other inch of wall and floor space on three sides of the room seemed to be taken up with filing cabinets and shelves. Clip folders of various different colours lined the shelves.

On the back wall was nothing but monitors. At least thirty of them, Maggie guessed. Each one showed a different part of the house and its grounds. She looked round with interest as Seymour led them into the room and sat down behind the desk.

'What is this place?' Mackenzie enquired.

'My head of security's office.'

Maggie glanced more closely at the bank of monitors, studying each screen quickly but intently.

'I would offer you a seat,' Seymour smiled, 'but, as you can see, there are none.'

'We're fine, Mr Seymour,' Maggie assured him, her gaze still flicking from screen to screen.

'Now, perhaps I can help you with your inquiries,' he

317

mused, his fingers flicking over the keys of the laptop. 'What was that man's name again? Phelan?'

'David Phelan,' Maggie said. 'P-H-E-L-A-N.'

'I'm surprised you don't have someone to do this kind of job for you, Mr Seymour,' Mackenzie added.

'I'm wealthy, detective, not paralysed,' Seymour replied. 'Too many men in positions like mine tend to suffer from an over-reliance on others. I like to do as much for myself as I can.'

He tapped the requisite keys and waited.

'What does Miss Crane do for you?' Maggie asked. 'Does she work for you?'

'She's a companion,' Seymour answered. 'Why? What did she tell you?'

'She said she was your partner,' Maggie said, watching a screen where two suited security men were talking animatedly in the garden of the house.

'Dear Stella.' Seymour shook his head gently. 'She does somewhat overestimate her role here. As I said, she's a companion for me. Most people need company of some description.' He brushed his cheek contemplatively. 'What's the phrase? No man is an island? That's true even for me, I'm afraid. Especially since my wife's death.'

Maggie and Mackenzie glanced at each other. Seymour's attention was still fixed on the screen before him.

'Nothing,' he declared. 'There doesn't seem to be any record of anyone called Phelan in my employ.' He looked expressionlessly at the two detectives.

'Can you double-check, please?' Maggie asked.

Seymour shrugged and repeated the procedure. Meanwhile Maggie gazed at the bottom row of screens. The first showed a deserted street, the next a pedestrianised square surrounded on all four sides by buildings. Beyond that there was a view of a church.

318

Maggie swallowed hard, trying to attract Mackenzie's attention.

There was something familiar about that view.

'How many cameras cover the grounds?' she asked, still eyeing the monitors behind Seymour.

'Thirty,' he told her.

Maggie finally caught Mackenzie's eye. She nodded towards the screens and her companion also ran his gaze over them.

Both the detectives saw the figures walking slowly through the pedestrianised square.

All three were wearing clown masks.

74

The floor of the warehouse was awash with petrol.

The thick, reeking fuel they had tipped from the cans had splashed across the concrete and dripped through the wire mesh to the cellar below.

Carla almost slipped in the liquid as she hauled another metal container towards the steps leading down into the cellar.

Chapman himself, carrying a can in each hand, hurried across the room, tipping the petrol all around him in the process.

The burst of automatic fire from below him caused the detective to duck backwards. He slipped in the petrol covering the floor and landed heavily on his back.

Carla dashed towards him but he waved her back, recovering and hauling himself upright again, his jeans drenched with fuel.

There was another blast of sub-machine gun fire, the 9mm slugs striking the edge of one of the rectangular holes in the floor.

Chapman looked round anxiously.

If one spark should ignite the already spilled petrol then the whole room would go up like a torch.

And he didn't want that yet.

He fired back down one of the holes, the bullets singing off the metal and concrete below, his ears ringing from the retort. Smoke drifted around him and he could smell cordite in his nostrils.

There were shouts from beneath them, the angry yells of the armed men who still inhabited the subterranean area where the generator continued to thump and pound like a huge mechanical heart.

'We need a fuse,' Chapman said breathlessly. 'Something to stick in one of these cans.' He held up a petrol container. It'll give us time to get out before the whole place blows.'

She nodded and ran for the door.

Chapman was about to ask her where she was going when there was another burst of fire from beneath him. Bullets drilled into the concrete, blasting pieces of it away. Others ricocheted, screaming off the walls.

He fired back, gripping the MP5K in one bloodied hand. Empty shell cases sprayed from the sub-machine gun until the hammer slammed down on an empty chamber.

Chapman reached for a fresh magazine and slammed it into the weapon.

Carla returned moments later, gripping a piece of dark cloth. 'I cut it from that dead guy's trousers,' she said, pushing the material into her father's hand.

He took it from her and twisted it. Then he stuffed it into the neck of the container.

'Give me the lighter,' he said breathlessly.

More gunfire from below. They both flinched.

Carla fumbled in her pocket and pulled out the lighter, handing it to him.

'Right, get out of here,' he said, glaring at her. 'Go now. Run.'

'What about you?' she protested.

'I'll be right behind you,' he assured her. 'This material is only going to take five or six seconds to burn down. We haven't got much time. When it goes up it'll set fire to the petrol.'

Carla opened her mouth to say something but no words would come. Instead she turned and ran for the door that led out of the warehouse.

Chapman raised the petrol can before him and flicked at the lighter.

It sparked but the flame died immediately.

He could hear footsteps on the metal walkways below him now, getting closer. Heading towards the steps that led up into the room where he was.

He flicked again at the lighter.

Still it wouldn't light.

'Come on,' he hissed.

Out of petrol?

He looked down at the fuel lapping around his feet.

Again he flicked the lighter.

A flame burst into life and he moved it towards the rag. It ignited immediately and the detective swung the petrol can backwards and forwards a couple of times, testing the range.

He was aiming for the rearmost hole in the floor, the one closest to the generator.

He released the can and saw it arc upwards into the air. Whether it hit its chosen target he didn't stop to see. He turned and moved as quickly as he could towards the door out of the warehouse.

As he ran he fired three more short bursts from the

322

machine-gun, raking the top of the stone steps to discourage those below from coming up.

Chapman crashed through the door and out of the warehouse, stumbling on the uneven ground, swallowed by the blackness.

He saw Carla gesturing to him, urging him to join her. He fell but hauled himself upright, anxious to be as far from the petrol-filled warehouse as possible.

Carla was still hesitating, waiting for him to reach her.

Chapman waved frantically at her to move back.

Then came the blast.

75

Chapman felt as if an invisible hand had grabbed him and lifted him off his feet.

The explosion that destroyed the warehouse illuminated everything within two hundred yards, lighting it with a hellish yellow and orange glow for endless seconds.

He pitched forward, thrown to the ground by the concussion blast. Pieces of stone, metal and wood showered down all around him like shrapnel, fragments of a building that had been virtually vaporised by the ferocity of the blast. He shielded his head as a large lump of stone thudded into the ground only feet from him.

A wave of heat rolled over him like an unfurling blanket and, for a split second, he feared that the raised temperature might ignite the petrol that was soaking his jeans. He rolled over, partly propelled by the explosion. A few feet away from him, Carla had also been jerked off her feet by the force of the blast, thrown backwards like a puppet whose strings have been tugged sharply. She landed heavily, rolled over then looked in awe towards the maelstrom of flame and smoke that now filled the space where the warehouse had been.

Chapman dragged himself across to her, the sub-machine gun still gripped in one hand. He too looked back in the direction of the blast, the heat strong on his face.

Tongues of flame were leaping fully fifty feet into the air and a choking mushroom cloud of black smoke was already beginning to form high above them. Every breath they took was filled with millions of tiny cinders and Chapman wiped his eyes with the back of one hand, trying to clear his vision. His one good ear was ringing from the blast and it sounded as if someone had wrapped a towel round his head when he finally spoke.

'Are you OK?' he gasped.

Carla merely nodded, her eyes still fixed on the leaping flames. She had cuts on her cheek, forehead and left hand but none of them looked serious. There were some trickles of blood but nothing to suggest she was badly hurt. Flying glass or debris, the detective guessed.

He rolled over and sat up, checking the magazine of the MP5K. There were about fifteen rounds left plus the fresh clip he had in his pocket. He nodded to himself and got to his feet, looking round anxiously to see if the blast had attracted any more of Seymour's men.

He knew it was only a matter of time before it did.

'Dad, look,' Carla gasped, grabbing his arm and pointing beyond the flames.

Chapman squinted to see what she was indicating.

Illuminated by the roaring tongues of fire, he could see something gleaming. There was a large metal door about twenty yards beyond the remains of the ware-house, although he couldn't make out any detail of the wall in which it was set.

'Come on,' he said, hurrying towards the fire.

As they got closer, Chapman noticed that the flames were bending and bowing towards them.

The smoke that had been pouring upwards was shifting slightly, the thick black column now quivering in places. As if blown by a breeze.

He hadn't felt a breath of wind since he'd entered the vast set but now, as they skirted the flames, he felt cool air against his face.

They reached the door and Chapman tugged at it, delighted when it opened.

A blast of cold air met them. The detective looked up and saw a set of stone steps rising before them, but it was what he saw above those stairs that forced a wavering smile on to his lips.

High above, thick clouds scudded across a watery moon.

'It's the way out,' he gasped, pulling Carla along with him.

They stumbled up the stairs into the fresh air.

He dropped to his knees on damp grass, the night air closing around him like a chilly fist.

'We're outside,' he panted. 'We've made it.'

'What the hell was that?'

Mackenzie spoke the words but Maggie felt the tremor too.

Somewhere beneath their feet it felt as if the world had split in two.

Two of the clip files on the shelves in the office toppled noisily to the ground.

Seymour looked up from the computer, his face expressionless.

'It was an explosion,' Maggie said quietly.

Seymour said nothing.

The man who appeared at the door of the office a moment later Maggie recognised as the individual who had greeted the two policemen when they'd first arrived at the house.

'Mr Seymour, we've got a problem,' he said agitatedly. He was trying not to look at either of the detectives. 'It – er – it would be simpler if you just came.'

'What's going on?' Mackenzie asked.

'That's what I'm about to find out,' Seymour said flatly, standing up.

'Can we check your records ourselves, Mr Seymour?' Maggie asked.

'Certainly not,' Seymour snapped. 'You'll have to wait until I get back.' He was already heading for the door. 'I'd appreciate it if you'd wait in the sitting room.'

'We haven't got time to hang around here all night,' Maggie protested.

'I've tried to co-operate with you,' said the millionaire. 'Don't test my patience too far.'

'If you don't let us check tonight we'll be back first thing in the morning with a warrant,' Maggie snapped.

'Then that's what you'll have to do, detective,' Seymour told her coldly. He turned to the suited man. 'See them out, then come to me.'

Maggie looked at Mackenzie, who could only shrug.

Both detectives hesitated, watching as Seymour walked off towards the wide marble staircase that led to the first floor of the house. Then they followed the suited man to the front door and went out on to the gravel drive.

'Get the car,' Maggie said.

'Just like that?' Mackenzie challenged. 'That's it? We just drive away?'

'Get the car, Mack,' she insisted, turning to look at the towering façade behind them.

Mackenzie hesitated a moment, then trudged off across the gravel to fetch the car. He returned a moment

327

later and pushed open the passenger door for her to climb in.

Maggie slumped in the seat, running a hand through her hair.

Mackenzie eased down on the accelerator, muttering under his breath, watching the house in his rear-view mirror. 'All this way for nothing,' he said.

'No, not for nothing,' she told him. 'Drive another hundred yards down the driveway then pull into the trees.'

He smiled thinly.

'You saw those monitors in that security room. Did they look like familiar settings to you, because they did to me. And what about the guys in the masks?' Maggie said defiantly. 'We're not leaving here until we find out what Seymour's hiding.'

76

'Where are we?' Carla looked around in the gloom, a growing breeze ruffling her hair.

Chapman shook his head, his eyes also scanning the darkness. 'I haven't got a clue.'

He looked behind him, towards the flight of steps they'd just climbed. The stone stairs seemed to disappear into the very depths of the earth itself.

'Jesus Christ,' he breathed. 'It's underground. The entire set is underground. We've been under the ground since we got here.'

Carla wiped some blood and cinders from her eyes and focused on a copse of trees about twenty yards away. She pulled her father towards it, suddenly feeling very exposed out in the open. The grass they trudged through was knee deep and it slowed their progress a little but they finally reached the trees. Beyond them, Chapman could see lights.

'There's something over there,' he said. 'It could be a house. You should try to reach it. Get help. Call the police.'

'And what are you going to do?'

'I'm going to find Seymour. He must be close.'

'You don't know that. You don't even know where we are.'

Chapman brandished the sub-machine gun before him.

'And what are you going to do if you find him?' Carla persisted.

'I'm going to empty this fucking gun into him,' he said, gripping the MP5K more tightly.

She looked at him defiantly for a moment. 'I'm not going anywhere without you.'

He sucked in a weary breath. 'All right,' he said finally. 'We go together. When I know you're safe, then I'm going after Seymour.'

They set off through the trees.

'Stop here.' Maggie glanced over her shoulder and saw that the house was a good three hundred yards behind them.

There was a dirt track off to the left of the driveway and Mackenzie turned the car down it, feeling the tyres bumping over the ruts and crevices in the earth. He brought the vehicle to a halt and shut off the engine.

'Now what?' he asked.

'We go back to the house and when we're inside we have a good look round. Without Seymour peering over our shoulders.'

'You saw his security, Maggie. How the hell are we supposed to do that? They'll spot us before we get within a hundred yards. They'll know we never left the grounds. They'll have been watching on CCTV. Why don't we just call for support?'

Maggie's only answer was to swing herself out of the car. She stood beside the vehicle, waiting.

A moment later, Mackenzie followed her example.

'Ready?' she asked.

He nodded wearily.

'He blew up the warehouse. And he took a machine gun from one of your men.'

Detective Sergeant Michael Bradley stood up, pointing agitatedly towards the bank of monitors, as Seymour entered the room.

'They're out,' he went on frantically. 'Chapman and the girl.'

'Where are they?' Seymour demanded.

'They're in the grounds somewhere,' the suited man said, following him into the room. 'We haven't located them yet, but they can't have got far.'

'Then find them,' Seymour snapped irritably. 'Contact all units and tell them to be careful. Tell them that Chapman's armed.'

'And if they're found?' the suited man asked.

'Kill them both,' Seymour said flatly. 'Shoot them on sight.'

77

'It is a house.' Carla jabbed a finger in the direction of the monolithic building about two hundred yards away. Both she and Chapman could see lights in several of the downstairs windows and others in the first and second floors of the huge edifice.

'Seymour's house,' the detective murmured under his breath.

'What? Are you sure?'

'I came here enough times after his son was attacked. It's not the sort of place you forget easily.'

'It's huge,' she said, awestruck. 'It looks like a fucking castle.'

He grabbed Carla by the arm and pulled her round to face him.

'If you set off that way,' he told her, stabbing a finger off to his right, 'you'll come to the drive. About half a mile down that is the entrance to the estate. Hide somewhere near the gates and wait for me to come.'

'I told you, I'm not leaving you alone.'

'I'm not asking you, I'm telling you.'

She pulled free of his grip. 'He tried to kill me too,'

she reminded him. 'Or are you the only one allowed revenge?'

Chapman didn't speak.

'You saw what happened to me,' Carla went on. 'You saw what those three blokes were doing to me when you found me. They were Seymour's men too. They were there because of him. I was raped because of him.'

The detective raised a hand to silence her.

'I want to kill him as much as you do,' she snapped.

'Are you going to use that on him?' He nodded in the direction of the nail gun she still held in her right hand.

'Whatever it takes,' she said quietly.

Chapman regarded her silently for a moment longer before walking off in the direction of the massive house, the ground sloping away gently before him. Carla hurried to join him.

About twenty yards ahead of them, Chapman could see the regimentally straight lines of privet that made up the maze. Great long topiary boundaries of hedge turning at right angles for five or six hundred yards in all directions forming a barrier to the rear of the building. Beyond the maze lay some neatly manicured lawns and well-tended flower beds. Then the stone steps leading up to the back of the house itself.

'Can we go round it?' Carla enquired. 'If we get inside we might never find our way out.'

Chapman put a finger to his lips.

Carla saw and understood the gesture. She also heard the footsteps.

A torch beam cut through the darkness on their left.

Chapman grabbed her arm and they both ran like hell for the maze entrance. Only moments later, two of Seymour's dark-suited security men emerged into the grassy area where they'd been standing.

Chapman turned to see the two men pointing in their direction; then the smell of privet and damp earth filled his nostrils. He dashed to his right, Carla close beside him.

One of the men ran after them, while the other spoke into a two-way radio.

'They're in the maze,' he said.

'Seal it,' said the voice on the other end of the two-way. 'Make sure they don't get out. This has gone far enough. Move in and finish them off.'

The ground was spongy beneath Maggie's feet. A carpet of leaves and moss made progress through the densely planted wood agreeably noiseless. Other than the unseen rustlings of nocturnal animals, there were few sounds to distract the two detectives as they made their way back towards Seymour's house.

Maggie climbed over a fallen tree trunk, almost over-balancing when she realised that the slope on the other side of the log was steep. She shot out a hand and grabbed at a branch for support. Mackenzie, a foot or so to her left, also slid on the slippery footing. He cursed under his breath, his arms pinwheeling for a moment as he struggled to retain his balance. Both of them managed to stay upright and pushed on, the lights from the front of the house now clearly visible.

Maggie touched her companion's arm and pointed to a marshy area off to their right. A toad croaked loudly in the stillness, its call echoing within the confines of the wood.

'Shit,' murmured Mackenzie, his feet sinking several inches into glutinous mud close to the murky water of the pond they were skirting.

There were several white plumes of vapour over the rank surface.

'Marsh gas,' Maggie murmured, glancing at the wraith-like clouds hovering above the water like phantoms. The rotten egg stink stung her nostrils and the back of her throat.

The croaking toad landed with a dull plop in the water and, once more, the sound reverberated inside the wood.

'This should take us round the side of the building,' Maggie assured her companion. 'We're covered until we get there. The CCTV cameras won't be able to pick us up. We can find a way into the house from there.'

'Why the hell don't we just call for some support?' Mackenzie asked.

'Because if we go back in there mob-handed then we'll never find what we're looking for. Seymour will destroy everything before we get a proper look at it.'

'We don't even know what we're looking for,' Mackenzie reminded her.

Maggie didn't answer.

They moved on.

78

'This way,' Chapman gasped, running as fast as he could on his injured ankle.

He turned to his left then left again, glancing over his shoulder to ensure that Carla was close by.

'How do you know this is the right way?' she panted, hurrying along with him.

'I once read that, supposedly, all mazes are built on right-hand paths,' he told her. 'If we keep turning left we should find a way through.'

'You're fucking kidding,' she said indignantly, slowing her pace. 'That's the only reason we're going this way? Because of something you once read?'

'You got a better suggestion?' he challenged.

They both slowed down to a walk, their feet crunching loudly on the gravel path that ran through the maze. Too loudly for Chapman's liking.

The privet walls of the maze were at least eight feet high and so thick that they might as well have been made of concrete.

Chapman ran one hand along the perfectly trimmed surface as he walked.

They turned to their left again.

Dead end.

'Shit,' the detective hissed.

'So much for your theory,' Carla sniffed.

They walked back the way they'd come and took the right-hand path instead.

Chapman stopped walking, leaning against one of the privet walls to support his weight. He sighed and looked down at his ravaged left ankle. It was throbbing painfully and he didn't even want to think what kind of infections he might have in the wound caused by the dog's saliva. Carla moved on a few more paces, peering round another corner to ensure their passage was clear.

'Do you think they'll follow us in here?' she said quietly as Chapman caught up with her.

He nodded. 'Probably. Although all they need to do is cover the exits and wait. They know we can't stay in here for ever.'

The path turned once more, branching off to the left and right.

They hesitated.

'You choose,' Chapman said.

Carla was about to step to her right when they both heard voices from behind them. Chapman heard the harsh crackle of a two-way radio.

'Come on,' he urged, pushing his daughter towards her chosen pathway.

A beam of torchlight cut through the gloom.

'They can't be far behind,' he said, looking anxiously over his shoulder. He gripped the sub-machine gun in his fist and looked round for anywhere to shelter. Take their pursuers by surprise. Ambush them. It seemed the only answer.

But how?

The torch beam penetrated a hedge near to them. They both heard heavy footfalls on the gravel path on the other side. Whoever was chasing them was gaining.

The pathway branched in two directions again. Chapman shoved Carla to the left while he took a few steps into the right-hand path, and turned. From where he stood, he could see that she was enclosed on three sides by the tall privet. There was no way out down that pathway.

'Stay there,' he mimed, indicating that she should move further back into the thick shadows. He himself readied the MP5K, flicking the selective fire switch from automatic to single shot. He didn't want to waste an entire magazine with one over-enthusiastic jerk of his finger. He'd have more control over the weapon with it on single shot.

The footsteps drew nearer.

Chapman gripped the machine-gun more tightly, holding it before him. Ready to fire.

He saw another flash of white light. Heard another hiss of static on a two-way radio.

Then silence.

Their pursuer had obviously stopped in his tracks just round the corner from where the detective and his daughter now waited.

Chapman could see Carla crouching in the gloom, the nail gun held in her fist, her eyes wide with fear. His own heart was hammering against his ribs so hard he felt sure that the pursuer must surely hear it.

Why wasn't he moving? Was he listening out for their movements as carefully as they were listening to his?

There was still only that cloying, overpowering silence.

Chapman edged forward slightly, trying to see through the densely grown privet, attempting to catch a glimpse of the man who hunted them. He could see nothing.

He ducked down, crouching so that he was barely ten inches off the ground. Then he moved forward carefully until he reached the fork in the path.

Now or never.

He rolled into the open, swinging the sub-machine gun up towards whoever might be standing there. His finger tightened on the trigger.

The pathway was empty.

Chapman scrambled up on to his knees, the MP5K still held at arm's length.

There was no sign of their pursuer.

The detective got to his feet, eyes still searching the gloomy interior of the maze for any signs of movement. He took a couple of steps along the pathway.

He didn't even hear the shot that blasted off his left middle finger.

It came from behind him. Fired from a pistol equipped with a silencer. Apart from a dull thud, all he was aware of was agonising pain in his left hand as the 9mm bullet sheared effortlessly through bone and sent the severed digit spinning into the air, trailing blood.

Chapman spun round, pumping the trigger of his own weapon, squeezing off five shots.

Two of them hit their target, one slamming into his attacker's stomach, the other drilling through his chest where it punctured a lung before erupting from his back. The dark-suited man dropped like a stone, the air hissing in his lung wound. Chapman knelt beside him, pushing his fingers against the man's throat to feel for a pulse. There was one there but it was weak.

'Where are the others?' Chapman demanded, glaring down at his fallen assailant. 'How many are there?'

The man's lips moved but no sound came out. A thin ribbon of blood trickled from his mouth and down his chin. Carla scrambled over to look at the stricken figure lying before them. She pulled the torch from his belt, flicked the on switch once, then jammed it into the pocket of her joggers.

'Come on, leave him,' she urged Chapman.

The detective hesitated a moment longer, then snatched up the fallen Glock 26 from the ground where it had been dropped and shoved it into his belt.

'Come on,' Carla hissed.

Behind them they heard more heavy footsteps drawing closer.

79

Maggie and Mackenzie both heard the shots. The staccato retorts echoed through the still night air. The two detectives looked at each other, aware that the sounds had come from the rear of the house. From where they now sheltered behind a low stone wall, they could clearly see a paved area leading to one side of the building. Beyond that was their objective. A set of stone steps leading down towards what they assumed must be a cellar. They'd spotted it fifteen or twenty yards back, and wondered how they were ever going to get past the two men who stood sentinel there.

When the shots sounded, both figures dashed off round the corner of the house, leaving the steps unguarded.

'Go,' Maggie snapped.

As they ran across the open area towards the steps, they heard more shots echo through the night.

'What the hell's going on?' Mackenzie hissed, reaching the stone steps a second or two behind Maggie.

She didn't answer him but, instead, made her way swiftly down the stairs towards a stout-looking wooden door.

Mackenzie followed, grabbing the handle and twisting it.

Unsurprisingly, the door was locked.

He dug in his wallet and pulled out a credit card, sliding it between the lock and the frame. Maggie watched intently as he pulled it back and forth, simultaneously twisting the handle again.

It wouldn't budge.

'As a police officer, I'm disgusted you know how to do that,' she said, a smile touching her lips.

Mackenzie merely raised his eyebrows. 'It only works in films,' he grunted, pulling the card free. He pushed it back into his pocket and retrieved another small object that Maggie recognised as a Swiss Army knife. She watched him pull the blade free and jam it carefully between the lock and the door frame. Again Mackenzie worked the metal back and forth until, with a triumphant grin, he heard a loud click. He pushed the door gently and it swung open.

Maggie stepped past him into the room beyond. Mackenzie followed her, glancing back up the steps to ensure they hadn't been spotted. He closed the door behind them.

Chapman felt as if his hand was on fire.

The pain from the bullet-blasted appendage seemed to have enveloped the whole of his left arm. Blood had stopped flowing so freely from the wound, and some had congealed darkly around the shattered stump. Otherwise it looked as if someone had dipped his left hand in red paint.

But still he ran on, his head spinning from the effort, the breath rasping in his lungs.

Just ahead of him, Carla moved with almost feline

grace, ducking randomly left or right through the maze. Cursing when she found their path blocked by another high privet wall, gasping triumphantly if they were able to proceed unobstructed.

They passed through the middle of the maze and moved on, always aware that they were being followed. Chapman had seen torches ahead of them too and realised that there were men entering the labyrinth from both directions in an effort to trap them. Shots had already been fired at them through the hedge barriers, one missing Carla's right shoulder by inches.

Chapman had fired back, slipping the selective fire switch back to automatic and raking the privet barriers with bullets, not even sure if he was hitting anything or not.

They turned to the right and found their path blocked.

Quickly they doubled back, spun left and ran on, Carla almost dragging her father along with her now.

They turned another corner.

One of Seymour's security men stepped out into the pathway directly in front of them, his sub-machine gun lowered and ready.

Chapman swung the MP5K up and squeezed the trigger.

The hammer slammed down on an empty chamber.

The security man smiled thinly and prepared to fire.

Carla raised the nail gun and pumped the trigger three times.

The first nail drilled into the man's left eye, bursting the orb and tearing through into his brain. The second hit him in the left cheek, driving into the bone. The third powered into his forehead and he dropped like a stone.

Carla hurdled the fallen figure and Chapman hurried

343

on behind her, pulling the empty magazine from the sub-machine gun and slamming in the last full clip. They burst free of the maze at last.

Ahead of them, the lights of Anthony Seymour's mansion beckoned. Chapman even managed to forget the searing pain in his left hand and ankle. There was nothing between them and the house. The detective gritted his teeth and ran on, his fist closing more tightly around the sub-machine gun as he went.

80

The wine cellar was enormous.

As Maggie and Mackenzie made their way between the racks of dusty bottles, neither of them could help being struck by the size of the subterranean chamber. However, despite the fact that many of the bottles were covered by a sheen of dust, the stone floor on which the two detective sergeants walked was clean.

They could both see a set of steps leading up towards another door just ahead of them. Maggie ascended first, Mackenzie glancing around anxiously as he followed her.

She looked back at him, her hand resting on the knob.

He nodded, and she turned it.

Beyond the door was a kitchen.

Lit only by a couple of fluorescents, it was almost as big as the cellar beneath it. Maggie poked her head round the door and scanned the large room. There didn't appear to be anyone inside and she took a tentative step forward. Mackenzie followed.

They were halfway across the kitchen when they heard pounding feet both ahead of them and above. Undaunted by the hasty movement, the two detectives moved on.

There were two doors in front of them.

Maggie headed for the nearest; Mackenzie went towards the one on the right. He opened it, glanced inside, then turned back towards Maggie and shook his head.

'Storeroom,' he said quietly.

She nodded and pushed open the door by which she stood.

It opened out on to a wide, brightly lit corridor. As in the rest of the house, the decor was impressive and there were more expensive paintings adorning the walls on both sides. Thick carpet covered the floor and Maggie stepped tentatively out into the passage.

'Up there,' Mackenzie hissed, jabbing a finger in the direction of a CCTV camera just above the door.

They both stepped back inside the kitchen, pulling the door almost closed.

No sooner had they retreated than they heard movement outside.

Footsteps, muffled slightly by the thick pile of the carpet, were moving towards them.

Maggie eased the door open a little wider, attempting to get a glimpse of whoever was passing.

It was a man in a brown jacket and matching trousers. A man she recognised.

'Bradley,' Maggie uttered, stepping back slightly.

Mackenzie looked puzzled.

'Bradley's here,' Maggie repeated. 'What the hell would he be doing in Seymour's house?'

'Perhaps he's looking for the same answers we are,' Mackenzie offered.

'Let's ask him.'

She stepped out from the kitchen into the corridor.

'Bradley,' she called. 'When did you get here?'

The other detective sergeant turned and saw her. For a moment he didn't move, and then he took a step towards her. 'What are you doing here?'

'I was just going to ask you the same thing,' Maggie said. 'Why didn't you contact someone? Let anyone know you were here?'

'It was private business,' he said, smiling crookedly.

Maggie frowned and stepped back towards the kitchen door. 'What sort of business?' she demanded. 'What the hell's going on here, Bradley?' She saw that he was now reaching inside his jacket.

'I told you, some private business between me and Mr Seymour,' he rasped. 'Nothing to do with you. Why couldn't you keep your fucking nose out? You shouldn't be here, you interfering bitch.' His faced contorted to match the venom in his words.

He pulled the Glock 19 from his belt and swung it upwards, firing as he did so.

Maggie hurled herself to one side, crashing through the kitchen door as the 9mm bullet drilled a hole in the wall close to her, blasting some of the plaster away.

She rolled into the kitchen, the sound of the gunshot reverberating in her ears. Mackenzie, his eyes wide with fear and confusion, backed off.

'He's coming,' she hissed, scrambling to her feet and looking for somewhere to hide.

Bradley burst through the kitchen door and saw Mackenzie. He fired twice.

The first bullet hit Mackenzie in the chest, shattering a rib and ripping through his lung before exploding from his back. Gobbets of pink lung tissue sprayed on to the wall behind him, propelled by the force of the bullet. The second shot clipped his right shoulder as he dropped to his knees. It smashed the clavicle and the detective fell forwards, blood puddling around him.

Maggie managed to reach the door of the storeroom and she wrenched it open, diving inside in an effort to escape Bradley. He drove a foot against the wood as she slammed it shut and Maggie gripped the door handle, fearing that he would break in.

She jumped back as two bullets tore through the wood, one almost catching her in the face.

Again he kicked the door and it flew backwards on its hinges with such force that Maggie was sent flying. She crashed into some shelves behind her, toppling them. Packets of food crashed down upon her as she lay helplessly on her back, trying to scramble away as Bradley barged into the room, the Glock levelled.

'You should have stayed away,' he snarled, looking down at her.

'Don't, Bradley,' Maggie said breathlessly, her eyes fixed on the yawning barrel of the automatic.

'Fuck you,' he hissed, and fired once.

From such close range he couldn't miss.

The bullet slammed into her face. It shattered her bottom jaw, blasting several teeth from their sockets before powering from the base of her skull. Maggie slumped backwards and didn't move.

Bradley looked down at her body for a moment longer, then turned to leave the storeroom.

He saw two of Seymour's security men standing in the kitchen.

'We heard shots,' the first one said.

'She's dead,' the detective sergeant told them, hooking a thumb over his shoulder.

'Who is she?'

'She was a colleague,' Bradley explained, a slight smile on his lips.

'Did she come here looking for you?' the second man asked.

'How the fuck do I know?' Bradley snapped.

'Mr Seymour said she did,' the security man continued. 'He said you could have compromised the entire operation.'

'I told Seymour, she didn't even know I was here,' Bradley hissed. 'No one did.'

'Mr Seymour said you were a risk,' the first man added. 'He told us to take care of it.'

Both men opened fire simultaneously.

The staccato rattle echoed loudly in the room. Spent cartridge cases sprayed into the air then landed noisily on the tiles beneath.

The two blasts of automatic fire from their sub-machine guns tore into Bradley. He staggered backwards, wounds stitched across his chest and stomach. His eyes rolled upwards in their sockets and he fell to the ground, the Glock slipping from his hand. A thin curtain of smoke hung in the air.

The first security man crossed to him and jabbed his body with the toe of his shoe. Bradley's head lolled to one side, blood streaming from his mouth.

The man was about to repeat the procedure with Mackenzie when there was another explosion of gunfire from beyond the kitchen. It was close, too. Both security men turned and hurried towards the corridor outside, the door closing behind them.

Detective Sergeant James Mackenzie tried to take a breath but the pain was excruciating. Blood spurted from his chest wound as he tried and, for a second, he thought he was going to faint again. Waves of nausea swept through him and his stomach contracted violently, but the feeling passed and he managed to haul himself upright.

'Maggie,' he croaked, more blood spilling from his wounds.

No answer.

He dragged himself to his feet, his head spinning violently for a second. Close by, he saw Bradley's body, the Glock only inches from his hand. Mackenzie reached down and picked the pistol up, closing his fist around the butt. Trying to ignore the pain that enveloped his upper body, he moved towards the stockroom and pushed open the door.

He could see immediately that Maggie was dead and he closed his eyes so tightly that white stars danced behind the lids.

'Fuck,' he groaned, reaching towards a pile of freshly laundered tea towels stacked on the worktop close by. He put the cloth to his chest wound and pressed hard. Blood began to soak rapidly into the material.

Mackenzie swayed uncertainly for a second then turned and headed towards the kitchen door. He almost reached it before he fell.

81

'Where's Seymour?'

His face contorted with rage and spattered with blood, Detective Inspector Joe Chapman gripped the fallen security man by the throat and slammed his head against the wall behind.

The man didn't answer.

'Where is he?' Chapman rasped, slapping him hard across the face.

'Fuck you.'

'Give me that,' Chapman snarled, pulling the nail gun from Carla's hand. He pressed the weapon against the left thigh of the security man, his finger pressed against the trigger.

'Where is he?' he repeated.

The security man swallowed hard but merely shook his head.

Chapman fired once.

The nail pierced the man's thigh and thudded into the bone. He shrieked in pain, his body twisting wildly, but Chapman held him down, using all his weight to keep his captive pinned beneath him.

'Where's Seymour?' he said again, moving the barrel of the nail gun until it touched the back of the security man's outstretched right hand.

Again no answer.

Chapman fired again. The nail tore through the man's hand and thudded into the wooden floor beneath.

'I'll fucking crucify you,' Chapman rasped, dragging the man's left hand on to the floor and pressing the nail gun against the back of it. He fired again, the nail slamming right through the outstretched hand, effectively pinning the man to the ground.

At the door, Carla was peering out anxiously, watching for any signs of movement in the corridor beyond.

'You'll never get out of here,' wailed the security man, tears of pain now staining his cheeks. 'You're dead.'

'Not yet,' Chapman breathed. 'Now, you tell me where Seymour is or I'll nail your bollocks to the floor.' He pressed the nail gun hard to the man's groin.

'I don't know,' the man said desperately. 'I swear to God.'

'Liar,' Chapman snapped.

'Please. I'm telling you the truth. I don't know where he is.'

Chapman's eyes narrowed.

'I swear,' the security man screamed. 'Please.'

Chapman fired once.

The 30mm nail pierced the man's scrotum before ripping into his left testicle. It tore through the bulbous sphere, cutting effortlessly through the veins. Blood burst from the wound and the security guard screamed madly as the passage of the nail was abruptly halted when the flattened head stopped it, pinning him.

'Where's Seymour?' Chapman roared, his face inches from that of his captive.

'I don't know,' wailed the man helplessly. 'Jesus Christ.' He slammed his head against the wall behind him in his agony.

Chapman prepared to fire again. To drive a nail through the man's other testicle.

The guard had already fainted.

Chapman slapped his face hard, trying to revive him, aware of the slick of blood that was spreading out around his riven scrotum.

The man opened his eyes and babbled something unintelligible.

'Where?' Chapman demanded.

'Control room,' the man whimpered. 'First floor.'

Chapman drove the man's head back against the wall then staggered away from him.

At the door, Carla heard movement drawing closer.

'They're coming,' she said, closing the door.

Chapman joined her, pushing the nail gun back into her hands. She saw that there was blood on the metal.

'We've got to get upstairs,' he told her, himself easing the door open to peer beyond.

There was another suited figure out in the corridor.

Chapman opened the door quickly and squeezed off three shots from the Glock 26.

The man in the suit dropped like a stone, his body quivering slightly.

Chapman and Carla stepped over him, looking round for the staircase that would lead them up to the first floor. It was ahead of them to the right.

'What if he was lying?' Carla asked frantically.

Chapman didn't answer.

They reached the bottom of the stairs and began to climb.

★   ★   ★

Anthony Seymour regarded the bank of monitors before him expressionlessly.

He had a clear view of Chapman and Carla ascending the staircase but if it bothered him, it didn't show on his face.

Alone in the control room, he waited.

82

Chapman drove his foot against the first door he came to, the wooden partition slamming back against the wall behind.

A bedroom.

Nothing more.

He ran on, Carla close behind him.

The next door he also kicked open.

Again nothing but an immaculately decorated bedroom beyond.

'Try the others,' he snapped, jabbing a finger at one of the doors across the spacious landing. 'Be careful.'

Carla dashed off to complete his instructions, herself shoving doors open but, like her father, finding little of interest behind them.

As he moved to the next door, Chapman looked up and saw the CCTV camera above him change position, the single, cyclopean eye fixing him in its glassy stare. The detective looked up briefly at the camera, knowing that the man he sought was watching the images it captured. He kicked out viciously at the next door and blundered into the room.

Another empty bedroom.

'Where are you, Seymour?' he hissed, backing out on to the landing.

Anthony Seymour got slowly to his feet and walked to the rear of the control room. He paused before the door there, glancing one last time over his shoulder at the banks of monitors he'd been watching.

There was a panel on the wall next to the door and Seymour tapped in a four-digit code, selecting each number carefully. He heard a low electronic buzz and turned the handle of the door, stepping through.

Beyond it, there was a narrow carpeted staircase, flanked on both sides by bare stone walls. He waited for the door to close behind him, then ascended.

Chapman steadied himself before yet another white-painted door, the MP5K gripped in one hand, the Glock 26 in the other. He glanced back to see Carla on the other side of the landing, brandishing the nail gun before her, her face set in determined lines.

The detective kicked out at the door and stepped into the room beyond.

'Jesus,' he murmured, glancing round at the array of monitors that greeted him. He could see every inch of the house and its grounds on them but it was the bank of screens directly in front of the control panel that interested him the most. He saw the inside of the holding cell where he'd first woken. The deserted street he'd walked along. The abandoned tennis court. Every part of the huge underground set he and Carla had been forced to battle their way through. On a number of the screens, the masked figures he'd come to recognise so well moved about silently. He felt a sudden surge of fury sweep through him, and he was still glaring at the monitors when the images upon the screens suddenly disappeared.

They were replaced, in each and every case, by an image of Anthony Seymour.

From every corner of the room, the face of the multi-millionaire stared out at Chapman.

'The game's nearly over,' Seymour said evenly. 'I suppose I should compliment you on your resilience.'

Chapman looked at the dozens of screens, every one bearing the face of the man he sought. He raised the sub-machine gun, ignoring the pain in his left hand.

'Not far to go now,' Seymour continued. 'Up the stairs behind you and you'll find me waiting.'

Chapman tightened his finger on the trigger.

Bullets spewed from the machine-gun, ripping across the control panel and the monitors, blasting holes in the screens. They shattered the glass of the monitors and pulverised the metal innards. Sparks flew from the blasted hulks and, as the detective continued to rake them with fire, the smell of cordite stung his nostrils. The recoil on the weapon made his hand numb. When the hammer finally slammed down on an empty chamber he merely dropped the gun then swung the Glock up with both hands and shot out the four remaining screens, each discharge blasting in the glass, destroying the set and wiping the image of Seymour away.

Chapman's ears were ringing. He coughed as the gunsmoke drifted like a veil before him, joining with that rising from the bullet-blasted remains of the monitors. Sparks, too, crackled in the riven shells of the shattered sets. There was broken glass everywhere and it crunched beneath Chapman's feet as he moved closer to the destroyed monitors.

Carla appeared in the doorway of the control room, surveying the destruction within.

Chapman was already making for the door at the back of the room.

'Stay here,' he told her, putting his weight against the door. 'I'm going to finish this.'

When it didn't open he stepped back, raised the Glock once more and fired two shots into the panel. There were more sparks as the 9mm slugs drilled into it. The detective kicked at the door again and it opened. He glanced up the short flight of stairs.

'Call the police,' he said, pointing at the phone on the desk next to the control panel. 'Tell them where we are. Tell them to hurry.'

Carla hesitated.

'Do it,' he snapped.

She nodded, watching as he disappeared through the door.

She waited until she heard his footsteps on the stairs then snatched up the receiver and jabbed the digits she needed. At the other end of the line, the phone rang.

And rang.

83

He recognised the smell.

As Chapman gently pushed open the door at the top of the narrow flight of steps, his nostrils flared. The odour reminded him of the disinfectant smell of a hospital. And yet, as he looked round at the white-painted corridor on either side of him and his feet sank into the thick carpet, the scent in his nostrils seemed even more alien within these surroundings.

He moved slowly down the corridor, noticing that it turned at right angles about twenty feet ahead. The smell was stronger now and it made him wince.

Chapman stopped, glancing up.

There were no cameras here. If Seymour was waiting for him, then he didn't appear to be watching his progress.

Why?

The detective gripped the Glock more tightly and moved on, his back pressed against the wall of the corridor. Blood from his wounds smeared the pristine paintwork as he slid along it.

He peered tentativly round the corner, his breath rasping in his throat, his heart thumping harder. The smell was growing stronger, it seemed, making it difficult to breathe comfortably.

The corridor extended about fifty feet away from him towards another white wall. To his right there was a dark wood door. A little further down on his left he could see a second door.

Seymour could be in either of them. Ready and waiting.

Chapman edged out into the corridor and approached the first door.

He closed his fist over the handle and turned it gently.

It was unlocked.

The stench was almost unbearable now and, finally, he realised what it was. Not the disinfectant stink of a hospital but something far more pungent. More repellent.

It was formaldehyde.

And, as he stepped into the room, he saw why.

There were five severed heads mounted on the wall opposite him.

All men. Ages ranging from twenty to fifty.

Men he recognised.

He knew their faces from the snuff movies he'd viewed. The snuff movies made by Anthony Seymour.

'Oh, God,' he muttered, moving another step into the room. He crossed to the row of mounted heads and inspected them more closely. Each one had been severed just below the base of the skull. Most bore wounds to their features. One had an eye missing. The flesh of all five looked waxy, as if they'd been lifted from Madame Tussaud's. An effect of the preservation process, he guessed.

He stepped back, glancing around at the rest of the room. The bare wood floor with the expensive rugs. The leather furniture. In particular at the high-backed swivel chair that faced away from him in one corner of the room.

The chair turned and he saw Anthony Seymour sitting before him.

He was smiling.

'Welcome to my trophy room,' he said.

Chapman extended his arms, the Glock aimed at Seymour's chest.

'You're insane,' he breathed.

'No,' Seymour told him. 'Madmen aren't capable of organisation on the scale that's been required here. I told you before, what I wanted was justice.' He nodded towards the row of severed heads. 'Those are the tangible evidence of that justice. When your head is alongside them then I'll be able to stop.'

'The police are on their way. This is over.' His finger tightened on the trigger.

'Why did you save the girl?' Seymour asked. 'I was watching. You could have left her to her fate. You didn't have to bring her out with you. Why did you?'

It was Chapman's turn to smile. 'You don't know, do you? Because you couldn't hear us talking. You could only see us.'

Seymour nodded.

'She's my daughter,' Chapman said.

'How touching.' Seymour smiled again. 'So, you've been reunited with your child. Perhaps you understand why I wanted justice after what happened to my boy. After you failed to bring his attackers to account.'

'I tried.'

'You didn't try hard enough,' Seymour snapped.

'Too bad,' Chapman rasped, lifting the barrel of the Glock slightly so it was in line with Seymour's head.

He felt a thunderous impact on the back of his skull

and he pitched forward, unconsciousness flooding through him like a black tide. As he hit the ground the Glock fell from his grasp. He tried to rise once, then slumped back down in front of Seymour.

The multi-millionaire got to his feet, glanced down briefly at the prone figure of the detective, then looked at the other occupant of the room, the one who had dealt Chapman a hammer blow with the metal bar he carried, and smiled.

'Good boy,' he said.

Thomas Seymour grinned, a thin ribbon of spittle hanging from his bottom lip.

'Bring him,' Seymour said, picking up the Glock.

Thomas nodded and swept Chapman's immobile form up in his arms as easily as a child would lift a doll.

He followed his father out of the room.

84

Detective Inspector Joe Chapman awoke suddenly, his eyes jerking open as if the lids had been shocked with electricity.

He tried to stand but a combination of the appalling pain in his skull and the fact that he was tied to a chair prevented even so simple a movement.

It took him a few seconds to realise that his arms and legs were secured with thick lengths of gaffer tape. As he struggled against the sticky bonds, he felt the hairs on his arms being pulled out. The pain from his ankle wound also restricted his movements and he gritted his teeth against the agony and his anger.

'This is what they did to my son,' Seymour announced, touching the figure next to him gently on the shoulder. 'This is what the men you couldn't catch turned him into.'

Chapman ran appraising eyes over the hulking figure of Thomas Seymour. 'And all your money couldn't help him,' he said dismissively.

'Don't think I haven't considered that,' Seymour rasped. He looked at the helpless detective and sneered. 'I thought it would be more fitting if he himself ended your suffering, Chapman.' Seymour pushed the Glock into Thomas's hand, keeping his own fingers closed over his son's fist.

Thomas looked at the gun and then at his father, an expression of incomprehension on his face.

'This man deserves to die, Tom,' Seymour said gently. 'And to die by your hand.'

Thomas smiled at his father, allowing his fist to be pushed towards Chapman's face. He held the Glock, his finger touching the trigger.

The barrel was inches from Chapman's forehead now.

'When he's killed me, why don't you get him to put the gun in his own mouth, Seymour?' Chapman hissed. 'Do everyone a favour.'

'Shut up,' the multi-millionaire snapped.

'He's no good to anyone, is he?' Chapman continued. 'A useless fucking retard.' He strained against his bonds and felt some of the tape round his right wrist come free.

'Shut up,' roared Seymour, smashing his hand across Chapman's face. Blood trickled from the cut on the detective's bottom lip.

Thomas stepped back, frightened by the sudden explosion of sound.

Seymour took a step towards his son, trying to coax him back towards where Chapman sat.

'It's all right, Tom,' he said quietly. 'Come here. Let me hold your hand.'

Thomas shook his head.

'Looks like he doesn't want to do your dirty work, Seymour,' Chapman said. 'Perhaps he's not as fucking stupid as he looks.' Again, the detective flexed his right arm.

'Tom,' Seymour called.

'Deaf as well as brain dead,' Chapman mocked, feeling the tape round his right wrist beginning to give.

Seymour grabbed his son by the arm but Thomas pulled away. He dropped the gun.

Chapman grunted derisively. 'Fucking idiot,' he snorted.

Seymour snatched up the Glock and stepped towards the detective.

'Go on then,' Chapman snapped. 'Do it, if you've got the balls. Pull the trigger. Kill me. You're finished anyway. You and your halfwit son.'

Seymour shook his head and pressed the Glock to Chapman's forehead. 'That's enough.'

Thomas Seymour covered his face and whimpered quietly.

Chapman gritted his teeth, his eyes open defiantly, staring at the multi-millionaire who held him at gunpoint.

Anthony Seymour smiled.

Three sharp reports filled the room.

Three shots from the nail gun.

The first hit Seymour in the base of the skull. The second ripped through one of his ears, shearing off part of the lobe then drilling into his cheek. The third hit him in the back.

As he turned, Carla advanced, her finger pumping the trigger. She fired four more nails into Seymour. Two into his left eye. Another into his mouth. A fourth she hammered into his eyebrow. As he dropped to his knees she pressed the nail gun against his forehead and fired two more of the 30mm steel spears into his skull.

As he dropped face down at her feet she clicked the trigger again.

The last nail slammed into his skull just below the right ear.

Carla dropped the weapon, tears running down her cheeks.

Chapman sat motionless, looking first at Seymour's body, then at his daughter. She pulled the knife from her belt and cut easily through the tape that held her father in the chair. He bent and snatched up the dropped Glock.

Thomas Seymour shook his head and backed away, whimpering to himself.

'Kill him,' Carla hissed.

Chapman shook his head.

Thomas Seymour went towards his fallen father, looked down at the body, then knelt beside it. He moved with surprising grace for such a big and ungainly man. Chapman saw him stroke his father's cheek, puzzled by the blood that covered it.

The detective walked towards the door of the room, pulling Carla with him. More than once, he stumbled, the pain from his ankle now almost intolerable. When he staggered, Carla lifted his arm on to her shoulder to support him and he leaned on her gratefully. Glad of the help. Thankful that she was there to aid him.

As they reached the control room, both of them heard the sound of sirens from outside the house.

They struggled on.

85

As they stepped through the open front door of Seymour's house, Chapman felt the cool breeze sweep over him. He took several deep breaths, trying to clear his head.

The night seemed to be filled with flashing blue lights. There were police cars and ambulances parked everywhere outside the huge house. Uniformed men ran backwards and forwards in a scene of apparent chaos.

Chapman murmured something quietly and slipped his arm from Carla's shoulder. She helped him to sit down on the steps leading up to the front door of the building.

They could see people being helped into ambulances or pushed into the backs of police cars.

'What'll happen now?' Carla asked wearily.

Chapman could only shake his head. 'That's not our problem.' He winced as he put weight on his left ankle.

There were two uniformed policemen approaching, eyeing the pair of them suspiciously.

'It should be fun trying to explain to them what's happened here,' Chapman murmured.

'I thought we were going to die,' she admitted, tears beginning to form in her eyes.

'To tell you the truth, so did I.'

She gripped his right hand and held it tightly. He looked at her and smiled.

'You don't get rid of me that easily,' he said quietly.

She moved nearer to him, tears now running freely down her cheeks.

'I could murder a cigarette,' he told her.

'Me too,' she confessed, managing a smile. She looked at him. 'When do we go home, Dad?'

'I don't know,' he confessed, gazing at the approaching policemen. 'I really don't know.'

He put his arm round her shoulder again and pulled her close.

'Thou wilt be condemned into everlasting redemption for this.'

Much Ado About Nothing, Act IV, Scene ii

'I am a plastic man. Wish I can be the one you could be proud of.'

Seether